D0198126

MEAN STREAK

Carolyn Wheat

BERKLEY PRIME CRIME, NEW YORK

For Margaret and Malice IV
With friends all things are possible

MEAN STREAK

A Berkley Prime Crime Book / published by arrangement with the author

PRINTING HISTORY
Berkley Prime Crime hardcover edition / May 1996
Berkley Prime Crime mass-market edition / January 1997

The Putnam Berkley World Wide Web site address is
http://www.berkley.com/berkley

ISBN: 0-425-15577-3

Berkley Prime Crime Books are published
by The Berkley Publishing Group,
200 Madison Avenue, New York, NY 10016.
The name BERKLEY PRIME CRIME and the BERKLEY PRIME CRIME
design are trademarks belonging to Berkley Publishing Corporation.

PRINTED IN THE UNITED STATES OF AMERICA

10 9 8 7 6 5 4 3 2 1

CHAPTER ONE

"You know when it's over?"
I didn't wait for an answer, just said the words that occurred
to me as I scanned the *Daily News*. "When you stop looking for his horoscope in the morning paper."

"Riordan, you mean," Dorinda interpreted. She lifted
the plastic cover from a tray of pastries and squeezed a
doughnut to test its freshness. It was fifteen minutes before
the Morning Glory Luncheonette was due to open its doors
to the public. I sat in my privileged seat by the window
sipping my first cup of the day.

"Those okay?" I tipped my head toward the pastries.

"They'll do. Maybe the crullers are a little hard,
though." She gave me an amused look. "Want to test
one?"

I shrugged assent. The cruller, homemade in a bakery
over on Henry Street, was spun of sugar, flour, and air.
Even a day old, they melted in the mouth. "They'll do,"
I agreed.

"I never had much faith in you and Riordan," Dorinda

said. She walked to the back, toward the kitchen, and returned with a rack of newly washed juice glasses. She set the rack on the counter and emptied it as we talked, the clink of glass punctuating our conversation, while the early morning sun lit the sky behind the Court Street storefronts.

"What makes you say that?" I had my own reasons for thinking Dorinda was right, but like any good cross-examiner, I wanted the witness's own version.

"You said it yourself, Cass," she replied with a smug little smile. She poured herself a glass of orange juice, took a quick sip, and explained. "The horoscope. You're Sagittarius and he's Scorpio. It was bound to fail."

"Sagittarius and Scorpio," I muttered, gazing into the depths of my coffee as though looking for something. "I should have known."

"You should have," Dorinda agreed, unaware we were on different wavelengths. "The Scorpion has a way of lashing out with his poisoned stinger," she said, her blue eyes intense. "And of course the arrows of truth aimed by Sagittarius can—"

"Can annoy the hell out of a saint," I finished. I'd heard this one before. "And as we both know, Matt Riordan is no saint."

"Have you read it yet?" Dorinda asked, carefully polishing one of her vintage juice glasses. This one was printed with gaily colored oranges that diminished in size as they reached the narrow bottom.

The question was not the *non sequitur* it sounded at first hearing; my ex's picture graced the cover of this week's *New York* magazine.

"It's in my briefcase," I mumbled. "I'll read it in court while I wait for the court officers to produce my client." The truth was, I was afraid to open the glossy cover, afraid to learn things about Matt Riordan I didn't want to know.

"Besides," Dorinda went on, bringing the discussion back to the personal, "he was too"—she broke off and gave an awkward shrug—"too driven, too involved in his career, too—" Another pause. "I never thought he wanted a relationship, just somebody to ball when he needed a—"

"Ball," I repeated. "I haven't heard that expression in a long time. I never really understood it; I mean it isn't the balls that do the—"

"And you aren't much better," my old friend went on, disregarding my excursion into anatomy. "If you had to choose between your main squeeze and your career, the guy'd be gone so fast his head would spin."

"Which made my relationship with Riordan perfect for both of us," I pointed out. "We were both driven, both ambitious, both selfish, each of us using the other for sexual release. We were made for each other."

Dorinda began shaking her head somewhere in the middle of my recitation. "You knew from the beginning it wouldn't last," she said. "In fact, I would have sworn you were getting ready to dump him."

I swallowed a hit of coffee and let the dark roast linger in my mouth. Then I spoke the truth that branded me a totally shallow, ego-driven woman: "That's not the same as him dumping me."

I looked down at the Formica counter. "For a lemon-haired lady," I added under my breath.

"Whatever happened to Dory Previn, anyway?" Dorinda asked.

This was a *non sequitur*. "What are you talking about?"

"That's her song. 'Lemon-haired ladies.' I just wondered what—"

"God, I don't know. I forgot that was hers." I stopped a minute as the irony struck me; if the song was Dory Previn's, then the original lemon-haired lady was Mia Farrow. What goes around, and all that. Which meant that somewhere along the line I was getting what I deserved for all the times I'd been the dumper instead of the dumpee. Not to mention those times when I'd been the Younger

Woman. Times now far in the past; for me to qualify as a Younger Woman these days, the guy would have to be collecting Social Security.

"Not that Taylor's hair is really lemon-yellow," I mused aloud. "More an ash-blond. Cut like Hillary's."

"She's younger than you, isn't she?"

"Younger, slimmer, blonder, better dressed—you name it, Taylor has it. Including the name Taylor. She's like someone on a nighttime soap opera. She even has a soap opera job; she designs interiors."

I swallowed the last of the coffee and stood up. I squared my shoulders and prepared to do battle in the only interior I knew anything about—the interior of the Kings County supreme court.

It was pushing eighty degrees, and the sun wasn't even over the three-story brownstones yet. It was going to be another scorcher. I wore a silk camp shirt and a cotton skirt and had my all-purpose linen jacket slung over my arm. I'd need it in the arctic air of the supreme court building.

Riordan and I had never promised each other fidelity. The thought hit me as I stood waiting for the light to change so I could cross Atlantic Avenue, home of Arab spice stores and warehouses filled with antique furniture. Also the home of the Brooklyn House of Detention, another building whose interior I was all too familiar with.

We had never promised anything.

Then why did it hurt so much?

I want my secrets back. The thought came unbidden as I strode along the steamy street. I wanted my secrets back. I wanted to unsay things I'd said as we'd lain in bed on delicious Sunday mornings when neither of us had a trial to prepare for.

That was the worst part about breaking up with someone. You'd told them things you'd never told anyone else. And now he wasn't your confidant anymore; he was a stranger, and he knew things you no longer wanted him to know.

In Brooklyn, the supreme court is decorated in blond wood, very fifties, with the added touch of carved slogans behind the judge's bench. The one in Part 57 said "Let Justice Be Done Though The Heavens Fall." It's shorter and pithier in Latin: *fiat justitia, ruat coelum.*

I tossed my files on the defense table. It was 12:30; I'd hit every courtroom on my schedule and if I could finish this case before the lunch break, I'd have the afternoon to catch up on office work.

I looked up at the slogan on the wall and reflected that today we were going to do very little in the way of justice; the heavens were safe from me.

I walked up to the court clerk and pointed to my case. "Do you think we can get my client down before lunch?" I asked, a wistful note in my voice. I really didn't want to come back; I had pleadings to draft on a breach of contract suit my Atlantic Avenue antique-dealer clients were bringing against a mirror restorer. Who knew there were people that spent their whole lives resilvering old mirrors?

God, the things you learn practicing law.

"I'll send the court officers right away," the clerk promised. "But if we can't get him down in ten minutes, I'll have to put it over. Judge Rossi doesn't like it when we go into the lunch hour."

I nodded, then walked back to the front row, traditionally reserved for lawyers and reporters. No reporters today; no other lawyers—until the door opened to admit Murray Singer.

He was a natty little man, if your idea of high style was formed in 1955. Balding, gray-haired, pink-cheeked, he was the constant butt of judicial humor, and had been known to contribute some of his own to the otherwise dull proceedings. I'd been on trial with him once, and in response to my making motions *in limine*—motions for a ruling on the admissibility of evidence before the jury hears it—he suggested to the judge that we make our motions in Bimini instead.

No one, least of all the very scholarly Judge Baumgartner, had laughed.

He was a Court Street hack, pure and simple. The kind of guy who stood in the lobby of 120 Schermerhorn Street, the Criminal Court building, and handed out his cards to perfect strangers. The cards were printed on light pink cardboard so that an illiterate defendant could flash it at the arraignment judge and be recognized at once as a Singer client. Guys like Singer didn't retire. Someday he'd grab his chest and go down like a tree in Jury One, having had The Big One at last.

When I'd stormed the male bastions of law school back in the Year One, I had envisioned a future as a female Perry Mason. Hell, why not say it: a female Matt Riordan.

There was every possibility I'd end my days as a female Murray Singer instead.

On that depressing note, I opened my briefcase and took out my copy of *New York* magazine.

The man I'd slept with, off and on, for four years stared out at me from the glossy page, his fading summer tan artificial-looking, his startling blue eyes an advertiser's dream. Every wrinkle, every gray hair, only added to his mature masculine charm.

I missed him. I missed his hands, well-scrubbed and manicured, like a doctor's. I missed the little fold at the corner of his deep blue eyes. I missed the way those eyes shot fire as he laid a particularly complex evidence question in front of me at the dinner table.

What was interesting was that I didn't particularly miss the sex. I missed the friendship I hadn't bargained on.

The article began by describing the old movie poster on the wall of Matt Riordan's office—a poster I'd given him after we discovered we both thought Jimmy Cagney's best dramatic performance had come in a movie called *City for Conquest*. It was less well known than *White Heat*, but it was a gritty black-and-white gem.

The article went on:

"It was a city for conquest"—and Matthew Daniel Riordan was just the man to conquer it. Young, freshly graduated from Fordham Law School, he stepped into his first big case by sheer accident. He was called into night court to represent Thomas F. O'Hara, a night watchman charged with drunk driving. Instead, he ended up assigned to Thomas P. O'Hara, notorious hit man for the Westies, an Irish mob working out of Hell's Kitchen. He got O'Hara released on one hundred thousand dollars bail—which may seem high, but the gangster was charged with a particularly brutal double murder (when the Westies say "heads will roll," they aren't speaking figuratively).

He buys his suits at Barney's, his shoes at Gucci's, his shirts at Brooks Brothers. But he still buys his Irish whiskey at The Bells of Hell, a neighborhood bar in Inwood, at the northern tip of Manhattan. There they call him Matty, or even Robbie Riordan's son—his father, a New York City bus driver, has been dead these ten years, but the people of the neighborhood have long memories, and stories of Robbie Riordan could fill an entire evening of drink and song at The Bells. Robbie, they say, was a darlin' man, a darlin' man. A wee bit too fond of the sauce, but a darlin' man nonetheless.

What they mean is that Robbie Riordan was an inconsequential man, a man whose life and death made little difference to other people. A man of charm and laughter and jokes and gentleness, but not a man to be greatly feared or respected. A darlin' man.

Matthew Riordan is not a darling man.

In the four years I'd known him, Matt Riordan had told me less than nothing about his father. I'd gathered it was a sore subject and had learned not to ask. And now he was telling the world whatever it wanted to know about the most personal side of his life.

He was in trouble. Deep trouble.

Which was what the article went on to say. It was a neat summary of all the ways the United States attorney's office for the Southern District of New York had tried to break Matt Riordan. First, they had him disqualified from representing Frank Cretella, successor to the notorious Donatello Scaniello. Then they forfeited a hefty fee he'd received from a Colombian client, on the grounds that it represented the proceeds of drug crimes.

The latest skirmish: an about-to-be-voted indictment for bribery. They claimed he paid cash under the table for secret grand jury minutes.

I could believe a lot of things about my former lover, but getting caught in a nickel-and-dime hustle like this wasn't one of them. I was willing to bet he'd beat the rap.

"Counselor, we've got your client," the court offer said. I jumped up; time to go to work. I stepped lightly past the desk where the court clerk was explaining to Murray Singer that he'd have to come back after 2:15.

I gave my client the bad news; I'd been on the phone to the D.A. the day before, and the offer was ten to twenty. No room for negotiation. This was his third armed robbery and he was going to do serious time.

"I can't be doin' no ten to twenty," Rafael Guzman moaned from his side of the bars. "The whole crime ain't took but three minutes."

"Unfortunately, the fact that you've perfected the art of armed robbery to where you can pull a gun and get away with the cash register receipts in a mere three minutes is not—"

"Oh, Jesus," my client continued, drawing out the syllables in what was almost a genuine prayer. He dropped his head into his hands and moaned again.

He sat on a bench in a metal holding pen. The walls were stone, but painted gunmetal gray; there were bars between us and a cold green metal table on which I rested my elbows and waited. My client was going to have to understand that he'd be spending at least the next ten years in rooms no more comfortable than this one. That gray would be the color and hard clanking the sound.

"I went out to see the complaining witness," I went on. "I took an investigator with me; we talked to her for a good twenty minutes. She saw you, Rafael. She remembered the tattoos on your arms, the—"

"Lots of guys got these tattoos," he protested. He rolled up a gray-green sleeve to show me. "They get them in jail all the time." He pointed to the crudely drawn snake on the inside of his forearm and to the teardrop at the corner of his eye.

"Great," I said, shaking my head. "I can see myself now, standing in front of a jury. 'Ladies and gentlemen, Rafael Guzman didn't commit this crime; some other jamoke with a jailhouse tattoo did it.' Think about it, Rafael; the only way to defend you is to admit you've got a record the size of the Staten Island phone book."

"Man, I don' know," he said, shaking his nearly shaved head. "All's I know is I can't be doin' them double digits."

I looked at Rafael. Junkie-skinny, the shaved head showing nicks and scars where he'd sustained injuries. Wearing torn jeans that weren't distressed in a factory for yuppie kids, and cheap sneakers worn down at the sides by his pigeon-toed feet. He was a mess. A mess who committed felonies for a living.

What the hell was I going to use for a bargaining chip to get him a plea he could live with?

I'd hoped my visit to the complaining witness would turn up something. Something like the fact that she was ninety-six and wore glasses with lenses the thickness of—

She was in her fifties, with eyes sharp enough to see the tiny teardrop on Rafael's cheek. If we went to trial, the ten to twenty he was being offered would seem like a dream; he was a persistent violent felony offender, in the words of the Penal Code, and he'd go away for life.

A sentence he richly deserved. A sentence I was being paid to reduce as much as humanly possible. But how? I thought about it as I made my way back into the courtroom.

I looked up as the judge entered and took the bench. I was already standing at counsel table, so I nodded instead of rising. Judge Rossi nodded back. He was a plump, genial man who liked long lunch hours and fast pleas. It was twenty minutes to one; if I could get him out of here in time to make it to Armando's before the rest of the court-house crowd, he'd be a friend for life. Or at least for the next ten minutes, which was all I needed.

"Well, Counselor," he said, fixing me with impatient eyes. "Have we got a plea?"

I rolled the dice. I walked up to the bench and heaved a theatrical sigh. "We're very close, Your Honor," I said, lying through my teeth. "Very close. There's just one little problem."

Pause for effect. Tease him. Make him ask.

"And what's that, Ms. Jameson?"

I sighed again and gave him a wide-eyed stare. "My client says he can't be doin' them double digits."

It could have gone either way. He could have slammed his fist down on the bench and roared at the court officers to take my stubborn client back to the cells to think over his misspent life, and then lectured me about frivolity in the courtroom. Or he could have thrown back his curly head and let out a good strong laugh.

Fortunately for Rafael and me, he laughed. Then he turned to my opponent and said, "How about it, Mr. D.A.? Ms. Jameson says her client can't be doing those double digits. Can we come down a little on this one?"

Howie Rosenthal pursed his thin lips. "If Ms. Jameson's client can't do the time, he shouldn't—"

"Do the crime," I finished. I rolled my eyes; Judge Rossi said the words that were on the tip of my tongue.

"Cut the clichés, Mr. Rosenthal. What about it?"

Howie drew himself up to his full height—two inches shorter than me—and filled his lungs with air. He was preparing for a speech; Rossi glanced at his watch and gave a small sigh of resignation. He saw his table at Armando's disappearing before his hungry eyes.

Rafael and I were about to unleash the second weapon in our meager arsenal: Howie had absolutely no sense of humor and was much given to pompous prosecutorial speeches.

"Your Honor, the people have offered a very reasonable plea under the circumstances," he began, "and we think—"

"Counselor," Judge Rossi cut in, "nine to eighteen will punish him just as effectively as ten to twenty, and we can get that today. We can get it in two minutes, can't we, Ms. Jameson?"

I nodded eagerly. "They don't call me the fastest mouth in Brooklyn for nothing," I tossed in. Howie glared at me; he'd lost the judge and he knew it. He could insist on ten to twenty and take the case to trial, but if he did, he'd be in Rossi's black book for weeks to come. Maybe months; Armando's had a way of running out of its most mouth-watering specials. If Rossi missed the *osso bucco* there was no telling how long he'd hold a grudge.

I sailed back over to Rafael and put my mouth next to

his ear. He smelled of sweat and fear.

Good.

"We got it," I said. "And the only reason we're getting nine to eighteen is that you gave the judge his only laugh of the day. Maybe the week. So my advice is to jump on this plea before he loses his sense of humor. You admit everything and you won't do double digits."

He jumped on it. We were out of there by ten to one; Rossi made it to Armando's and Rafael and I achieved a victory of sorts.

As I left the courtroom, Murray Singer's gravel voice echoed in my ear. "So then the rabbi said to the chorus girl . . ."

I wondered when I'd start telling Borscht Belt jokes to court clerks.

One of my very favorite things about Matt Riordan was his voice. It was as rich and dark as fine Belgian chocolate; it soared into various registers like a well-played bassoon; it was lithe and playful, like a sleek otter. And it was on my answering machine for the first time in two months.

All he said was: *Call me.* Two words; no name, no phone number. I was supposed to recognize the voice and remember the number.

What pissed me off was that of course I did. The voice sent a shiver of anticipation through me. Absence might not have made the heart grow fonder, but it had definitely enhanced the libido.

As for the number, I recalled from memory not only his home number but his office number, his fax number, and his beeper number. This from a woman who has to look up her own mother's—

But would I call? That was the question.

I looked at the phone. The phone looked back at me. Not good. Not good at all. The quintessential female situation: looking at a phone and thinking about Him.

What did he want? Had he realized Taylor was too young for him? Had he too missed our Friday night dinners, each of us telling war stories and judge stories and swapping notes about our respective weeks in court? Did he want to know what I thought of the *New York* magazine article?

There was only one way to find out. I picked up the phone and dialed quickly, before I had time to change my mind. On the first ring I hung up.

If there's one thing in this world I hate, it's feeling like a teenager. I wasn't crazy about it when I was a teenager, but in my forties I really thought I should be able to call a man on the phone without wondering if my voice would sound too eager.

I dialed again and this time I stayed on the line until I heard that voice. "Riordan."

"Matt?" Why my voice rose inquiringly when the man had just said his name was beyond me. It's the same reflex that makes you push the elevator button even when you've just seen the person next to you push it first.

He didn't make that mistake. "Cass," he replied, filling the single syllable with a flood of warmth, as though hearing from me was a wonderful surprise.

Terse. To the point. That was the best approach. "I got your message," I said. "What do you want?"

Was that terse or just rude? I opened my mouth to add something, anything, but I didn't have a chance.

"Would you be free for dinner?"

"Tonight?"

"It could be tonight," he said. I had a mental picture of him consulting his Rolex. "Shall we say an hour from now, at Tre Scalini?"

An hour. An hour to shower, do my hair, change into a silk blouse—and of course the one I wanted would need ironing, and were my black jeans back from the cleaners? And then there was the subway ride to Little Italy.

"Make it two hours," I said. He agreed.

I was twenty minutes late. Not only were the jeans at the cleaners, so was the blouse. I tried on four others before I found one that picked up the teal in the embroidered vest that matched my favorite cloisonné earrings.

Date behavior. I was exhibiting definite date behavior, something I hadn't done with regard to Riordan in a long time.

He was sitting at a quiet table in the corner, his face ruddy in the pink light of the tiny lamps on the rose-painted wall. Tre Scalini looked like the inside of an old-fashioned valentine, all lace and Victorian colors and dainty, delicate embellishments.

"One thing about eating with you," I said, sliding into the seat next to his, "you always know where to get the best clam sauce."

He laughed. It was an old joke between us, but he laughed anyway. "I guess when your clients are named Scaniello and Cretella, you tend to eat Italian."

"Good Italian," I amended. I opened the menu, which was a huge hand-scripted parchment affair. My eyes bypassed the real food and went straight to the section headed *Dolci*. "Does this place still have *tiramisu* to die for?"

He smiled. It was an intimate, amused smile such as a fond father might bestow on a precocious daughter. It took me back to the early days of our acquaintance, when he treated me precisely that way, even though he was only twelve years older than I. As a result, I'd tended to exaggerate the adolescent brashness, while he leaned heavily on the avuncular. We'd outgrown those roles over the years, but we'd returned to them now that things were once again awkward between us.

It wasn't until we had steaming plates of *linguine alla vongole* and an enormous *insalata verde* in front of us that he revealed the purpose of this meeting. I choked on a clam and had to be pounded on the back by an overenthusiastic waiter before I could speak.

"You want me to *what*?"

"You heard me. I want you to represent me. Nick Lazarus is going to have that indictment voted and filed any day now and I need—"

"Riordan, you don't need me. You need Alan Dershowitz. Maybe F. Lee—"

"No, I don't," he cut in, an amused smile on his face. At least it was meant to be an amused smile; there was a strain around the edges that told me to stop kidding around. "I need you. I need you because you're smart and tough. You don't run away from a fight and you don't think prosecutors walk on water."

For a wild moment, my heart filled with pride. The pride a daughter feels when Daddy praises her. I let myself slide into fairyland; I pictured myself standing before the federal bench, cross-examining witnesses with laserlike acuity, pleading before a jury with an eloquence that had Juror Number Four dabbing tears from her eyes. Saw myself hitting the big time at last, all thoughts erased of ending my days as a female Murray Singer.

CHAPTER TWO

I'd come prepared on some subconscious level for Matt to ask me to resume our relationship. I hadn't come prepared for this. I went into stall mode, tap dancing until I thought my way clear.

"I haven't done much federal work," I remarked, as if that were the biggest obstacle to my taking the case.

He waved the objection away with a languid hand gesture; the red stone in his Fordham class ring gleamed in the subdued light of the restaurant. "Courts are courts," he said. "I can advise you on the more arcane aspects of federal procedure."

"You sure you don't need someone with a name?" I parried. "Someone with clout," I went on. "What about Litman? What about Slotnick?" I named the two most prominent, most aggressive Manhattan criminal lawyers I could think of.

He'd begun shaking his head before the first name left my mouth. "No and no," he said with a finality that had me wondering if he'd already asked and been turned down.

"I need a woman, for openers."

A little warning bell went off in my head. He needed a woman. Why? Because asking a male peer to defend him would be tantamount to stepping down as king of the hill? Because he couldn't let a male lawyer see him scared and vulnerable?

If that was his reasoning, it was not a sound basis for an attorney-client relationship.

He kept talking. "I need someone local. I need someone who doesn't have a reputation as 'the lawyer of last resort'—which is another way of saying 'a lawyer who represents the guilty.' I need—"

"You need a woman?" I broke in. "Why?"

"Because Davia Singer is the lead lawyer for the prosecution," he replied. "She's young, ambitious, a tiger on cross—and she looks great in a tailored black suit."

"Which is one thing I've never been known to wear," I countered. "If you're trying to answer femininity with femininity, I'm not your woman."

"Cass, I'm not asking you to be anything but yourself; I just don't want to present the image of a big, tall man pushing Davia around the courtroom."

"Whereas if I push her around, the jury thinks it's a fair catfight?" A nice double bind; if he said no, he'd be lying. If he said yes, he'd brand himself a sexist.

This time the smile was genuinely amused. "You've got it."

I smiled back. His deep blue eyes connected with mine and a surge of sexual energy filled my body. God, he was good-looking, full of masculine power.

I was glad I'd dressed. The silk felt sensual next to my skin, and I knew the teal blouse and brightly colored vest looked good on me. I rested my chin on my hands and gazed into his hypnotic eyes, pretending if only for a moment that the night might end in bed, that his manicured hands might unbutton my blouse and reach inside to unhook my Victoria's Secret bra.

It wasn't going to happen. His eyes might have a spark of sex in them, but his words were all business.

"Cass, Nick Lazarus would give his left nut to see me convicted and disbarred. He's had a hard-on for me ever since my first Scaniello trial." I had to smile; the phallic images only served to confirm my earlier notion that the bull elephant wasn't about to ask a rival bull to stand up for him in court.

I started a checklist in my head. One column was headed *Take the Case*; the other said *Hell, no*. I put a great big check mark in the *Hell, no* column; I didn't want a client who'd hired me on the basis that I wasn't a man.

I spoke a truth I'd known for a long time, but had never said aloud, at least not to Matt. "Lawyers like you have a limited lifespan," I remarked. "Like dancers."

I looked down at my plate, at the sea of virgin olive oil and the stray linguine strands and the one lone clam. I decided what the hell and stabbed the clam with a fork.

"You had to know it would happen someday," I pointed out. "You had to know the prosecutors couldn't stand to lose all the time, that one day they'd come after you the same way they came after your clients. The question is, did you do anything that would give them the ammunition they need?"

"You mean, did I sit around the Ravenite Social Club and discuss taking out a hostile witness?" he countered. His tanned face reddened as he spoke; the words collided with one another as they left his lips. "You mean, did I accept fees in cash handed to me on the street in a paper bag? Did I act as go-between in a drug deal?"

"Look, Matt, everything you've just mentioned was done at one time or another by a lawyer who swore up and down he was just representing his clients," I shot back. The one constant in our relationship was that I was determined not to be bullied. In the past, he'd always liked that about me; it was one reason he was considering putting his future in my hands. "I know you're not dumb enough to do those things, but did you do anything that might have blurred the line between acting as counsel for Mob clients and getting on the payroll?"

"I am not a Mafia lawyer," he pronounced, as if speaking for the record. "I have represented some clients who've been accused of—"

"Save it for the next time you're on *Charlie Rose*," I cut in. All thoughts of date behavior were forgotten. He'd come to me for some kind of truth, and he was going to get it, whether he liked it or not. "The last time out, Lazarus managed to get you bounced off a Frankie Cretella case on the grounds that you were, and I quote, 'house counsel to organized crime.' True or not, Judge Schansky bought it and the Second Circuit affirmed. That decision set the stage for this indictment; it served notice that you were no longer immune by virtue of having a law degree."

Matt reached for the after-dinner brandy he'd ordered. He lifted the snifter to his nose and swirled the liquid around. I could smell its potent aroma from my side of the table. He took a bigger sip than I would have. Then he took another.

He'd had a Scotch in front of him when I'd arrived, and since I was late, I doubted it was his first. Together we'd finished a carafe of Chardonnay, with him drinking three glasses to my one. Now he was plowing through the brandy.

The Matt Riordan I'd known had liked his liquor, but he'd always, always limited his intake. He was a man who needed to be in control the way other men need to surrender to the oblivion of intoxication. I'd never seen him drunk, never even seen him slightly tipsy.

Until tonight. Tonight the spider veins in his nose stood out like a roadmap. Tonight the famous voice slurred ever so slightly. Tonight he was drinking more than the self-imposed limit he'd always so rigidly set for himself.

"What have they got?" I asked, keeping my tone crisp and businesslike. I wanted to reach over and give his hand a reassuring squeeze, to stand up and knead his tense shoulders. To bring back the urbane, witty, controlled Matt Riordan I'd known, and banish this worried shell of a man.

"They say I bribed a court clerk, bought grand jury minutes."

"What's bribery worth in the federal system?" I asked, keeping my tone professionally detached.

"Fifteen years max," he replied. "That's the going rate for bribery. Of course, I doubt the judge would send me away for that long, but if I lose this case, I'm ruined even if I never see the inside of a jail cell."

I nodded. That was a given in a case involving a lawyer; a felony conviction would lose him his license, and the notoriety might lose him his clientele no matter how the case came out.

"And, in case you were wondering," he said with a sarcastic edge to his voice, "I did not put money in Paul Corcoran's pocket in return for the grand jury minutes of Nunzie Aiello."

He said it crisply, decisively, unambiguously. I put a mental check mark in the column headed *Take the Case*.

"Nunzie," I mused aloud. "He's the guy who—"

"Please, Cass," Riordan said, holding up a restraining hand, "let me tell this in my own way."

I nodded; interrupting people is one of my besetting sins. It's just one more example of my resistance to the concept of patience.

"Nunzie was a low-level Mob guy," Riordan explained. "He pretty much ran errands and talked tough. There were rumors he was involved in street drugs, which Frankie Cretella hates like poison. But nothing was ever proved."

I ran the risk of Matt's displeasure by saying, "I never believed that crap about the Mafia being down on drugs. It always struck me as sentimental nonsense.''

"It isn't sentiment," Matt disputed. "It's self-preservation. Guys could do serious time for drug-selling, and a guy facing serious time could decide to cut a deal and sell out the bigger fish. So the big fish made a hard-and-fast rule: Deal drugs and you're dead. They didn't want to risk going down because of something they couldn't control."

"And this Nunzie broke the rules?"

"So I heard," Riordan replied. "But that's another story. He got caught up in Frankie Cretella's garment union case; Lazarus charged him with being the one who threatened Lou Berger with a strike that would cripple his business. I represented Nunzie on that case."

He paused. I decided a question wouldn't be out of order. "As I recall, Cretella himself wasn't charged with anything."

Matt shook his head. He signaled the waiter for another brandy, making a little circle with his finger to indicate the need for another round. In my case, that meant a refill of insipid coffee. I schooled my face to show nothing; this wasn't the time for a temperance lecture.

"Lazarus wanted Frankie in the worst way, but he just didn't have the evidence. The only one Berger could identify was Nunzie. One day Nunzie hands me an airline ticket and a hotel receipt that put him in Barbados on the day Berger said he was threatened. I presented the evidence to the jury, but they convicted Nunzie anyway." Riordan's face was troubled; I could see why the conviction bothered him. If a jury was prepared to discount such seemingly strong evidence of an alibi, it meant they believed it was a fake. Riordan's reputation as a miracle worker was catching up with him; people were beginning to wonder what was really inside the magician's hat.

"Did you check this alibi out?" I asked. "Did you call

the hotel employees to back up Nunzie's story? Did you—''

"Cass, I took what appeared to be genuine documents from my client's hands and I entered them into evidence. It was for the jury to decide whether—"

"But you had your doubts," I persisted. "It's obvious from the way you're talking now—you didn't believe Nunzie's alibi, but you presented it to the jury, anyway.'' This called for two check marks in the *Hell, no* column. At least.

"Cass, please, haven't you ever presented evidence that you weren't one hundred percent convinced of yourself? Do you always act as judge and jury?"

I opened my mouth to retort that I would never have permitted a client to slip bogus documents past me, but then I remembered Bobo.

Bobo wasn't my client. My client was Jaime Ortega, late of Puerto Rico. He swore on a stack of Bibles that the car he was accused of stealing was sold to him by a guy on the street named Bobo. I explained to him that he was going to be convicted of possession of stolen property unless he produced a bill of sale proving that he'd bought the car in good faith. I was confident that he had no such bill of sale, and would be taking the eminently reasonable plea offer extended by the assistant district attorney.

Instead, on the next court date Jaime proudly presented me with a bill of sale. In the space marked "Seller's name" was scrawled the single word: "Bobo." No last name, no address. Just "Bobo."

The anxious lines around Riordan's mouth disappeared as I told the story, and his booming laugh filled the room. "So what did you do?" he teased. "Throw the bill of sale back into the guy's face and call him a liar?"

"He might not have been the liar," I said defensively. "Maybe some guy on the street really gave him a bill of sale in the name of 'Bobo.' "

"At least that's what you told the judge," Matt surmised.

"There were two possibilities," I explained. "Either my client was a very stupid man who was taken advantage of by an unscrupulous seller, or he—"

"Or he was a very stupid man who stole a car and didn't have the brains to fill out a bogus bill of sale with a believable seller's name," Riordan finished. "I take it you didn't see fit to present the judge with that alternative."

"I told the judge my client was a cane-cutting peasant from Puerto Rico who got ripped off by a city slicker named Bobo," I admitted.

"What happened to the case?"

"God, I don't remember. This happened years ago."

"But you tried to get your guy a better deal on the basis of a bill of sale you had some reason to believe he might have forged. That might be penny ante stuff compared to Nunzie's trip to Barbados, but the principle is the same. Does a good defense attorney look a gift horse in the mouth?"

"He does if the horse might turn around and bite him."

He considered that remark in silence; this horse had bitten Matt with a vengeance. But I did erase one of the two check marks I'd placed in my mental *Hell, no* column.

"And then?" I prompted, bringing him back to the matter at hand.

"And then Lazarus, the snake, put the squeeze on Nunzie," he said. "He promised him a walk if he'd incriminate me in the phony alibi. Word on the street is that Nunzie bought the deal and told Lazarus that he was given the documents by my investigator."

"This is Fat Jack Vance, the bail bondsman?" He was a legend in Manhattan court circles; the fat man and Riordan went back a long way together.

Matt nodded. "The next word I hear is that Lazarus sent Nunzie into the grand jury to get an indictment for subornation of perjury against Jack and me."

"And right after that, Nunzie Aiello went missing," I

finished. Nunzie's disappearance right after his grand jury appearance had been the subject of a certain amount of press speculation. Half the reporters in town thought he'd taken a strategic trip to the Old Country, while the other half had him swimming in the East River in cement shoes. Either way, his absence was Riordan's reprieve. There could be no trial without the chief witness.

"Lazarus was steamed, I take it."

"Lazarus was rabid," Riordan amended. "Now there was even wild talk he was going to prove I killed Nunzie to prevent him from testifying against me."

I finished the story for him. "And then, last October, the Department of Sanitation towed a derelict car from under the Williamsburg Bridge. The car was in the pound for a month. It was about to be auctioned, when the guys inspecting it smelled something rotten. They opened the trunk, and there was Nunzie. One bullet to the head, another in the mouth."

"Classic," was all Matt said. "The bullet in the mouth is a traditional way of marking an informer."

"Do you think Cretella did it?" I asked. This was, strictly speaking, irrelevant to Matt's defense. But I had decided that if the answer was yes, Matt would have to keep looking for counsel. I could represent Matt himself without becoming known as a Mafia lawyer, but if there were deeper Mob crimes underlying Matt's troubles, I preferred to stay on the Brooklyn side of the bridge.

Matt's eyes narrowed; at first, I thought he resented the question. But his thoughtful tone told me that he was thinking the matter through. "If Nunzie was *shtupping* me," he said in an uncharacteristically tentative tone, "then he was probably sticking it to Frankie too. I've represented Frank Cretella for almost fifteen years now, and this isn't the first of his former associates to be found with a bullet in his mouth."

"You didn't know beforehand, but you'd have defended

Cretella if he were charged with the murder.'' I tried to say the words dispassionately, but a hint of disapproval must have been there, because Matt suddenly exploded. He banged his open hand on the table with a force that had the glasses jumping and the waiter running over with a look of alarm on his face.

''Goddamn right I'd have defended him,'' Matt said. ''And that's what Lazarus wanted to prevent. That's why he wants me indicted and convicted. Because as long as I've been Frankie Cretella's lawyer, he hasn't been able to convict the man of anything. But with me defending myself, Cretella has to get new counsel, and Lazarus finally has a chance to get the conviction he needs for his political career.''

I gave the agitated waiter a conciliatory smile and waved him away. ''I'd say you had a pretty good opinion of your own legal talents,'' I remarked to my companion. ''Of course,'' I amended with an air of judicious consideration, ''in this case, your assessment is pretty close to the truth. You have kept Cretella out of jail for a long time. But is that necessarily a good thing for the rest of society?''

''My job is to defend my client,'' Matt replied. ''Society has another lawyer.''

''But Cretella is a—'' I broke off as my mind ran through the various terms that could be used to designate a man reputed to be the new head of the Scaniello crime family.

''That's exactly my point,'' Matt said. He settled back in his chair like a man victorious in argument. ''Because of Frankie's reputation, you and everyone else in this city are willing to believe he clipped Nunzie. But we do not convict people of murder in this country solely on the basis of reputation.''

It came to me that reputation was at the heart of the case against Matt. He was the aging gunslinger all the up-and-coming shootists wanted to best. He was the bull moose whose magnificent antlers the hunters wanted gracing their walls. Convicting him would make Nick Lazarus a famous man, a man who might rise politically the same way Tom Dewey and Rudy Giuliani had risen.

I'd been spooning *tiramisu* into my mouth as I listened to Riordan tell the story. Now I put the tiny silver spoon down with a clatter as I realized what else I was doing: writing my summation in the case of *United States of America* v. *Matthew Daniel Riordan*.

My mental checklist was forgotten; I no longer remembered how many check marks were in each of my columns. It no longer mattered.

I had taken the case.

To a Brooklyn lawyer, a trip to lower Manhattan was like a shopping spree on upper Fifth Avenue. The courthouses were more imposing; the people on the crowded streets were more important and better dressed. And the prices were higher.

I passed the Municipal Building—a huge wedding cake on the outside, a rat's maze on the inside—and kept going along Centre Street. If I kept moving, I'd come to 100 Centre, the huge monolith that housed the supreme court and criminal courts, as well as the infamous Tombs prison. If I stopped a little short of that, I'd be at 60 Centre, the picturesque old civil courthouse they always show on television when they want to display New York jurisprudence.

But today I was headed for the big time, for the federal courthouse that was home to the Southern District of New York, the gold-topped building that sat in Foley Square like a duchess. There were police barricades on the sidewalk in front of the long stone staircase that led up to the door; reporters with minicams milled around, smoking and waiting. Waiting for what? I wondered; I had a quick frisson of anticipation as I realized they might recognize me as Riordan's lawyer and pepper me with questions I wasn't ready to answer. But then I laughed at myself; they weren't here for me or Riordan—yet. They were here because Riordan's former client, Frankie Cretella, was on trial in a RICO case. The reporters were waiting for Cretella's new lawyer—who just happened to be Riordan's former associate, Kurt Hallengren. Kurt was riding the case for all it was worth; he was well on his way to supplanting his old boss as the preeminent criminal lawyer in New York.

Come next week, when I showed up for Riordan's arraignment, the reporters would beg me for a sound bite; today, they didn't know me from Eve, and that was fine with me. I wrapped myself in anonymity and strode up the stone steps, then pushed open the heavy door that led to the lobby.

The ceilings were higher than St. Patrick's Cathedral, and decorated almost as elaborately. Gold-edged bas-relief flowers painted in blue and rust-red, long-stemmed chandeliers, and windows which let the light through in shafts that illuminated the building like well-placed track lights. I looked up and stifled the quick feeling of awe, the sense of being dwarfed by a place of quiet power. What I was feeling was exactly what the architect of this building wanted me to feel, which was reason enough to resist the emotion.

I pulled out my lawyer's identification and showed it to the uniformed guard, then bypassed the metal detectors and made my way to the elevator banks. There were two sets, one to the tenth floor and the other from ten to twenty. I pushed the button for the second bank and waited.

In Brooklyn, they say it is better to know the judge than to know the law. Here in federal court, I knew neither the judge nor the law; I'd come to get a sneak preview of what I'd be up against the next time I walked through the gilded doors.

My old friend Lani Rasmussen, who'd transferred from Brooklyn Legal Aid to Federal Defender Services, sat behind her desk, stockinged feet propped up on a half-open file drawer, loafers on the floor next to three huge piles of file folders. She wore a drip-dry khaki blazer and a shapeless navy skirt with an Oxford-cloth shirt. A female version of the standard Legal Aid uniform. Clothes for the woman who hates clothes.

"I guess you want some idea of what you're up against," she said by way of greeting. She stood up and slipped her shoes on.

"I also want lunch," I said, nodding assent. "Where shall we eat?"

"I know just the place," she said with a grin. "You'll love it. You can have any kind of food you want, and the atmosphere can't be beat."

I couldn't believe it when my old pal marched me down the stone steps to the row of food booths that were set up every summer in the plaza between the courthouse and the Municipal Building.

True, you could get any kind of food you wanted, from Greek salads to Chinese lo mein to Ferrara's tart lemon ices. But you had to sit at metal picnic tables that were chained to the ground so that enterprising New York thieves didn't haul them away in pickup trucks during the night. And the food was just short of fast-food bland, for all the pretense to ethnic diversity. Why were we eating here when the neighborhood held such a wealth of really good restaurants?

"I have a client coming by in a half hour," Lani explained. "She has to sign an affidavit for me on a motion to suppress. I think I'll go for a black bean burrito," she went on, making her way to the line of customers waiting at the booth marked "The Whole Enchilada."

A black bean burrito sounded good; I stepped into line with her. "Anything you can tell me about Lazarus' case against Riordan," I began, "even the most off-the-wall courthouse gossip, could help. What have you heard?"

"I know what everybody knows," Lani replied. "That

the minute Eddie Fitz said he could bring down Matt Riordan, Nick Lazarus had him transferred out of Brooklyn and assigned full-time to the Court Corruption Task Force.''

"Eddie Fitz," I echoed, thinking aloud. "This is Detective Fitzgerald, I take it." My friend nodded. "He's the one who testified before the Mollen Commission? The one who started all this bullshit about corruption in the courts? I don't remember running into him in the courthouses in Brooklyn. What precinct did he work out of?"

"I don't know," Lani replied. "Someplace black. Brownsville or Bed-Stuy. The kind of neighborhood that just loves young Irish cops from Long Island coming in like centurions occupying Gaul."

"I should be able to get the skinny on him," I said. We were at the head of the line; we placed our orders and watched the man behind the counter wrap black beans and pork in a huge flour tortilla. "My contacts in Brooklyn are second to none. What I need from you is Manhattan dirt."

"If it's dirt you want," Lani said, making her way through the crowd, paper plate in one hand, giant soda in the other, "you need to concentrate on Fat Jack Vance."

She led me to a table in the shade. I slid onto the metal bench and set my plate down. For a moment I wondered whether it was prudent to have our conversation in such a public place, then realized there were very few people who looked like lawyers eating here.

"Riordan's co-defendant?" I asked; a dumb question. How many Fat Jack Vances were there in Manhattan, anyway?

Lani nodded. "His crimee, as we used to say in Brooklyn."

I smiled the obligatory answering smile, but I didn't like the implication. *Crimee* meant that two defendants had committed a crime together, and I wasn't about to begin Riordan's defense by believing he was guilty.

"What about Fat Jack?" I asked. I unwrapped the burrito

and lifted it to my mouth. It was hot and squishy and tasted dark and satisfying. Maybe booth-food wasn't so bad, after all.

"Fat Jack is a sleaze," Lani said matter-of-factly. "He doesn't just handle bail bonds, he acts as an investigator—which means he produces phony alibis and pays off corrupt cops who want to sell their cases. And he's worked for Matt Riordan for about twenty-five years. So when Eddie Fitz says the money he handed Paulie the Cork came from Riordan through Fat Jack, I for one have no trouble believing him."

She fixed me with her clear brown eyes, eyes that sat in her makeupless face and challenged me. "And when Fat Jack says he got the money from his boss, I have no trouble believing that either. Nor do I find it outside the realm of possibility that the reason Nunzie got dead in a car is that he crossed Matt Riordan and Frankie Cretella. Is this really," she asked in an uncharacteristically solemn tone of voice, "the kind of guy you want for a client? I know you and he had a thing for a while, but that doesn't mean—"

A thing. Yes, that was what you called it when it wasn't love and it wasn't exactly an affair either. A friendship with extras, I'd called our relationship when I tried to describe it. A friendship with bed privileges. A thing.

And now it was over.

Or was it?

"That has nothing to do with my representing him," I said firmly, hoping to hell I was telling the truth. "I can't stand the way they're all ganging up on him. This is part of the war against the defense bar," I went on. "If Lazarus has his way, every defense lawyer who's any good will find himself facing indictment on something or other."

"Cass, come on," my friend remonstrated, the effect only slightly spoiled by a mouthful of black beans, "you can't really believe the only reason Matt Riordan is facing indictment is that Lazarus has a vendetta against him. He's played fast and loose with the system for a long time—and you're running a risk of being tarred with the same brush if you take his case.''

"Oh, that's nice," I shot back. "You mean I'm supposed to stand back and let Riordan get railroaded so I can keep my skirts clean? This does not sound like the Lani Rasmussen I used to know.''

Lani finished her burrito and took a swig of soda. It caught in her throat, producing an unladylike burp. She laughed. "Why did you take this case, anyway?'' she asked.

This was a question to which I'd given a lot of thought since I'd sat across from my client at Tre Scalini. And all the reasons I'd come up with really boiled down to one.

"Have you ever heard of a place called Cedar Point?'' I asked. Lani shook her head. "It's a big amusement park in Sandusky, Ohio," I explained. "We used to go there every summer when I was a kid. My brother, Ron, and I would ride the roller coaster, a big old wooden thing called the Blue Streak.'' I leaned back on the picnic table and cupped my knee in my hand.

"We thought that roller coaster was the scariest thing in the world," I said, letting reminiscence wash over me. "We'd sit in the front car and scream bloody murder when the coaster went around curves. Sometimes it felt as if all the cars were going to run right off the tracks and land us in Lake Erie. We loved the thing.''

"What's this got to do with—''

"Patience," I said, holding up a restraining hand. "I outgrew Cedar Point for a while," I went on. "But then I went with a bunch of college friends one summer. I couldn't wait to show them the Blue Streak. Only a funny thing happened—they'd built a new roller coaster, bigger and faster and scarier. They called it the Mean Streak.''

I smiled at the memory. Next to the Mean Streak, the old Blue Streak was a kiddie ride. Or so I bragged to my friends as I made my way to the front car of the big new roller coaster.

"I thought I was going to die," I told Lani, recounting my first trip. "By the time it was over, I was sobbing with terror and relief. The Mean Streak had lived up to its name."

Brooklyn state court, where I knew all the plunges, all the curves, all the acceleration points, was the old Blue Streak. The Southern District, the federal court, was the Mean Streak. It was bigger, scarier, with curves I didn't anticipate, speeds I might not be ready for. But I had to try it. I couldn't spend my life on the kiddie rides, afraid to test myself on the big one. I explained this as best I could to Lani, and then we sat in silence, a silence I broke by asking, "What else have they got on Riordan?"

"Word on the street is that Fat Jack is on tape telling Eddie Fitz the money came directly from Matt Riordan."

Tape. They had a tape. Maybe tapes plural.

"Is Riordan himself on tape?" I tried to keep my voice neutral, but the panic edged through. Lani's smile was one part pity, two parts innocent malice.

"I hear your client's golden voice is on at least two of the tapes," she replied. "But the bulk of their case is Eddie Fitz and Fat Jack."

My defense jelled as I sat across from my old buddy. I saw myself at counsel table, flanked on one side by Matt Riordan—and on the other by the slimeball known on the street as Fat Jack.

Ladies and gentlemen of the jury, the evidence is clear that Jack Vance, known for obvious reasons as Fat Jack, knowingly and deliberately paid money to a corrupt court clerk in return for grand jury minutes. This was a crime. This was wrong.

And we have Fat Jack's word—and only Fat Jack's word, ladies and gentlemen, because Eddie Fitzgerald was only repeating the words Fat Jack said to him—that the money came from Matt Riordan.

It would be a mudslinging contest between Fat Jack and Matt Riordan—and there was little doubt in my mind that the jury would have no trouble choosing which man to trust.

Our whole defense would depend upon the fat man sitting next to Matt.

I could handle this, I decided; the Mean Streak wasn't as scary as it looked.

CHAPTER THREE

"You *said* there wouldn't be a little black suit," I protested through clenched teeth. "You *said* I could be myself."

"I forgot that your idea of dressing for success is a hand-sewn Afghan smock from the Daily Planet catalogue," Riordan replied with a wry smile. He sat on a red plush stool; I stood before a beveled three-way mirror in my stocking feet. An Ann Taylor suit in a deep charcoal with faint chalk stripes hung from my frame like a burlap sack.

"It's too boxy," I said. My voice held exactly the same shade of sullen resentment I'd used at age ten when shopping at Horne's with my mother.

"True," Riordan agreed in a cheerful tone that steadfastly refused to acknowledge my mood. "A woman in a suit should always look as if she's not wearing anything underneath. There should be a provocative little hint of cross-dressing, of feminine charms hidden under a deceptively masculine wrapping."

"When the hell did you start writing for *Women's Wear*

Daily?'' I shot back. I felt like a fool. Worse, I felt like Julia Roberts in *Pretty Woman*, like Eliza Doolittle, like the original Galatea, like every woman who has ever let a man dictate to her how she should present herself. Riordan had hired a lawyer, not a mannequin, and it was about time I—

"Everything counts," my client said in a low voice. The testiness in his tone was overlaid by an intense conviction. As much as Matt Riordan was capable of speaking directly from the heart, he was speaking that way now. "I know you think it's enough to know the law, to be quick on your feet, to care about your cases. But when I say everything counts, I mean everything, including physical appearance. And yours," he went on, "could stand a little improvement. More Manhattan, less Brooklyn. More Wall Street, less Legal Aid."

"More Jane Pauley, less me," I muttered. But the sullen edge left my voice; I was just bantering now.

Everything counts. That was Riordan in a nutshell. His own appearance was a matter of constant, meticulous concern. I'd given him a tie one Christmas; he'd never worn it, and when I asked why, he told me. At length. He was only doing to me what he'd always done to himself.

"Just try on the next suit," Riordan begged. "I think the amethyst raw silk has possibilities."

It did. Believe it or not, I looked great in the thing. It had a peplum and a rounded forties collar with rhinestone clips. Very period, nipped at the waist with a straight skirt that ended just above the knees. Short enough to show leg; long enough for a woman who hadn't worn a miniskirt since the last time they were in style.

Pearl-gray pumps, gray hose with just a touch of lavender, silver earrings, and a haircut that cost more than my last year's entire beauty shop budget—and I was finally ready for prime time.

We grabbed a cappuccino at a little place on Madison Avenue. I had six shopping bags filled with silk items, two shoe bags holding Louis Jourdan pumps, and a wardrobe of scarves in colors like eggplant and teal. I was also under orders to wear only my most conservative, absolutely real jewelry. No craft fair finds in hammered silver, no hand-made Navajo turquoise, no images of animals.

I had appointments for a facial, a leg waxing, and a man-icure. Was I preparing to try a case or enter the Miss Amer-ica contest? I absentmindedly raised a hand to my hair, intending to run my fingers through it, but instead of the real thing, I now had a headful of doll hair, sprayed into plastic straw. I grimaced and lowered my hand.

Would Riordan have done the same—minus the leg wax-ing—if he'd hired a male lawyer? Looking at his razor-cut hair, well-groomed nails, and impeccable wardrobe, I knew the answer: He sure as hell would. And that, somehow, made it all right.

Halfway through my first cup of the foamy, caffeine-laden brew, Matt began to talk about his father. I was so surprised, I put the cup down onto the saucer with an au-dible clatter and stared at my companion. He had never, but never, mentioned his parents or his childhood to me in all the years we'd been together.

"We were living in Hell's Kitchen back then," he said. "In those days, wives didn't work unless their husbands were seriously deficient."

I nodded; my own mother hadn't begun her career in real estate until both her children were in college.

"So we lived on my father's bus-driver salary," he went on. "Which meant we were just a little bit poorer than some of the other people on the block, a little richer than others. My father used to lay bets with the bartender at the Shan-non Bar and Grill over on Tenth Avenue. Never won much. Hell, he never won a damned thing, which was why my mother used to cry when he'd come home with half his paycheck riding on some broken-down nag out at Aque-duct. He'd always tell her that one day his horse would come in, and when it did, we could move out of the neighborhood and go to the Bronx, where things were good.''

I laughed aloud. The idea of the Bronx, the city's most dangerous borough, being a good place to raise kids was a concept totally new to me.

"Hey, don't laugh," he protested, but the smile lines around his eyes forgave me. "In those days, moving to Parkchester was the best thing that could happen to an Irish family. My parents talked about the Bronx as if it were the Promised Land.''

It came to me that the reason Matt was talking to me about his family was that I was now his lawyer. What he'd kept hidden from his sometime girlfriend could be spoken about with his legal representative. We were closer as lawyer and client than we'd ever been as lovers.

"One day it happened. The horse he'd bet on came in first. Forty to one odds. He'd put down a thousand bucks, more than he'd ever bet before. He said it was because he had a tip from the jockey's second cousin's best friend, but who cared how it happened? The really important thing was that he'd won, that he was going to get forty thousand dollars and we were going to move to the Bronx.''

I happened to know Matt had never lived in the Bronx.

"Something went wrong," I guessed. "What was it?"

"The bartender who took the bet worked for the Westies," he said. "They were behind the whole betting operation. Not that we in the neighborhood ever called them Westies—that was a name the press made up. But forty thousand bucks was an amount they just couldn't see paying off on. They welshed on the bet, and when my father went to the Shannon to collect, they beat him up. Badly. He was in the hospital two weeks, and when he came home, he couldn't talk because his jaw was wired. The night he came home," Matt went on, his own jaw clenching with remembered anger, "the very night, he had us pack up all our things and move out. We slunk out of the neighborhood like a bunch of thieves, as if he'd done something wrong. He didn't have what it took to stand up to them.''

"Didn't he go to the police?" I asked. "Not about the bet," I clarified. "I know the cops couldn't have done anything to help him collect on an illegal bet. But beating someone up is a crime, right?"

"That's the part I could never forget," Matt said. His smooth-as-silk voice grew ragged as he finished the tale. "Or forgive. The neighborhood cop, Tommy Mackay, stopped by and talked to my father. Told him, sure, he could file a complaint, but he went on to say that the cops couldn't protect him twenty-four hours a day, and maybe it would be better for all concerned if he made a complaint that a couple of niggers beat him up. That, by the way, was his precise wording: 'a couple of niggers.' When Tommy knew what the whole neighborhood knew: that Pop was beaten up by the Westies because he'd dared to ask for his money from the bet. As we left the neighborhood that night, as all my clothes and toys went into a rented truck and we drove up Broadway to Inwood as if we'd done something wrong, I swore to God I'd never take that kind of shit in my own life. And I swore that I'd show cops like Tommy that they couldn't push people around like they pushed my father."

I said nothing for a full minute, then quietly asked, "So you think Nick Lazarus is a little like Tommy the cop? Pushing people around just because he can?"

"I do," my client replied. "And I'm counting on you to help me show him he can't. I'm not sneaking out of the neighborhood this time, no matter what the bullies try to do to me."

We went to court two days later. Nick Lazarus had filed his indictment and Matt was charged with bribing a federal official.

We were mobbed on the way into the courthouse. The

reporters and minicams behind the police barricades were waiting for me this time. No cameras were allowed inside the sacred precincts of the federal courthouse; they would have to garner their sound bites on the steps before trial began. Ginger Hsu of Channel Five thrust a mike into my face and asked, "What do you think your client's chances of acquittal are, Ms. Jameson?"

I mouthed a "No comment" and pushed past the crowd. I was almost at the top of the stairs when I felt a tug on my silk-clad sleeve. I turned; Matt had my arm. He stopped me and motioned toward the steps below us.

About halfway up, standing in the exact spot where the minicams would get a nice shot of the impressive courthouse columns behind him, stood Nick Lazarus. I couldn't hear the words, but every one of the reporters listened, microphones poised, as he spoke. Next to him, Davia Singer wore a carefully schooled expression of neutrality on her thin face. It was the kind of expression a wife wears in public when her husband flirts with the waitress, a wait-till-I-get-you-home look. It was the expression my face undoubtedly would have worn if my boss had hogged the cameras on my case.

Riordan stepped toward the knot of reporters. I wanted to grab his sleeve and pull him back, but he was too quick for me. By the time I caught up, he was at the edge of the crowd. I caught the last few words out of Nick Lazarus' mouth: "Matt Riordan is a cancer in this courthouse," he intoned, "and this trial will remove that cancer once and for all."

He's no Cancer, I thought with flippant irrelevance, *he's a Scorpio*. I had no idea what Matt was going to say, but it was clear to me he wasn't going to let Lazarus have the last word with the press.

Carlos Ruiz of Channel Seven stood next to Riordan. He nudged his cameraman, who turned the lens toward my client. Other reporters and camera people realized Riordan was nearby, and soon all the lenses were focused on him, all the mikes were poised and waiting for his reply to the insulting challenge just issued by the prosecution.

Ruiz was known for his cocky, street-kid style. Geraldo Lite. "So, Riordan," he began, "this Lazarus dude says you're a cancer. That true, or what, man?"

It was the perfect setup; if Riordan had paid Ruiz to ask the question, it couldn't have gone better. "A cancer?" he quipped. "At best, I'm a hernia. A pain in the you-know-what. And you want to know something?"

By now all the reporters had zeroed in on Matt; Lazarus stood alone, flanked only by Davia Singer.

Matt's resonant voice lowered just a tad, making them edge in a little closer. Emphasizing the fact that the reporters were hanging on his every word, Lazarus forgotten. "It's my job to be a pain in the you-know-what. And Nick Lazarus doesn't like it when I do my job, so he's trumped up this case to teach me a lesson. Well, you wait and see who learns a lesson here. Just wait and see. That's my advice to all of you."

There were more questions, but Matt waved them away with a friendly smile. He turned and strode back up the steps, without a backward glance to see whether or not I was following.

It wasn't until we reached the landing at the top of the stairs that he acknowledged my existence. He wheeled on me so suddenly, I took a step backwards. His face was a mottled red and the veins stood out in his neck. He shoved me behind one of the massive pillars and pinned me against the smooth marble with a sinewy arm.

"You will *never*, ever use the words 'no comment' again while you are my lawyer," he said in a thick voice, biting off each word. "This is a media case and the only way we are going to win is to play the media as carefully as we play the judge and jury. If you have a problem with that, say so now and I'll find somebody else to represent me."

When I'd agreed to take Matt's case, I had no idea I'd be riding the Mean Streak outside the courtroom as well as inside. I nodded, too upset to speak, but knowing he was right. As long as Lazarus intended to try his case on the courthouse steps, we had to do the same.

I had to do the same. I should have been the one to talk to the reporters, not Matt. It was my place, not his. He had only stepped up to the plate after I'd struck out.

I had to get a hit next time, or admit I wasn't ready for the bigs.

I pushed open the giant carved wooden door to the courtroom with the name Justice de Freitas on the identifying plaque, and stepped onto the big roller coaster.

I'd thrown up my popcorn and cotton candy after my first ride on the real Mean Streak; walking into my first-ever federal courtroom, representing the most famous defendant I'd ever had, I felt the same queasiness in my stomach. Of course, I reassured myself, this time I hadn't had five beers and two joints before getting on the roller coaster.

I reminded myself I'd gone back later for a second ride. By the time we'd left Cedar Point, the Mean Streak was my new favorite. I hoped I'd feel the same way about high-profile federal cases sometime before the verdict came in.

Davia Singer sat at the prosecution table with her file spread out before her in neat, orderly stacks of paper. I gazed at her as I made my way up the aisle toward the defense table. What kind of lawyer was she? I wondered. How would we play against one another at trial?

Davia. A soft, evocative name. A name that promised loose curls framing an olive-skinned face with huge dark eyes. A name that promised a soft, slightly accented voice. A name that held mystery, femininity, yet conveyed the strength of a David.

Which left me playing the uncoveted role of Goliath.

Lazarus stood aside and smiled as Riordan and I walked

through the heavy door. It was the smile of a predator who sees his prey coming within claw range. I smiled back, beaming confidently. If there was one thing I'd learned from the man who was now my client, it was to radiate confidence no matter what. In fact, the more scared you were, the more important it was to make people think you had the world by the tail.

I stepped up to the defense table and set my briefcase on its shiny surface. I opened it and pulled out a yellow legal pad and a nearly-empty manila folder. I set them carefully on the table, marking my territory as instinctively as a cat.

I had to make the courtroom as much mine as Davia Singer's. I opened my card case, took out a card with my name and address on it, and walked up to the court reporter. I handed it to him with a smile and told him I'd want the arraignment minutes as soon as possible. "I'm willing to pay rush rates," I added.

This was Riordan's idea. It was the legal equivalent of handing the maitre d' a big tip to insure good service.

The courtroom was filling up. The reporters were print people, for the most part; without cameras in the courtroom, the television types were limited in their coverage. I recognized *Village Voice* columnist Jesse Winthrop, the grand old man of New York City muckraking, in the first row. He still resembled an urban Jewish John Brown, with deep-set eyes that burned with indignation.

The rest of the rows were occupied by well-dressed young lawyers. Probably Singer's cheering section; baby U.S. Attorneys eager to see the aging gunslinger Matt Riordan brought down by one of their own. She was a new import from Brooklyn, I'd recently learned. She'd transferred from the quieter precincts of the Eastern District to the goldfish bowl of the Southern.

The huge door swung open and a grossly fat man waddled up the aisle, trailed by a ferret of a man with a bald pate and a furtive glance. Fat Jack Vance, Riordan's bail bondsman, had arrived, along with his lawyer, a Baxter Street hack named Sid Margolies.

"All rise. The United States District Court in and for the Southern District of New York is now in session. All those who have business before this court draw near and give your attention."

I rose, my heart thudding with anticipation. Judge de Freitas stepped forward and took the bench. He was a small, neat man with liver spots on his bald crown. With his sad eyes and sagging jowls, he bore an uncanny resemblance to the late Adlai Stevenson. He had taught Evidence before his elevation to the bench; one of his prize students at Fordham Law School had been a young Matt Riordan.

The bailiff called the case. I felt a jolt of doubt and fear as the words were spoken out loud: "United States of America versus Matthew Daniel Riordan and John Anthony Vance."

I was used to having the state of New York lined up against my client, but this time it was the whole country.

We began the ritual.

"Mr. Riordan, you are charged with violating Title 18, Section 201 of the United States Code. How do you plead?"

"Not guilty, Your Honor," Matt said in ringing tones. As the lawyer, I usually answered on my client's behalf, but with the reporters avidly taking in every nuance, we'd decided Riordan should proclaim his innocence early and often.

"Ms. Singer," the judge went on in a thin, dry voice I knew was going to get on my nerves at trial, "do you have Rule 16 material to turn over to defense counsel?"

Singer nodded and handed me one of the massive piles of material on her table; I acknowledged receipt for the record and tried not to look as daunted as I felt. There was an envelope on top, bulging with hard, rectangular objects: tape cassettes.

They had him on tape. Lani had warned me, but it still felt as if the roller-coaster was taking a hundred-yard plunge, leaving my stomach on the platform.

The bailiff turned his attention to our co-defendant. I breathed a sigh of relief.

"Mr. Vance, how do you plead to these charges?"

The roller-coaster swerved, nearly knocking me out of the seat. Instead of the "not guilty" I'd been expecting, Sid Margolies replied, "Your Honor, Mr. Vance pleads guilty to the crime of aiding and abetting a bribery."

I shot a quick glance at Davia Singer. She was wearing a catlike smile, a smile that said she knew she'd scored the first points in this game. She'd done something I hadn't anticipated, for starters, and she'd taken away one of my most important weapons in Matt's defense.

I needed Fat Jack at trial. I could have made a motion under Rule 14 to sever Matt's case and try him separately from the bail bondsman. I hadn't made the motion because I needed the fat man sitting next to Riordan, looking gross and slimy, in sharp contrast to my client's dapper appearance. I needed him as the jury's focus, as the man who'd really done the bribing, using Matt's name but without authority to do so. A guilty plea took him out of the case and left Matt facing the music alone.

It got worse. My stomach churned as I listened to Fat Jack enter his plea. Aiding and abetting—and in order to plead to aiding and abetting, he had to recite chapter and verse regarding exactly whom he'd aided and abetted. And that meant Matt.

According to Fat Jack, Riordan had given him money to give to Eddie Fitz in return for the minutes of the grand jury testimony of one Annunziato Aiello. He'd been the go-between, and he made it very clear that he'd received money from Matt and delivered the grand jury minutes directly into Matt's hands.

Which explained the plea. The prosecution was letting

Fat Jack cop a plea in exchange for his testimony against Matt. Singer would call Vance to the stand, and I'd have a shot at showing the jury he'd cut a deal to save his oversized ass at my client's expense. It was a standard prosecution ploy, and one I was increasingly certain I could deal with at trial.

I could handle this, I told myself, as my stomach settled down. The Mean Streak wasn't so different from the old wooden roller coaster I was used to.

When Fat Jack was finished, Davia Singer assured the court on the record that no consideration had been offered for this plea. It was legalese for "there was no deal."

I gave what I hoped was a ladylike snort of derision; of course Fat Jack had cut a deal; he was going to catch a break on sentence, the U.S. attorney was going to put him on the stand and turn him against Matt, and I was going to have a field day explaining to the jury just how far they could trust a man who'd copped a plea in return for his testimony.

What was Singer thinking? Fat Jack Vance as the linchpin of the government's case? The same Fat Jack who had apparently just pled guilty to fraud? Matt had assured me that Vance's troubles in Brooklyn were wholly unconnected to our case; they involved a construction company and a multimillion-dollar negligence claim. If Singer intended to put Fat Jack on the stand against Riordan, I'd have a cross-examination made in heaven.

I tuned back in; they were talking sentence. "The government will make no recommendation as to sentence, Your Honor," Singer was saying, "except that it is to run concurrent with whatever sentence is imposed in the Eastern District of New York on the unrelated charge of criminal conspiracy to defraud."

It was a cute trick. By avoiding any recommendation on the record, by deferring to the Eastern District on sentence, Singer was laying the groundwork for denying a deal in front of Riordan's jury. She would be able to tell them she hadn't offered Fat Jack a cut in sentence in return for his testimony against Matt because the sentence that counted was being imposed in an unrelated case across the river and had nothing to do with her or her office.

It was a cute trick, but it wasn't going to work. No jury could listen to this and believe there was no deal. Fat Jack on the stand was something I was very much looking forward to.

I made a mental note to follow up on something Matt had told me: that Davia Singer had begun her prosecutorial career in the Eastern District, under Dominick Di Blasi. Did that mean she and her old boss were up to something regarding Vance? I intended to find out.

And then the roller coaster took another sharp swerve. "Mr. Vance will not be called at trial by the prosecution," Singer announced. She gave another one of her enigmatic smiles; she was enjoying this. It was as if she'd anticipated every turn my mind would take—and then shot down all my assumptions, stymied all my strategies. Of course, that was her job as a lawyer and a prosecutor. I just wished she wasn't so damned good at it.

I stood as straight and still as a redwood tree. And just about as intelligent; I was having a hard time adjusting to the concept of a trial without Fat Jack as a co-defendant and/or witness for the prosecution. My entire defense strategy depended on Fat Jack, and now the prosecution was letting him walk. And trying to convince the judge there had been no deal.

But why let Jack take a walk unless they could squeeze him to testify against the man he'd worked for?

There had to be a deal. But how were we going to prove it?

I stepped out of the courtroom feeling almost as queasy as I had the first time I'd ridden the real Mean Streak.

Riordan maintained his coiled-spring cool until we

jumped into a cab on Centre Street, and then he exploded.

"That fucking bastard," he burst out, the consonants hitting the air with hard little sounds like a bullet fired through a silencer. "That unscrupulous scumbag, that—"

"I take it you're referring to Nick Lazarus," I said mildly.

"He lets Jack cop a plea, then tries to sell the judge that there's no deal. Of course there's a deal, for God's sake. What does he think we are, stupid?"

"We've got three weeks to prove there's a deal," I pointed out. "Three weeks to prepare our defense. Of course," I went on, thinking aloud, "we could always ask for an adjournment if we can't—"

"No adjournments," my client announced. "Adjournments are for losers."

I shelved the discussion; it would only be important if we actually needed to put the case over. But Matt wouldn't let it go. He turned to me in the back seat of the cab and locked onto my eyes. "Lazarus will jump like a cougar on any sign of weakness," he elaborated, "and I'm not going to give him anything he can jump on. He smells blood in the water, he'll be like a shark, taking bites out of us. So no adjournments no matter what. I don't care if the judge calls us tomorrow and wants to pick a jury at ten o'clock, we're ready. Got that?"

I nodded. The cab had snaked its way through traffic and was facing horn-honking gridlock at Canal Street. Crossing Canal during rush hour was like fording the Mississippi; it would take a good five minutes just to get through the intersection, and the Israeli cab driver would be leaning on the horn all the way. Conversation, however important, was no longer possible.

I leaned back in my seat and enjoyed the reprieve. It would last, I knew, only until we reached Riordan's midtown office. Then we'd resume my postgraduate course in federal criminal practice.

Ten minutes later, we took a right on Forty-second, and went around the block. The cabbie let us off in front of an imposing office building with rococo gold trim. The Helmsley Building, it was called, and its choicest offices had panoramic views of Park Avenue.

Matt paid the cabbie and I hopped out into the overheated air. I waited for him on the sidewalk, which was so hot it burned the soles of my feet through my thin shoes. I nodded at the doorman, who smiled broadly as he held open the gilded door. Riordan always got first-class service, thanks to the hefty tips he handed out at Christmas.

You entered Matt's office in three stages. First, the waiting room, with its Daumier legal prints on the wall, its dark green leather couch, its exotic flower arrangement with pale peach lilies and deep mauve chrysanthemums. Tasteful but not personal, a waiting room that deliberately said as little as possible about Riordan's true personality.

The next room was the one Matt called the parlor. It was decorated in the same deep green and pink-peach tones, but here the effect was welcoming, homey. The green was the background color of a chintz pattern that covered two armchairs, placed at angles for easy conversation. A small drop-leaf table was set between the chairs, and a reading lamp stood behind one of them. It was a cozy nook where two people could engage in the most intimate kind of discussion. It was where Matt routinely accepted the most sacred confidences from his clients.

The inner sanctum was Matt's own personal office. The desk was clear and the green leather office chair was shiny and new-looking, but it was a working environment. Piles of transcripts sat on side tables, open law books rested on chairs, and the art on the walls reflected Matt's personal taste.

Matt led me to the office, bypassing the parlor area. "I don't know about you," I began, trailing him through the rooms, "but I could use a drink."

"Got just the thing, babe," he called over his shoulder. Opening the door of a mini-fridge, he took out a chilled bottle of pepper vodka, poured a generous slug into a heavy old-fashioned glass, and handed it to me. The combination of fire and ice was like drinking a melted diamond.

Matt heaved a sigh and flung himself into his leather chair. He looked tired and old, jaws sagging, eyelids drooping. I glanced at a framed courtroom sketch of him as a fire-eating young trial honcho and the contrast stabbed my heart.

I decided getting down to business was the only thing that could cheer Matt. "Okay," I began, "we play the tapes. Since you never gave Jack money for the grand jury minutes, there won't be anything that can really hurt us. Then we investigate this plea of Jack's across the river."

I stopped and locked eyes with my client. "What I'd like right this minute," I began, keeping my tone conversational, "is one more assurance that whatever Jack did to get himself indicted in Brooklyn is not going to affect this case."

He returned my stare with a steady gaze. "Nothing to do with me," he said. He lifted his glass to his lips and tossed back the vodka with a practiced movement. "But I'd give a lot to know what the hell Di Blasi's up to over there. It's obvious why Lazarus wants to let the Eastern District handle the sentence; they want deniability. They want to be able to say they're not going easy on Jack. But why is Di Blasi going along? He hates Lazarus—everyone knows that—and word is he was pissed as hell when Singer left the office to take a job with Lazarus. She was his protégée, and her walking out was a hell of a blow to his ego."

"So why is he making it easy for them by taking Fat Jack off their hands?" I mused aloud, finishing his thought. "I'll see what I can find out," I promised. "Then I'll use my Brooklyn contacts to find out all I can about Detective

Edmund Fitzgerald. We should be able to do a lot of damage on cross.''

My client had begun shaking his head somewhere in the middle of my recital. ''No, babe,'' he said in a more-in-sorrow-than-anger tone of voice. ''No, that's not how this game is played. I don't play not to lose. I play to win.''

''And that means—what?'' I didn't bother to conceal the annoyance I was feeling. I had every intention of winning, and if Matt didn't realize that, then he might as well fire me right now.

''Did you ever hear of Cato the Elder?'' Matt asked. I shook my head; the name was vaguely familiar, but I could see Matt had a story he wanted to tell.

''He was a senator in ancient Rome,'' Matt explained. He leaned forward in his chair; the sag had left his jowls and his eyes had regained their spark. ''Rome was at war with a city called Carthage, and every time Cato the Elder stood up to speak in the Senate, he said the same thing: '*Cartaga delenda est.*' Carthage must be destroyed.''

''Which means?''

''Which means I want more out of this case than a 'not guilty' verdict,'' my client pronounced. ''As far as I'm concerned, Lazarus *delenda est.*''

Lazarus must be destroyed. I looked at Matt's face, and saw there what the ancient Romans must have seen on the face of Cato himself: implacable determination. My client wasn't kidding. Lazarus must be destroyed—and he wanted me to do it.

CHAPTER FOUR

The next issue of the *Village Voice*, which appeared a week after Matt's arraignment, featured Detective Edmund Fitzgerald, whom columnist Jesse Winthrop named the Hero Cop, on its cover page. For once, Winthrop's sarcastic knife wasn't out; he called Eddie "the last cop in this cesspool of a city with honor and integrity."

Eddie's face, his Irish-cop, grownup-altarboy face, stared up at me in gritty black-and-white. It was a face, I reflected glumly, that any jury would love: boyish and open, with a winning smile.

I looked from the newspaper to my client, comparing Eddie's youthful face to Matt Riordan's—the face that had launched a thousand acquittals. It was a handsome face, but it was also one that had known guile, a face that concealed hidden agendas. A face it would be easy to distrust.

We were in my office, on my turf. I'd insisted on that; it would be all too easy to let Matt run the show if we continued to discuss the case on Park Avenue. So he'd come to Brooklyn, still impeccably dressed, in a golf shirt and creased pants. I wore an old T-shirt with the slogan "A Woman Without a Man Is Like a Fish Without a Bicycle." In the months since Matt and I had broken up, that T-shirt had left my closet a lot more often.

"We've got to do something about this Eddie," I said. I wasn't crazy about the wistful note in my voice; I'd said the words as if the prospect of "doing something about Eddie" was a dream that might never come true. Not exactly the attitude of a winner.

The door opened and Angelina Irrizary, my investigator, bustled in. She tossed her oversized bag on the couch, and sat next to Matt with an eager expression on her small, heart-shaped face. "What's the story?" she asked, an anticipatory gleam in her eyes. "What's this case all about?"

I let Matt tell it. "I was stupid," he began. "I see now I was unequivocally stupid. I never should have let Jack talk me into meeting Eddie Fitz in the first place."

Angie nodded; with Eddie's face on the front page of the *Voice*, she had no reason to ask who Riordan was talking about.

"The first I knew about any of this," Matt went on, "Jack called me and said he wanted me to meet a friend of his, someone who might have heard something about Nunzie. I said I didn't want to hear any more. I blew him off."

He paused. I raised an eyebrow; if that had been the whole story, we wouldn't be here now preparing his defense to federal bribery charges.

"Jack called again. Again, I said no to a meeting. But then the rumors about Nunzie's disappearance began floating around the courthouse. People were saying Lazarus was trying to put together a case against me for murder. It was crazy talk, but this time when Jack called, I agreed to meet this guy Eddie."

"You knew he was a cop?"

"Hell, I counted on his being a cop," Matt said with the kind of disarming honesty that just might win points with a jury. "And, yes, we talked about the rumors around the courthouse. We talked about Nunzie. But I never told him I'd pay for grand jury minutes, and I never saw grand jury minutes."

"Wait a minute," I said, holding up a hand to stop the question hovering on Angie's lips. "Something just occurred to me." I turned to Matt. "What made you think Eddie Fitz could help you with information about Nunzie? Eddie was a Brooklyn cop," I explained, as much to myself as to my audience, "and Nunzie was part of a federal RICO case. Eddie had no reason to know about the inner workings of Lazarus' office, unless—"

I broke off and looked at my client expectantly. He sighed, and finished my sentence. "Unless I had reason to believe Eddie Fitz had a connection to Nunzie above and beyond just being a cop," he said.

"You said Nunzie was into drugs," I reminded him. "And Eddie Fitz was a member of an elite narcotics task force in Bed-Stuy," I continued. "Do I take it that Nunzie's drug empire was headquartered in the same neighborhood?" My voice quickened with anticipation; maybe there was something we could do about this Eddie after all.

Matt nodded, then sighed. "I knew a few things about Nunzie I didn't particularly want to know," he said in a resigned tone. "I had reason to believe his drug empire had more than a few Brooklyn cops on the payroll. When Jack mentioned Eddie Fitz, I remembered hearing Nunzie talk on the phone to someone he called Fast Eddie. I got the impression this Fast Eddie was a kind of partner in Nunzie's drug deals."

"A partner? Not just a cop who looked the other way, but a partner?" This was too good to be true: Lazarus' star witness was a drug dealer with a badge. Of course, we had yet to actually prove it, but it was definitely worth following up.

"That was how it sounded to me," Riordan said, then added, "But all I heard was the name Eddie. There could be six cops in that precinct named Eddie for all I know."

"But only one of them is Lazarus' star witness against you," I reminded him. "If there's a snowball's chance in hell that dirty cop was Eddie Fitz, we've got to get solid evidence and bring it into court."

"I'll start digging into the precinct," Angie promised. She began ticking off her prospective tasks on her polished fingernails. "I'll also check into Eddie Fitzgerald's finances, find out whether he lives like a cop or spends like a drug dealer."

"I'll get onto the Legal Aid grapevine," I said. "If there are rumors floating around Brooklyn about Eddie Fitz, I'll know someone who's heard them all." I gave my client a reassuring smile. "You do the organized crime," I said. "Leave the disorganized crime to me."

"Eddie Fitz on cross. God, this is a Brooklyn lawyer's wet dream," Deke Fischer said two days later. We sat at a little round table under an umbrella at a sidewalk cafe on Montague Street, sipping wine. Ten years earlier, we'd have held down the bar at Capulet's-on-Montague, a beery establishment we used to hit every Friday night, after a grueling week in court. Now it was white wine and mineral water and a table out of the sun. And instead of swapping tales of our adventures in court, we'd spent the first ten minutes comparing notes on health, our own and that of our acquaintances. Ah, middle age.

"I don't remember this Eddie," I complained.

"You left Legal Aid," Deke reminded me. "You've expanded your horizons. Oh, sure, you still take criminal cases, but you don't live in the narcotics parts the way we lifers do. If you did, you'd know Eddie Fitz, all right."

"Why? Why would I know Eddie Fitz?" I sipped the spritzer and made a face. I wanted real booze, but I also wanted to keep my head while talking to Deke.

"He's a mainstay of the Brooklyn war on drugs," my old friend replied. He ran a hand through a thinning thatch of kinky black hair. "He testifies in a lot of cases, and a lot of us think he perjures himself on a regular basis to get convictions. Some of us even go so far as to wonder which side of the drug war he's on."

"You mean you think Eddie's a bent cop," I confirmed. Deke nodded. "But can you prove it?"

"Hell, Cass, if I could prove it, I'd have won my last three trials. He put away three guys on drug deals I'd be willing to swear he took a cut from."

"You're saying he's a drug dealer?" Disbelief edged my voice; this was too good to be true. And Deke himself admitted it was sheer speculation, nothing I could take to a jury. Yet.

"Everybody in Brooklyn knows he is," Deke replied. This was hyperbole; what he meant was, everybody at Legal Aid was convinced they were losing cases because Eddie was a liar. "His partners are no prizes, either," he went on.

I fished a notebook out of my tote bag and took down names: Dwight Straub and Stan Krieger. Then I went back to the task at hand.

"You know as well as I do," I reminded Deke, "that what 'everybody in Brooklyn knows' is not admissible in evidence. What I need are solid facts. What I need are witnesses who'll come to court and tell the jury what Eddie Fitz is really all about. Can you help me with that?"

Deke laughed. It was a derisive laugh that held a tinge of self-disgust. "Sure, Cassie, for you, anything. The only problem is that all the witnesses I can get you are doing time. If you don't mind a little thing like that, I can give you six, seven names of people who'll roll over on Eddie Fitz.''

''Are they all junkies?'' I asked, my tone reflecting my disappointment. Deke was right; his former clients were unlikely to convince a jury to discount the testimony of the Hero Cop.

He nodded. ''Junkies are usually the people who tend to buy drugs,'' he said. ''Of course, they might have kicked in prison,'' he went on. His face brightened. ''They might have found Jesus or Allah and turned over a new leaf.''

''That'll help a lot,'' I mumbled. The trouble with Deke was that he was quite possibly serious in his assertion that getting religion in jail would turn a junkie felon into a credible witness against a member of New York's Finest. This level of denial was one reason I felt I could no longer practice law for the Legal Aid Society.

''There's a guy called TJ,'' Deke said. ''A black dude, lives in Eddie's precinct. Word on the street is that they're very tight, that TJ is Eddie's front man.'' He lifted his wineglass to his lips, then put it back down on the scarred table. ''If you could get TJ on the stand, you might have a chance of convincing a jury that Eddie's more crook than cop.''

''Why?'' I countered. ''Why should the word of a drug dealer carry more weight than that of a user?''

Deke's answering smile took ten years off his age. He sat back in his chair with the annoying self-satisfied look that had always pushed my buttons, and replied, ''Because this particular drug dealer happens to be a registered narcotics informant.''

''And I suppose Eddie was the cop who registered him?'' I demanded. ''God, what balls!'' I went on, lost in admiration. ''A cop who goes into business with a drug dealer covers his partner by registering him as an informant. That way if a cop who's not on the take busts the dealer, the bad cop can just step in and say, 'let him go, he's my snitch.' Perfect."

"Not exactly," Deke replied. "Eddie's partner, Stan Krieger, actually did the registering. But it comes to the same thing: TJ has credibility, and it was given to him by the cops themselves."

I thought about it. "So if I put TJ on the stand as a registered informant," I said, "the only way Singer can tear him down is to show he's a dealer—and if she does that, she admits that Eddie's own partner, this Krieger, is a bent cop."

"A nice double bind," Deke approved.

"So where can I find TJ?" I asked.

"I had a client who might be able to help," Deke replied. "I'll bring him down from upstate on a writ, and you can talk to him."

I paid for the drinks and walked home down Clinton Street—named for DeWitt, not Bill—with visions of destroying Eddie Fitz on the witness stand dancing in my head.

I'd met Jesse Winthrop once before; he'd looked just like the picture that headed his column: a fanatic's eyes, a mane of hair down to his shoulders, a handsome-craggy face. A New York face, full of dashed hopes and wry humor.

He looked old. Not just older, but old. The hair was still a good deal longer than most men wore in the nineties, but it was all white now, and hung limp and lank. The face was craggier than ever, but the fire in his eyes had banked. He looked tired; it was hard to put this old man together with the exposés that had electrified the city.

"Mr. Winthrop," I began, taking the chair nearest his and tossing my bag onto the floor. I wasn't sure exactly why I'd felt compelled to call him, to make an appointment to meet him and talk about Eddie Fitz. I just knew I somehow owed it to this man to let him know his Hero

Cop might take a big fall from the pedestal he'd placed him on. After two weeks of digging, I was beginning to see that Eddie Fitz had feet of very muddy clay indeed.

"Jesse," he amended. "And you are, as I recall, Cass instead of Cassie."

I nodded. "Good memory."

"Part of the job." He shifted his gaze to the window. We were seated at a window table at The Peacock, one of the Village's best coffeehouses. The tables were tiny wooden affairs that just barely managed to support coffee cups; the chairs were eclectic leftovers from Grandmother's attic, the atmosphere was dark and quiet, and they played good classical music. And the window seats looked directly out onto Greenwich Avenue, so you could sit for hours people-watching and sipping cappuccino.

It was a good place for a rendezvous, a place where you could tell secrets and the people at the next table wouldn't even give you a glance; they were busy arguing about the Czech movie they'd just seen at the Quad or doing their homework for NYU, scribbling on notepaper with a huge book open on the spindly table. Or they were in love; two twentysomething girls dressed in black held hands and gazed into one another's eyes at a table near the huge brass and copper coffee urn the owners had brought from the Old Country.

I'd once broken up with a boyfriend in here, and nobody noticed or cared that I stormed out in a flood of noisy tears.

"If a beached whale washes up on Coney Island," Jesse pronounced in his gravelly New York voice, "it's news. If a shark does the same thing, it's not. Nobody cares what happens to the shark, and nobody cares what happens to Matt Riordan."

"This is not the Jesse Winthrop I used to read," I said, letting my tone carry all the very real disappointment I was feeling. I'd hoped he'd be at the least a neutral observer of the trial, rather than a shill for Lazarus. "In the old days,"

I went on, "you would have lambasted Lazarus for bending the rules to nail Riordan. You would have reminded your readers that even a guy like Riordan deserves the Constitution, that the authorities can't convict him just because of his reputation. Hell," I said with a rueful smile, warming to my theme, "I can just see the article now. You'd have called it something like 'Even Sharks Can Be Endangered,' or—"

"How about 'Sympathy for the Devil'?" Winthrop cut in.

"I like it."

"Well, you're not going to see it in print anytime soon. I can't say I approve of everything Nick Lazarus has done on this case, but one thing I do know is that Eddie Fitz is a straight-arrow cop who did the right thing." The salt-and-pepper beard was now all salt, and the magnificent head of hair was a halo of white. Winthrop looked like an Old Testament prophet, but his prophecies had grown increasingly irrelevant as the sixties receded from the popular mind.

"You're very sure about that," I remarked. I opened my mouth to ask whether he had ever heard his Hero Cop mention a guy named TJ, but Jesse beat me to the conversational punch.

"I'd better be sure," he said. "I've got a book deal pending."

Why did this surprise me? Why did I rock back in the little wire chair and look at the man with new eyes?

Because on some level I'd still believed in Jesse Winthrop, the incorruptible journalist, the one lone guy who would never sell out, no matter what.

He caught the look; how could he not?

"Don't give me any self-righteous bullshit, Cass. I get enough of that from the little shits at the *Voice*, the ones who still think they can change the world with one more exposé on rotten landlords. I've been writing articles and columns for forty years now, and what have I got to show for it? I still live in a rent-controlled apartment, I drive a ten-year-old car, I take my vacations in what is euphemistically called a recreational vehicle and is really a sardine can on wheels. I keep going around and around on the carousel, but I never get close to the brass ring. Until now. Until I latched on to Eddie Fitz. I'm going to ride him to the big time, Counselor. My book will be another *Prince of the City*; my agent is already talking movie and I haven't written word one of the book. If Eddie Fitz is anything but a hero, I sure as hell don't want to know about it."

"Until after you've signed the contract," I amended.

His nod was firm. "Until after I've signed the contract," he repeated. His lips formed a smile, but to me it looked more like a rictus, which was appropriate. The Jesse Winthrop whose column I'd read for twenty years was dead.

I paid for the coffee and stepped out into the humid day with a heavy heart.

Deke's client, Shavon Pettigrew, was in shackles, which pleased the court officers no end. They loved it when state prisoners were brought in with leg irons and handcuffs chained to their belts. They marched him through the corridor to the lawyers' conference room and deposited him on a hard chair. They unlocked the shackles only when I asked; they'd have been happy to leave him trussed up like a dressed pig.

"Do I know you?" he asked with studied insolence. He sprawled in the seat, legs wide apart, the way some macho types sit on the subway, thrusting themselves physically into the space of the people sitting next to them. As if their status depended on the amount of cubic feet they could command.

"No, but I know you," I replied evenly. "Your lawyer said you might want to talk to me." It had taken me almost two weeks to pull the legal strings to bring him to Brooklyn. He *had* to talk—but I wasn't about to let him know how much I wanted his information.

"My lawyer," Pettigrew snorted. He corrected me with a contemptuous sneer. "You mean my Legal Aid. What that faggot got to say about me, anyway?"

Deke Fischer was practically born married, but I let the epithet go. In this guy's streetwise mind, any man who didn't wipe out his enemies with an AK 47 was a faggot, and it wasn't going to do me any good to argue the point.

"How you get me down here, anyway?" he continued.

"I had the court issue a writ of *habeas corpus ad testificandum,*" I explained, taking the question literally. It was my way of letting Shavon know I wasn't going to bullshit him or talk down to him.

He picked up on the implication at once. He probably couldn't have read the words I'd said, but he got the point. "If you mean testify, I ain't gonna," he said. He shook his head from side to side; his hair was so close-cropped as to appear shaved. "Not for you, not for nobody."

"Good," I replied. "Testimony from a double murderer I don't need."

"So I can go now?" he asked, moving his arms in the wide gesture of a rapper. "We finished here?"

"Well, there are a couple of questions I'd like to ask you," I said.

"Why you think I'm gonna answer, bitch?"

I let it go. Much as I would have enjoyed teaching Shavon Pettigrew some manners, this wasn't what our meeting was about. And in his world, just as all white men were faggots, all women, black or white, were bitches. The best I could do was show him I was a tough bitch.

"Well, for one thing, I did you a favor, bringing you down to the city. Your mother doesn't get up to Dannemora very often, and she can come to see you while you're at Rikers. And so can your girlfriends. So right there, I think you owe me a little something."

He mulled it over. "I didn't ax you to bring me down here," he pointed out.

"No, but I did call your mother and the three girls in your life, let them know where to find you. That ought to be worth a couple of answers."

"Depends on what kind a answers you talkin' about," he countered. I could see the wheels turning behind the sullen brown eyes. The ethics of the 'hood required repayment of debts, but the repayment would be carefully scaled to the size of the favor done him.

I nodded approval. "Good point. I'm not looking to hurt anybody and I'm not asking you to rat anybody out. But I do need to find a friend of yours." I leaned forward in the chair and locked eyes with the hard-faced young man across from me. "Now, don't go ballistic on me," I warned, raising a hand, "but I need to find TJ."

"Oh, shit," he cried, waving his arms and nearly leaping out of his chair. "You raggin' on me 'bout TJ, bitch? You expectin' me to give up that brother to a white bitch? Whatchou think I am, some kinda raggedy-ass—?"

"Chill, Shavon," I said. "Please. Sit down and listen. I already said I have no desire to hurt TJ. I just want to talk to him. I think it's possible he wants to talk to me. His partner, Eddie, is about to testify against a friend of mine, and I need TJ to take the stand and tell the truth about Eddie."

At the mention of the name Eddie, Shavon quieted down. "That Eddie be one mean motherfucker," he said. "I know for a fack TJ ain't wanted to have nothin' to do with that cracker. But that Eddie jammed him so bad, he ain't had no choice but to let the little faggot in."

"What I need to know is, where can I find TJ? Nobody's seen him lately. Is there anyplace he hangs out, anybody in the 'hood who might know how to get a message to him?" It was more than a little ironic to be asking a guy who'd been in an upstate prison for a year how to find a guy roaming the streets of the borough I lived in, but such were the ways of street life. A guy like Shavon, connected by a network of homeboys, could locate TJ from prison more easily than I could from white Brooklyn.

He gave the matter some thought. "Used to be a dude caught messages and shit," he said at last. "Don't recall his name, but he work in a place called the Ace a Spades, on Nostrand Avenue."

"Nostrand near Fulton? Near the subway?"

The look he shot back was full of the same contempt he'd showed at the outset of the meeting. "What's the matter, bitch, you afraid to wander too deep into the 'hood? You wanna know you can ride back to white-bread land on the subway?"

I had told him no bullshit, and I meant no bullshit. I looked him straight in the eye and said, "Damned right."

The shadow of a smile crossed the thick lips. "Say hey to the brother for me when you find him," Shavon said.

"Will do," I replied.

Matt was elated when I told him the results of my meeting with Shavon. He grabbed his suit jacket, without waiting for me, and headed for the door. I understood his haste—we were due back in court the next day, and this was the closest we'd come to a smoking gun. I followed, unable to picture Riordan's silver Jag parked at the corner of Fulton and Nostrand, in the heart of one of Brooklyn's most dangerous neighborhoods.

I was right about that; we raced for the nearest subway. It was too noisy for conversation; we both stared ahead of us in the see-no-evil fashion of New Yorkers in crowded public spaces until the A train pulled in at Nostrand Avenue. We emerged from an air-conditioned car onto a grimy, dimly lit platform with graffiti on every surface. We hiked the steps to the sidewalk and stepped into a steambath. The humidity had to be one hundred percent; my blouse stuck to my skin and we'd only been out of the air conditioning for three minutes.

The street was lined with little mom-and-pop stores: A record shop blared rap music; a clothing store had African fabric shirts on a rack outside; and there were four liquor stores on every block. A check-cashing place and the Ace of Spades flanked the corners.

Riordan made for the bar with a purposefulness that had me following blindly, like a little kid being dragged on a shopping expedition. I would have liked to pull his sleeve and ask a few questions, but he was moving too fast. If I wanted to know what his plan was, the best thing I could do was keep up with his long-legged stride.

We were two well-dressed white people about to enter a black bar in a black neighborhood and ask questions about a local drug dealer.

I did not feel optimistic. I did not feel safe.

Ordinarily when I came to ghetto neighborhoods to investigate cases, I brought someone with me. Preferably someone armed.

Was Riordan carrying?

If he was, he had one hell of a tailor.

He opened the door to the bar and strode in. I followed, the dimness making purple spots in front of my eyes after the bright sunshine outside. There were two guys at the bar, sitting apart; a big ex-boxer type sat behind the bar, hunched over a King Tut Dream Book.

"Got a good number today?" Riordan asked, nodding in the direction of the book.

The bartender gave a nod. "My woman dreamed about water last night," he explained. "She grew up down South and in her dream there was a great big river. It says here a river means you should play the number nine, but nine always been a curse on me, so I don't know what to do."

"It was your wife's dream," Riordan pointed out. "Maybe the number nine's lucky for her but not for you."

"Could be, could be," he said. "Still, when a dream comes by, you gotta take it. You gotta ride the sucker. So I guess I'll be playin' nine instead of my usual today."

"Smells great in here," Riordan said.

He was right; I hadn't noticed because I'd been tense about walking into someone else's territory, but the aroma of rich soul food permeated the little place.

"Fredda Mae's got smothered pork chops today," the bartender said. The hint of pride in his tone told me Fredda Mae was the woman who'd grown up down South, the woman who was going to win on number nine, if dreams were to be believed. "Pork chops and rice with red beans and a nice mess of greens. Y'all be wantin' some, I suppose."

It was ninety in the shade; this bar had no air conditioning. The thought of eating heavy, greasy food was nauseating, and yet the aroma was delicious.

"Absolutely," Riordan said with enthusiasm. I nodded agreement. The bartender made places for us at the end of the bar; it would be rude, I realized, to sit at a table here, apart from the other patrons.

I didn't see a kitchen. I whispered as much to Riordan, and the bartender overheard. "Oh, we ain't got no kitchen, not really. Fredda Mae cook on hotplates, in a little room used to be a coat closet. She cook pork chops on Mondays, chicken on Tuesdays, short ribs on Wednesdays, pigs feet on Thursdays, and fish fry on Fridays."

I said a silent prayer of thanks that today wasn't Thursday. My Midwestern upbringing hadn't prepared me for eating pigs feet, even in the interests of investigation.

Riordan ordered a whiskey and tossed it back in one gulp. I didn't think they'd have Perrier, so I had a glass of Mission cola over ice.

The food was fabulous. Fredda Mae, who was so skinny she couldn't possibly have eaten her own food, wore a kente cloth turban on her head and Birkenstock sandals on her feet. She brought steaming plates first to the two other men at the bar and then to us, setting them down with a clunk and then disappearing back into her closet without a word. I had the distinct feeling she disapproved of white folks she suspected of slumming.

The pork chops were smothered in cooked onions and gravy; the red beans and rice were spicy and rich, and the cabbage and greens were pungent. It was food to satisfy even the Wasp soul.

But it wasn't getting us information about TJ.

Riordan led up to it slowly. I listened with interest as by degrees he steered the conversation toward the existence of someone who might answer to the name of TJ. But every time he seemed on the verge of asking a direct question, he'd back off and raise another, more neutral topic. Then the talk would edge toward TJ again, but before the bartender could decide things were getting too close for comfort, Riordan would veer away.

It was a thing of beauty, but it was frustrating as hell to listen to.

"It's the cop I'm really interested in," Riordan said at last. "Anybody who might be talking to this TJ could tell him that for me. I just want to talk to him about the cop. Fast Eddie—the one they call Eddie Nino over in the Spanish neighborhood."

"Eddie Bigmouth, they call him over here," the bartender said with a tiny smile. I schooled my face not to smile back; this was pay dirt at last. If the bartender admitted knowing this much, it was only a matter of time before he admitted knowing TJ.

I wanted to talk, but Riordan gave me a hand signal that said he'd turn me into a smothered pork chop if I opened my mouth, so I sat and waited.

"You that lawyer," the bartender said in a conversational tone. It wasn't a challenge, but it was a demand that Riordan state his business honestly and openly.

"Yes," he replied. "And a cop named Eddie's trying to jam me up. I'm trying to figure out if this could be the same Eddie who works with TJ."

"Only one cop named Eddie I knows about," the bartender replied.

That was good enough for Riordan; he gave a crisp nod and plowed ahead. "Any chance of getting word to TJ that I'd like to talk to him?"

The bartender reached for a rag and wiped the bar. He slid our empty plates to the end and polished the wood where they'd sat in front of us. He made a gesture toward our drinks; we agreed to a second round.

Then he said, "I might could get a message to TJ. I ain't seen him in a while, though. Seems to me it's been near a month since he come in here last, and he was powerful fond of Fredda Mae's short ribs. Said they reminded him of his grandmother's cooking. Fredda Mae's food reminds a lot of people of their grandmothers, seems like."

Oddly enough, although neither of my grandmothers would have known a collard green from arugula, Fredda Mae's food had taken me back to Sunday dinners after church, to big meals cooked with love and eaten with gusto before the word cholesterol crept into our vocabularies.

"You think TJ would talk to me?" Riordan inquired. "You think maybe he'd tell a jury what he knows about Eddie Fitz?"

"TJ wasn't any too pleased when that little white boy started cuttin' hisself in on TJ's business," the bartender replied. I nodded; this squared with what Shavon had told me. "Leastwise, that's what I done heard. I can't be speakin' for TJ, mind, but I don't think he was any too happy 'bout that boy."

"It's one thing to be unhappy," Riordan pressed. "It's another to stand up in court and talk about another guy."

"Way I heard it," the bartender said, "TJ done already talked. TJ took a little trip to federal court a month or so ago, ready to tell them what he knew about Eddie Big-mouth, but they didn't want to hear no evil 'bout their golden boy. Sent him away with a flea in his ear, told him not to tell nobody what he knew.''

"Any idea who he talked to over there?" Riordan asked with a casualness that belied the weightiness of this information. Was this guy really saying that TJ had blown the whistle on Eddie Fitz, that the prosecution knew its Hero Cop was a part-time drug dealer?

"Guy with a name sound like the Bible is all I remember," the bartender answered.

A name from the Bible. A name like Lazarus.

CHAPTER FIVE

Armed with a subpoena for "any and all records naming or pertaining to or containing any reference to an individual designated as John Doe 'TJ,'" I made my way to the federal courthouse. There was a fine mist falling; the tops of the World Trade Center towers were shrouded in fog. You could open your mouth and drink the air. My new designer clothes clung damply to my skin and I feared for my expensive pumps.

I was as wired as if I'd drunk five cups of coffee, as buzzed as if I were running on speed. Today was D-Day, the day I'd stand up in court and begin the most publicized trial of my career. The day I'd come home to the six-o'clock news and see my face, rendered by an artist's pen, on the TV screen. The day I'd begin taking the test that would determine, once and for all, whether I could handle the big ones. Whether I could ride the Mean Streak without losing my lunch.

I had to eat. I'd downed my coffee while struggling with the curling iron, trying to get my hair to behave. I'd wasted my time; I could feel it frizzing with every step I took in the humidity. I turned onto Broadway from Chambers Street and opened the door to Ellen's. I stood in line behind a couple of suits and gazed at the autographed pictures on the wall.

The coffee shop was directly across the street from City Hall, so the photos were of political rather than entertainment celebs: Ex-Mayors Dinkins and Lindsay and Manhattan Borough President Ruth Messenger stood next to a smiling Ellen. She had been a Miss Subways; black-and-white posters of the various women who had held that title graced the walls. I smiled and relaxed a little as I looked at the pictures of the ordinary working girls from Queens or Brooklyn or the Bronx who had been honored with placards in the subways. They spoke of an earlier New York, a city of young women who wore white gloves when they "went to business."

I grabbed a seat at the counter and ordered coffee and a cheese danish. My hand shook as I reached for the steaming mug. Just what I needed, I thought as I took the first scalding sip, more caffeine.

I would never have admitted it to Dorinda, but my trial persona was built around the fact that I was born under the sign of Sagittarius. Honesty, that was my trump card. I admitted weaknesses in my case up front; I showed the jurors from the beginning that I was to be trusted, that I spoke truth. Then I slipped in bits and pieces of my own defense-oriented version of said truth, and hoped they bought it along with the rest. I used blunt, simple language. I spoke conversationally whenever possible, saving the arcane legal language for arguments outside the jury's hearing. I looked jurors in the eye, picking out the ones I thought were exceptionally sympathetic and roping them in as confederates, priming them to carry my arguments into the jury room.

As I bit into the creamy danish, I reviewed my theory of

defense. Somehow I would have to demonstrate to the jurors the strength of Nick Lazarus' obsession with bringing down Riordan. And I would have to do it without Lazarus ever taking the stand. I would have to extract admissions from the people who worked for him, from the FBI agents who'd wired Eddie Fitz for sound, that Lazarus would stop at nothing to nail a lawyer he thought was subverting the justice system.

And then would come Eddie. By the time the prosecution's star witness took the stand, I decided, I'd be in possession of the fruits of today's subpoena. I'd be able to rattle his cage with mention of TJ, with hints that TJ had told everything he knew to Nick Lazarus. And then I'd call TJ as a witness and watch Lazarus' face collapse as he realized it was all over, that we had solid proof that not only was Eddie Fitz a crooked cop, but that he, Lazarus, had known that fact and buried it in order to get Riordan. Matt would be acquitted, Eddie would be charged with perjury, and Lazarus would be fighting for his professional life.

Lazarus *delenda est*, Matt had said. And once we had TJ, we'd be well on our way to destroying Lazarus. The thought was as sweet as the danish.

It was a lovely dream while it lasted. But finally, I tossed a tip next to the empty saucer, paid my bill, and left the sanctuary of the coffee shop for the arena.

We were a long, long way from producing TJ—or any solid proof of Eddie's venality, for that matter. All I had for sure, I reminded myself as I hastened along Chambers Street, was my pathetic little parade of junkies willing to testify that Eddie Fitz dealt drugs with TJ and split the proceeds with the late Nunzie Aiello.

All that coffee had been a mistake. I realized that when I rounded the corner onto Centre Street and saw the mob of reporters camped out on the shiny-wet courthouse steps. All I wanted was a restroom, but I'd have to deliver a few sound bites before I'd be allowed to enter the building.

I had two minutes to shape my thoughts; I didn't dare slow my pace or turn back for a moment of thinking. They had to see a confident lawyer striding into battle without a second's hesitation, a lawyer so certain of the righteousness of her cause that she needed no time to compose herself for the cameras.

". . . new evidence that will expose the truth behind this vindictive prosecution," I heard myself saying into the large, fuzzy microphone. "Nick Lazarus is on a vendetta here," I went on, "and the defense will—"

"This is no vendetta," an angry male voice cut in. It was a thin instrument, not a good stage voice at all. But Nick Lazarus used it for all it was worth, raising it to a strident edge that cut through my words and grabbed the attention of the assembled reporters.

"This is justice, pure and simple," the U.S. attorney went on. He stabbed the air. "Matt Riordan has been jerking this court around for too long. He's played fast and loose with the justice system, and now—"

"And now you're going to jerk him around?" I demanded. "Now you're going to pervert justice in order to nail a guy you don't happen to like?"

I gave Ginger Hsu my biggest smile and opened my purse. "I just happen to have something here that I'd intended to serve in court," I said. Avid reportorial eyes lit up; all the mikes and minicams were positioned to catch my next words. I took the subpoena out of my designer handbag and handed it to Nick Lazarus.

"This is a subpoena," I explained, "for information pertaining to a man named TJ. I'll let Mr. Lazarus fill you in on who TJ is and why he's relevant to this case." With that, I broke away from the pack and stepped smartly up the stairs, leaving a sputtering Nick Lazarus to explain himself to the hungry pack. I concentrated instead on trying to remember exactly where the nearest ladies' room was.

Later, when an exultant Matt Riordan praised me with

the highest compliment he knew—that he couldn't have handled the moment better himself—I smiled demurely and neglected to tell him it had happened mainly because I'd had to pee.

We had a jury by lunchtime, in part because Judge de Freitas refused to hear argument on the subpoena. "Put it in writing, Ms. Singer," he'd said in a flat voice. "Make a motion to quash."

In federal court, the judge picked the jury. I was used to a lengthy *voir dire*, a time to get acquainted with the prospective jurors and to introduce myself to them, a time when the judge sat back and watched while the lawyers from both sides questioned the panel members. But here, the ball was squarely in the judge's court. Only he was allowed to address the jurors, although both sides could suggest questions to be asked. It was a bloodless, boring procedure, and it produced a final jury panel in far less time than I was used to. The Mean Streak was a fast sonofabitch.

Matt and I grabbed a quick lunch in Chinatown. We sidestepped the crowded tourist restaurants along Mott Street and found a nameless noodle shop that served hot tea in glasses and posted its menu in Chinese only. Years of practicing law in lower Manhattan had given Matt the ability to order two bowls of noodles with chicken in what the waiter took to be passable Mandarin.

The hot tea felt good going down my throat. Oddly enough, the Chinese theory that hot beverages cooled you off in summer seemed to have some basis in fact.

"So how's your investigator doing finding TJ?" Matt asked.

"If anyone can find him, she can," I replied, which wasn't a real answer to the question. "She's meeting us after court," I added. "I thought McSorley's."

"Good thought," Matt replied approvingly. "We'll both want a cold beer after today's session. And it's far enough away from the courthouse that we ought to be able to talk freely."

After slurping up the last of the noodles, we took a walk. Chinatown was its busy, bustling self as tourists, city workers, lawyers, and ordinary Chinese people jostled for a place on the narrow sidewalks. I steered Matt to one of my favorite places—the Chinatown Ice Cream Factory. Under his indulgent gaze, I ordered a cone with red bean ice cream.

"It's better than it sounds," I said defensively when Matt raised a single eyebrow.

"Just don't spill any on your silk suit," he warned.

I looked down at my mauve shell and murmured, "I'm not sure man was meant to eat and wear clothes at the same time."

When we stepped back into the courtroom at 2:15, it was like walking into an electronic nightmare. Huge cables criss-crossed the floor, and there were individual headphones at each juror's chair. A tape player with amplifiers sat next to the witness box. Government tapes were notoriously poor quality; you needed state-of-the-art players to get anything intelligible.

My anxiety rose another notch. Not only was the jury about to hear from the FBI, it was going to hear the tapes.

Matt and I had listened to them at least fifteen times. They were coming in; there was no motion to suppress that would keep them from the jurors' ears. And there was no smoking gun on the tapes themselves as far as Riordan was concerned.

So why was I so nervous?

Because there might be something I'd missed. There might be one phrase, one word that would convince the jury that Matt had authorized Fat Jack to give money to Eddie Fitz in return for the grand jury minutes. There might be a nuance I hadn't considered, a secret code I hadn't broken, an expression whose double meaning I hadn't known.

There might be things my client hadn't told me.

But there was nothing I could do about that now. I took my seat with an air of competent boredom, as if the playing of the tapes was just one more tedious task to get through before the really important stuff began. The second-last thing I wanted was to let the jury know I felt any anxiety about the tapes.

The last thing I wanted was to let Singer know.

Warren Zebart looked like an FBI agent. He was a beefy man in his mid-fifties with a ruddy face and iron-gray hair. He wore thick-soled wingtip shoes and an off-the-rack gray suit. Even his tie was gray, with navy rep stripes.

I took rapid notes as he told the jury how long he'd been a special agent, and how he'd come to be assigned to Nick Lazarus' task force. I leaned forward slightly when he told of his first meeting with New York City Detective Edmund Fitzgerald.

Was the slight, almost imperceptible curl to his lip when he mentioned Eddie Fitz a figment of my imagination? I hoped not; if I could show the jury that even the chief FBI man had reason to despise the turncoat cop, we'd be setting the stage for TJ's revelations. If we could find TJ in time. If we could find TJ at all.

I stifled those thoughts in case they began to show on my face, and gave my full attention to the FBI man.

"I was the contact agent," Zebart explained. He shifted in his seat and turned his face toward the jury box. Clearly a man who'd spent a good deal of his professional life on the witness stand. "That means that Detective Fitzgerald reported to me."

I made a quick note to ask Agent Zebart on cross if the contact agent wasn't also known as a "handler." The slang term would make Eddie Fitz sound like a wild animal, someone who needed to be kept in check by the cool heads at the FBI. Then I'd hit Eddie with the term, hoping the implication would rankle enough for him to say something he'd regret. Or at least something Davia Singer would regret.

"Agent Boatman was the electronics expert on the case," he continued. I jotted "Boatman-wireman" on my legal pad. Zebart went on to give a cursory overview of the surveillance techniques the FBI had used in the case; the details would be filled in when Harris Boatman took the stand.

According to Zebart, Eddie had met Fat Jack Vance at the round information booth in the courthouse at 100 Centre Street. Immediately prior to the meeting, Zebart had watched Agent Boatman tape a Nagra recorder to Eddie's naked torso.

It took another fifteen questions to lay the foundation for the playing of the tapes. I rose to indicate the defense's lack of objection, hoping my demeanor indicated a supreme indifference to whether the tapes were played. They were coming in anyway, Matt and I had reasoned, so why make a fuss that might indicate we had something to fear from them?

The first tape began with a huge amount of background noise from the crowded lobby at 100 Centre. The courthouse was home to both the criminal and supreme courts in Manhattan; during the lunch recess hundreds of people bustled past the information booth where Fat Jack and Eddie Fitz had arranged to meet.

The two men made for a restaurant in Chinatown. We listened to several minutes of dishes clattering, waiters bustling, and people chatting over their moo shu before Fat Jack got down to business.

The fat man's raspy voice said, "Maybe you could help us out on the Nunzie thing."

Zebart had already given the jurors the background; the name Nunzie wouldn't come as a surprise to them.

"Yeah, I heard something about that," the young voice that belonged to Eddie Fitz replied. "Something about Lazarus yanking this guy's chain pretty hard, trying to make him roll over on his lawyer."

"His own lawyer, can you believe it?" Fat Jack's wheezy voice trembled with indignation. "There's no loyalty these days."

"What I hear," Eddie Fitz said, "Lazarus is always pulling that shit, breaking some guy's shoes so he turns on his friends. Guy like that's gotta be stopped."

"I heard Lazarus went to see Nunz at the Federal Correction Center," Jack went on. The words were punctuated by a slurping sound that was probably Fat Jack inhaling a bowl of hot-and-sour. Two jurors giggled. I relaxed a bit; if I could get them laughing at the tapes, they might not take them as seriously as Singer wanted them to. "I heard they talked a long time. So, you heard anything, or what?"

Eddie echoed the fat man's George V. Higgins style of speech. "I heard something all right," he replied. "But the guys I hear things from, they don't do anything for charity, you know what I mean? They gotta know they're gonna be taken care of."

Jack chuckled. "And I suppose you're gonna want a little something for yourself?"

"Just tell me how much I can spread around and still have something left over," Eddie said.

"Hey, Matty takes care of his friends," Jack replied. I had carefully planned for the first mention of Riordan's name on the tapes. I was to look completely bored, completely unfazed, completely unruffled. As far as I was concerned, this was Fat Jack pretending to be a big shot, pretending he spoke for his sometime employer. It was not evidence of a conspiracy between my client and the soon-to-be-ex-bail bondsman.

"Don't worry about that. He'll see to it you're covered," Fat Jack promised. "Matty's got the bucks and so do the guys he works for. You'll be squared on this thing.''

End tape. And end Warren Zebart's tenure on the witness stand; from here on the tapes would be placed in evidence by the man who'd taped the wire to Eddie Fitz: Agent Harris Boatman.

I limited my cross of Zebart to pointing out, in several different ways, that he'd never met Matt Riordan and hadn't been present when the alleged payoff was made. The impression I wanted the jury to have was of a man doing his job, but doing it without the full benefit of the information they were going to have once this trial was over. On summation, I wanted to be able to discount Zebart, not as a liar out to frame Riordan, but as a man who'd been lied to by Eddie Fitz and used by Nick Lazarus. Sincere but uninformed, that was what I wanted the jurors to see when they looked at the FBI man.

Harris Boatman was a lithe black man with close-cut hair and pencil mustache. His suit was brown and his tie had flowers on it. What I'd learned from Matt Riordan about men's ties was that flowered ones were worn only by men whose wives picked out their clothes. How this was going to help on cross, I had no idea, but I filed the information in a corner of my mind.

He described at length the process of wiring Eddie Fitz for sound. And he told the court that there were nights when Eddie refused to wear the wire, nights when he'd been sure he'd be searched by the men he was meeting.

Matt and I had known there were meetings that hadn't been taped; this was the first time we learned why.

On the second tape, the food was Italian; Jack and Eddie were eating at Forlini's, a venerable institution located directly behind 100 Centre Street.

''Matty and I talked,'' Jack said, ''and we need to know where Lazarus is on this thing. If Nunzie testified in the grand jury, then we need those minutes. And we need the 3500 material. All of it, not just Nunzie's.'' Singer had already explained to the jurors that 3500 material meant witness statements, which were required to be handed to the defense after the witness testified at trial, but were not privy to the defense beforehand.

"I already talked to Paulie the Cork," Eddie boasted, naming the grand jury clerk of the federal courthouse. The clerk had pleaded guilty, and would be taking the stand to confess. "He says Lazarus walked Nunzie over to the grand jury personally. That's how bad he wants to hurt your boy. But don't worry," Eddie went on, his tone expansive, "I'll get this shit right out from under Lazarus' nose."

"Good," the fat man replied. "I'll tell Matty as soon as we leave here. So how soon can we see this stuff?"

I had my summation line ready. Fat Jack was blowing smoke, Fat Jack was doing what we in the trade called "puffing"—he was pretending to have contacts he didn't really have. He was playing big shot, throwing Matt's name into the conversation to make Eddie Fitz think he was a big man.

Paulie the Cork came to the table the next time out. The food was Italian again, but this time they were up in Little Italy, at the Luna.

And this time, Fat Jack insisted on frisking his new cop friend.

"Hey, what is this?" Eddie said. "Take your hands off me, you little—"

"Don't take this wrong, Eddie," the new voice identified as Paulie the Cork's pleaded, "but Jack says I gotta search you."

"Jack says, huh?" Eddie retorted. "Jack don't trust me, he can tell me so himself, not make you put your hands all over me like some faggot. I'll tell that fat sonavabitch what I think of him."

"Hey, Eddie, don't take this wrong," Fat Jack repeated. "It's just business, that's all."

"If that's the way you do business, you can keep your

business to yourself. I'm outa here.''

"Ah, sit down, Eddie," Jack told him, his voice coated with olive oil. "You're not going anywhere. You need us, we need you. The people I work for just get a little nervous about discussing business with cops, that's all. Too many stupid fuckers have hung themselves on tape—you know that.''

Considering that the entire courtroom was listening to the product of the wire Eddie had been wearing, Judge de Freitas had to pound his gavel a few times to stop the derisive laughter. Fat Jack and Paulie the Cork had hung themselves on tape, all right—but I made a note to remind the jurors that Matt Riordan hadn't even been in the room at the time.

"Yeah, you gotta admit—" Paulie started.

"Shut up, Paulie," Jack cut in. "Sit down," he went on, switching back to the cajoling tone he used with Eddie Fitz. "Have a little vino, some fettucine. You'll feel better after you eat a little something.''

Jack's idea of "a little something" for lunch had Juror Number Four stifling a giggle. By the time the three men had thoroughly discussed the respective merits of *zuppa de pesce* versus *tortellini in brodo*, most of the jurors were smiling.

Eddie apparently sat down at the table, but he wasn't about to let the matter of the frisk go. "You sure you want me to sit here, Jack? We're pretty close to the jukebox. All I'm gonna get is Sinatra, I sit over here.''

"Ah, just sit the fuck down, Eddie.''

Eddie wasn't about to let the joke die. "See that waitress over there?" he asked. "The one with the big tits. Wanna know why they're so big? On account of she's got a microphone hidden in the left one. Yeah, talk into the left one, you want Lazarus to hear nice and loud.''

"Ah, cut the crap, Eddie," Jack begged.

By the time the three men started in on the *zabaglione*,

a fee had been agreed to and another meeting set up to make the exchange.

Matt came to the next meeting. They were back in Chinatown; there was talk of ordering a whole carp in black bean sauce. There was also talk of another frisk, before Matt joined them.

"You gonna read me my fucking rights while you're at it?" Eddie demanded. "You're makin' me feel like a skel here, patting me down all the fucking time."

"Don't be like that, Eddie," Jack replied, his tone weary. "Matt says I got to search you, he's gonna come to the table."

"It's just business, Eddie," Paulie the Cork contributed, his voice a sycophantic whine.

"That's the way you mopes do business," Eddie retorted, "I'm outa here. You can keep your business to yourselves."

The argument ceased when Matt stepped up to the table.

"Word in the courthouse says Nick Lazarus wants your ass real bad," Eddie said for openers.

I allowed myself the ghost of a smile. This was precisely the theme my summation would center on. Lazarus wanted Riordan's ass real bad—and he wasn't above using a crooked cop to get it. How nice of Eddie Fitz to give me a line I could build my final speech to the jury around.

"Nick isn't fit to shine your shoes, Matty," Paulie the Cork chimed in. "He can't try a case, is his problem. So every time he loses, he puts the blame on you."

Nick Lazarus sat in the front row of the courtroom, directly behind Davia Singer's chair. A dull red crept into his sallow cheeks as he listened to the assessment of the former court clerk. True or not, those words were going to end up in the lead paragraph of every story to hit the papers tomorrow.

Nobody said Shut up, Paulie, but everyone at the table

was thinking it. I knew this because I was thinking it, just listening to the tape.

"I hear Nunzie may have made a deal with Lazarus," Matt said in his deep voice.

"What I hear," Eddie Fitz replied, "is that Lazarus promised him a walk. A clean walk, if he'd roll over on you. I hear he walked Nunzie over to the grand jury, and Nunz gave it all up. Told Lazarus everything he knows about you and Frankie C. and the Lou Berger thing."

Singer rose to explain to the jury exactly who Frankie C. was. In case the jurors were too stupid to realize that Eddie had just named Don Scaniello's successor, Frank Cretella, who just happened to be Matt Riordan's longtime client.

"I wish I knew exactly what Nunzie told them," Matt said.

I made a note: *Wish I knew not same as would pay to know*. But I wished I had something stronger than that to say.

Judge de Freitas cut us loose at precisely 5:00 P.M., with two more tapes to go.

I felt as if I'd run a marathon; I hadn't even stood up to cross-examine Boatman yet, and I was as wiped out as I'd ever been after a day of trial. I'd overdosed on adrenaline and I hadn't really begun to try this case.

It was pouring. All the pent-up humidity of the day had given way to a slashing rain that dumped a river onto the slick stone steps of the courthouse. I didn't want to walk down those steps in my expensive new shoes, but the minicams waited at the bottom, undeterred by the downpour. I shrugged at Matt and headed down the steps, unfurling my umbrella as I went.

"All we've heard so far," I told Ginger Hsu, "is that Jack Vance likes sesame chicken and Eddie Fitz prefers jumbo shrimp." Matt and I had decided never to use the nickname Fat Jack when talking to reporters; we didn't want to offend weight-challenged viewers.

"There has been nothing offered today to indicate that Matt Riordan had the slightest idea what Jack Vance was doing—and there won't be any evidence like that tomorrow, or the next day, or the next day," I promised. "This whole thing is exactly what the government's chief witness just said it was: Nick Lazarus wanting to nail Matt Riordan's you-know-what."

Behind me, Carlos Ruiz tossed a challenge at the United States attorney. "So, Lazarus," he began, "is it true what they say—you can't try a case?"

I didn't wait to hear the answer; the question itself filled me with elation. Matt shepherded me toward a cab—how he managed to snag an empty one in a rainstorm was one of those unexplained miracles—and in a matter of minutes we were on our way up the Bowery to McSorley's to meet Angie.

There was a certain irony in going to McSorley's. It had been a males-only tavern for over a hundred years, and had been integrated by women within my lifetime as a New Yorker. And now a female lawyer was going there to meet her female investigator, a former Housing cop.

The place was cool and dark and yeasty, a perfect sanctuary on a wet summer evening. Matt hustled me inside and ordered us both a Watney's. I picked up my mug and took a grateful sip, letting its malty flavor linger on my tongue.

"God, that was an ordeal," I said when half the brew had disappeared down my dry throat. And if it was dry today, when I'd done virtually nothing in court except listen to tapes, how would I feel after a bruising cross?

"I'm exhausted," I went on, "and we've just started this thing. How in hell do you do this, week in and week out? Year in and year out?"

I never got to hear the answer. The door flew open and a very soggy investigator pushed her way in. Her hair was sopping and her clothes hung on her as if she'd put them on straight from the washing machine, without benefit of dryer.

She was out of breath. She tossed her bag onto an empty chair and plopped down next to me.

"I found him," she said. Then she grabbed another lungful of air. "I ran all the way here from the subway," she explained. "No umbrella."

My exhaustion fell away at once; I felt alive again, ready to go. Should we abandon our beers and head for Bedford-Stuyvesant, nail down an interview with TJ as soon as possible? Had he admitted that he and Eddie Fitz were partners? Would he testify?

"Where is he?" I asked.

"When can we see him?" Matt demanded.

"You can't," my investigator replied decisively. "He's in the morgue."

CHAPTER SIX

Riordan slammed his fist down on the table so hard the beer mugs jumped. "I knew it!" he cried in a voice torn between anguish and triumph. "I knew that bastard would stop at nothing. He must have found out we were close to bringing TJ into court, and he—"

"Wait a second here," Angie cut in. "Not so fast, Jose." One of Angie's peculiarities was her penchant for giving everyone Spanish names. "This guy happens to have been dead a month already. Found in the trunk of a car over on Bushwick Avenue."

"Just like Nunzie," I murmured. "I wonder if the people who iced Nunzie also took out TJ."

"No way," Matt said in a decisive voice that brooked no argument. "No way this guy's death is a coincidence. He's the only credible witness who could prove Eddie Fitz is a lying scumbag, and he turns up dead on the eve of our calling him to the stand, and it's a coincidence?" He shook his head and repeated his earlier pronouncement: "No way."

"Look, I can see where our chief witness ending up wearing a toe tag is upsetting," I began, trying to sound more conciliatory than I felt, "but, face it, the guy was a drug dealer. A lot of people might have wanted him dead."

"You think his murder has nothing to do with this trial?" The edge in Matt's voice questioned my sanity; as far as he was concerned, everything about this case, up to and including the death of our intended surprise witness, was personal in the extreme.

"All I'm saying," I pointed out, "is that we didn't even know there was a TJ a month ago. If Angie's right, he'd been dead about a week when I first heard his name from Deke Fischer."

"That doesn't mean squat," Riordan pronounced. The trial was taking its toll on him. He didn't use vulgarity as a rule, preferring a rapier to a broadsword, but lately he'd been larding his speech with crude expressions, reverting to the Hell's Kitchen street fighter he'd been before Fordham Law.

"If we're right about TJ being Eddie's front man on the street, then he not only could have brought down Eddie Fitz, he could have blown Lazarus' whole career. Think about it, Cass," Matt went on, building his case as thoroughly as he would have in front of a jury. "TJ visits Lazarus, tells him what a piece of shit his star witness is, and then turns up dead. If we could prove it," he finished, "we'd have Lazarus on trial for his professional life."

I sighed. Matt's insistence that Lazarus must be destroyed was getting in the way. "Look," I said, not bothering to conceal my annoyance, "you may be right. Lazarus might personally have put a gun to this guy's head and blown his brains all over Bushwick Avenue. I don't know. What I do know," I went on, "is that I am going to appear before Judge de Freitas in less than fifteen hours. Eddie Fitz is going to step up to the witness stand, and I am going to have nothing—*nada*, zip, *rien*—to hit him with on cross.

TJ's getting dead doesn't do us a damned bit of good in court unless we can nail down his killer by tomorrow afternoon at the latest. And the reality is," I finished, "we can't."

We stared each other down like two kids on the playground. Mine were the first eyes to veer away. "Okay," I conceded with a sigh, "I'll get the police reports as soon as I—"

"I'm way ahead of you, Rosita," Angie cut in. She reached into the hand-woven Guatemalan basket she used as a briefcase and pulled out a piece of paper. "I got the M.E.'s autopsy report. You gotta remember who you're dealin' with, chica," she reminded me with a snap of her gum. "I don't come here with bad news and no sugar on the spoon."

Riordan grabbed the report before I could.

"Two shots," he read. "One to the head, one in the mouth."

I echoed the words he'd said after telling me how Nunzie Aiello had died: "Classic. A classic mob hit."

Matt raised his eyes from the page for a single second and retorted, "Or someone who wants the murder to look like a classic mob hit."

A waiter wandered over and inquired about a second round. Matt and I agreed, and Angie ordered a cuba libre with dark Jamaican rum.

". . . nine millimeter bullets," Matt murmured as his eyes scanned the report. "Mushroomed upon impact," he went on. He raised his eyes. "They must have used hollowpoints," he said.

"Did they find the gun?" I began, then withdrew the question. "I guess we won't know that until we get the police reports," I amended.

Angie shook her head. "No," she said, "I talked to a guy at the M.E.'s office. He told me that whoever shot your witness took the gun with him. No shell casings either.

They think the dude was shot outside the car, then shoved into the trunk. Not enough blood in the trunk, is what the medical examiner says.''

"Who investigated?" I inquired. "NYPD or the feds?"

"What I heard at the M.E.'s office," Angie replied, "is that the city cops had the case, and then the feds came in and kicked them off it."

"I'll amend my subpoena to include all federal reports on the investigation into TJ's murder," I promised. "And I'll draft a new subpoena for everything the NYPD has on the case."

"Meanwhile," Matt cut in, his tone as dry as the imported ale we were drinking, "as you rightly pointed out earlier, I now have no defense. What do we do about that?"

"In fifteen hours," I murmured.

"In fifteen hours," he agreed. "We might have enough here to get an adjournment for a day or two, but I don't want to ask for it unless we absolutely have to."

"Okay," I said, stifling any misgivings. Even a one-day adjournment would have been manna from heaven as far as pulling together a cross-examination strategy was concerned. "What about the other cops?"

"What other cops?" Angie put in. "You mean the ones who investigated TJ's murder?"

I shook my head. "No, not them. I mean the cops who worked with Eddie on the Narcotics Squad. The cops who have to be shitting bricks, wondering if Eddie's going to rat them out in the grand jury when he's finished convicting you."

"A good point," Riordan murmured. "Inelegantly put, but a good point nonetheless."

"You want elegant," I retorted, "get F. Lee. One of those cops might be willing to take the stand and tell the truth about Eddie Fitz," I went on.

"I don't know, babe," Riordan said with a shake of his

head. "These cops stick together. The Blue Wall of Silence, and all that."

Matt's gloom was catching. "And then there's the little matter of the Fifth Amendment," I added. "We can subpoena every cop who ever met Eddie Fitz, but—"

"But the minute they say the magic words, the judge bounces them off the stand," Matt finished. I nodded; it would have been nice if we were able to call Eddie's cohorts to the witness box and present the jury with the spectacle of New York's Finest refusing to answer questions on the grounds that the answers might incriminate them, but it was a good solid bet the judge wasn't going to let it happen. Instead, de Freitas would hold in camera testimony, out of the hearing of the jury, and the minute one of the cops took the Fifth, he'd strike their testimony and refuse to let us call them at trial.

"So what we have to do," I reasoned, "is scare these cops enough to make them want to sell Eddie out, but not so much that they'll see themselves going down with him."

"You're assuming these guys even know they're in danger," Matt objected. "Eddie probably told them he'd cover for them."

"But Lazarus can't really let them off the hook," I pointed out. "He's got political ambitions, remember. How's it going to look if he gives Eddie's cop buddies a pass? No," I went on, warming to my theme, "Lazarus is going to send Eddie into the grand jury some day, some time, and he's going to make Eddie name names, and the first name he's going to name is—"

"Stan Krieger," Riordan said, finishing my thought. "The cop who registered TJ as an official narcotics informant. I wonder," he continued, a thoughtful look on his face, "if we could catch him tonight. He could be working a late shift."

Angie walked over to the pay phone in the corner, put in a quarter, and came back forty seconds later. "He's working midnight to eight tomorrow,'' she said. ''You could stop by the precinct and see him before court in the morning.''

Wonderful. Not only could I eat, sleep, and breathe this trial from eight in the morning to midnight, I could get up at six A.M. and put in a solid hour of interviewing before getting to the courthouse. I stuck my tongue out at my oh-so-helpful investigator, but I would also add a substantial bonus to her fee for this one.

''Which gives us the entire evening to do something else,'' Matt said helpfully.

''Something else like what?''

''Something else like going out to Long Island to talk to the other cop in the picture: Dwight Straub.''

Once again, my investigator dug into her Guatemalan basket, fished out a quarter, and went to the phone. This time she came back with Dwight Straub's home address block-printed on an index card in her signature purple ink.

She handed it to me with a superior smile. ''I'm gonna owe somebody huge for this one, Juana,'' she said. ''Which means you're gonna owe me.''

''You're the best, Angelina,'' I said, pronouncing the name in the best Spanish accent I could muster. She grinned and popped her gum.

''I'm going home, then,'' she said, slinging the bag over her shoulder. ''Catch Jimmy Smits on TV. Why can't any of the cops in this city ever look like him?''

I slipped the card into my purse with resigned acceptance. When you're on trial in a big case, you don't expect the night off. You expect to work until at least midnight and then get up at dawn to add whatever new ideas you might have come up with in your sleep. But I'd thought my time would be spent preparing my cross-examination questions, not chasing down cops who'd probably refuse to answer questions, in or out of court.

I said as much as we drove along the Long Island Expressway, on our way to the North Shore, in Riordan's silver Jaguar. We'd picked it up from the garage underneath his First Avenue apartment building after leaving McSorley's.

"Face it, he's not going to talk to us."

Riordan gave a shrug that might have been dismissal or resignation. "We can't assume that. He might want to get it off his chest."

I made an unladylike sound. "He wants to get it off his chest, he'll go see a priest. He won't tell all to a defense lawyer he's been brainwashed to think of as the scum of the earth."

"We have to try," Riordan said with a finality that closed the subject.

"You're right," I agreed with a sigh. "I'm just getting tired of running into dead ends." It took a moment for my exhausted brain to realize I'd just made a bad pun; TJ was a very dead end, indeed.

Dwight Straub lived in Southhold, on the North Shore of Long Island, in a white house with an honest-to-God picket fence. It was a modest house, maybe three bedrooms, but it had a postage stamp yard of emerald-green lawn and neatly trimmed hedges. Marigolds and red impatiens bordered the shrubs, and a red-painted rowboat filled with flowers graced the front yard. It was a far cry from the mean streets he'd patrolled, from the drug dealers' apartments with their trapdoors cut into the ceiling so that narcotics could be passed upstairs in case of a raid.

I rang the bell. Riordan stood behind me on the concrete porch.

The woman who opened the door had a lived-in face. She was in her mid-thirties, but her face had seen a lot more life than most women her age; it showed in the wrinkles around her eyes and the set of her mouth. She had opened that door more than once with her heart in her mouth, praying she wasn't about to be told to come to the morgue to identify a dead cop who used to be her husband.

She didn't relax an inch when she saw it was me. I was bad news, not as bad as the news she reflexively stiffened against, but bad enough.

"My husband's not here," she said, beginning to close the door. "I don't know when he'll be back."

My foot was already wedged in the doorway; a lawyer learns all the techniques of a door-to-door salesman, being just about as welcome in most people's homes.

"Ms. Straub, my name is Cassandra Jameson," I began. I made a gesture that encompassed Riordan, and introduced him as well. That name she recognized. She took a step back from the door and said, "You're that lawyer."

She didn't mean me. I stood silent while Riordan stepped forward and exercised his formidable Irish charm. Within minutes we were inside, seated on the sofa, while Annie Straub poured us iced tea.

"Dwight wouldn't want me talking to you," she said, "but I can't see protecting Eddie forever. He wouldn't keep quiet to save Dwight, that's for sure."

Riordan decided he'd been silent long enough. "If you feel that way about Eddie Fitz," he said conversationally, "why not tell the world what he really is?"

The smile she turned toward him had all his Irish charm and more. "Because every word I say against Eddie is a nail in my husband's coffin, and I'm not going to see him taken down. Not even to nail Eddie. If nobody talks, everyone has a chance to walk." She lifted her chin in a defiant gesture. "At least that's what Stan says," she amended. Her eyes traveled to the piano in the corner of the room; a photograph of a group of men holding beer steins aloft in a drunken gesture of camaraderie sat atop the polished surface. It could have been a fraternity beer bust, except that most of the men were too old for college, and several wore sweatshirts with NYPD logos on the front. One logo read OCCB, the Organized Crime Control Bureau, which operated out of police headquarters.

The Squad. I squinted my eyes to try to make out Eddie Fitz, whose face I'd only seen so far in the newspaper. He sat at the center of the group, wearing the biggest grin and holding his beer mug higher than the others.

"Which one's Stan?" I asked, pointing to the picture.

"Oh, Stan the Man's the one in the back," Annie replied. "The older guy."

Stan the Man. I filed the nickname for future reference and asked, "Did your husband have a nickname, too?"

"Not at first," she said. "But then Eddie found out his middle name was David, just like Eisenhower. So he started calling him Ike." The twist of her lip said she'd never liked the nickname, but she didn't say why.

Riordan brought the conversation back to essentials. "Nobody's going to walk," he said firmly, putting all the considerable authority his voice was capable of behind the statement. "Lazarus is going to pick off the squad one by one. The only hope any of the cops have is to cut a deal before the others do. The same way Eddie did. The first guy to open his mouth can walk; the others are going to do time. So if you don't want to see your husband behind bars, Mrs. Straub, I advise you to convince him to be the one to tell the truth."

"To be the one to rat out his friends, you mean," Annie retorted. She crossed her arms over her chest. "My husband is not that kind of man."

The door opened. All three of us turned toward the man who entered.

My first impression of Dwight Straub was that he was a pale imitation of someone else. His hair was sandy, thinning on top and revealing a broad forehead. His hands fiddled with the keys in his pocket, they ran through his hair, they waved in the air as he spoke, making odd, jabbing gestures that had little or nothing to do with what he was saying. His voice was high-pitched and verged on a squeak in his agitation at finding us in his living room.

"What are you doing here?" he demanded. He turned to his wife. "Why did you let them in?"

Dwight Straub stood in the doorway, his eyes wide with fear. He was a deer caught in the headlights; I was the Cadillac.

"I won't talk about Eddie," he said, his tone truculent, like a toddler refusing to eat his nice oatmeal. "You can't make me talk about Eddie."

"Actually, I can," I replied. "I can subpoena you and make you come to court, and then—"

"Get the hell out of here," Dwight said. His face was red; he looked like a three-year-old about to hold his breath. "Get out of here right now."

"Honey, maybe it would be better—" Annie began, but her husband was having none of it.

"I'm not talking to any lawyers, and I'm not talking about Eddie," Dwight shot back. He still stood in the doorway, his short-sleeved sport shirt stained under the arms, clutching a spiral notebook as if holding onto a life preserver. His balding head added to the babyish, unfinished quality of his moon face and smooth skin.

He was an unlikely cop; he looked more like an accountant for a small, failing business. A man continually on the edge, a man growing an ulcer, a man who took his work home with him and fretted about it through dinner. A man ripe for exploitation by the likes of Eddie Fitz.

"But is Eddie going to return the favor?" I inquired with an air of innocent curiosity.

"What's that supposed to mean?" Dwight tried for menacing, but only achieved petulance.

"You know what it means. Do you really think Eddie's going to stop with Matt Riordan? Or is he going to step into the grand jury room and start naming names? Cop names?"

Ninety percent of my attention was on Dwight; the look

on his face told me this question had kept him awake nights. The other ten percent was focused on Annie; her face said she'd been thinking about this possibility longer than her husband. She'd seen the potential for disaster in Eddie's cooperation with Nick Lazarus for a long time; Dwight was just beginning to catch up.

"He's going to sink you," I pointed out. "He's going to pin everything you guys did with TJ on you and Krieger. He's already on record as telling Lazarus he saw bad stuff go down on the street, but he wasn't part of it. He's stuck with that now; if he admits he lied, Nick Lazarus can and will charge him with perjury. So his only hope is to hold the line and blame you and Stan for TJ."

Dwight blanched. I'd thought his face was pale already, but it went so white I thought he was going to faint.

"What do you know about TJ?" he asked. For the first time, his face reflected menace; he wasn't just scared, he was scary. He took a step toward me, fists clenched at his side as though he was restraining himself from striking me.

Not that I was really afraid he'd hit me. But I could see now where street junkies could find this baby cop from East Cupcake, Long Island, someone to fear. On the street, they might have the ability to strike back, but in his own world, armed with a badge, he had authority it would be all too tempting to misuse.

And all my instincts were telling me he had misused it, that Dwight had joined Eddie Fitz in taking a big bite out of the tenderloin Jesse Winthrop had described. And now he was scared as hell he'd be found out and disgraced. Maybe even charged with murder, if anyone could prove who shot TJ and put him in the trunk of a car, setting him up to be found the same way Nunzie Aiello had been found.

I held up a placatory hand. "Hey, I'm just the messenger here," I pointed out. "I'm not saying anything you haven't already thought about. Eddie can't get a pass as the Hero Cop without somebody else getting covered in mud, and you and Stan are the logical candidates. You worked with Eddie on the special narcotics task force and Stan put TJ on record as a confidential informant.''

"How in hell did you know that?'' Dwight demanded. He came over to the sofa and sat down at the other end, still glaring at me.

"Isn't it interesting," I remarked, answering his question with one of my own, "how Eddie never manages to take official responsibility for anything? How he gets Stan on record as TJ's contact? I'll bet you're out front on something else, something that was really Eddie's, but Eddie put your name on it." I paused to gauge the effect my words were having. And they were having an effect; I knew that because Riordan was silent. If he'd thought I wasn't getting anywhere, he'd have had no compunction about jumping into the conversation.

"He's really good at that, Eddie. And now he's a big hero, picture on the cover of the *Voice*, movie deals I'll bet. And where are you and Stan?'' I continued, jabbing the needle in a little further. "In the shitcan, Dwight, that's where you are. In the shitcan, while Eddie Fitz—''

"Shut up! Will you just shut up and get out of here?''

"I could do that,'' I replied. "Or I could stay and talk to you about how to improve your position in all this.'' I leaned back on the sofa to indicate my willingness to spend the night if necessary.

This was disingenuous at best, unethical at worst. I represented Riordan, and my interest in Dwight Straub was strictly that of attorney seeking a witness; I had no right to offer under-the-table counseling to a man who might be facing serious charges himself. But I could listen to Dwight and help him get a lawyer; he'd need one if he did what I wanted him to do, which was to take the witness stand and tell the truth about Eddie Fitz.

It would be the end of him as a cop. I knew it and he knew it and Annie knew it.

"I know what you're thinking," I said. "You think that keeping your mouth shut about what went on is being a standup guy. You think Eddie and Stan will respect you for that. You think if you tell the truth, other cops will consider you a rat and a traitor. But what you really are is a patsy, Dwight. You're letting Eddie Fitz take you down because you're afraid to do what he did and cut a deal."

"Eddie didn't make any deals," Dwight retorted. "He told me and Stan he didn't cut a deal and I believe him."

I said nothing. I just looked at him, letting my face reflect the very real pity I was feeling for the man on the other end of the white sofa. He was like a kid, with his magic thinking: *If I close my eyes real tight and believe Eddie's my friend, then he won't hurt me.* But even he was beginning to realize magic wouldn't be enough.

"Maybe you should listen, Dwight," Annie Straub whispered. The words were said so softly I could almost believe I hadn't really heard them.

"You keep out of this," Dwight shouted. "You never liked Eddie, and now you want me to rat on him. I won't do it. I won't talk about Eddie, not to you, not to anybody."

"You'd better go," Annie said. She rose from her chair and led us to the door. As I walked behind her, I reflected that if I'd been alone with Annie, if neither man had been present, I might have convinced her that her husband's best interests lay in telling the truth about Eddie Fitz.

"Counselor, don't waste your breath," Stan Krieger said with a world-weary tone straight out of ten o'clock television. "I got nothing to say to you about Eddie or anything else."

It was 6:38 A.M.; I'd had about four hours of troubled sleep, waking every twenty minutes or so with yet another penetrating question I should have asked Dwight Straub. I was on a sleep cycle that was all-too-familiar to lawyers on trial: fitful sleep followed by too much coffee and heavy doses of adrenaline, followed by another sleepless night that required serious caffeine the next morning, which led to tossing and turning the next night, and so on. I stifled a yawn that had nothing to do with boredom.

"So it's okay with you that Eddie goes down as the Hero Cop, and you just go down," I said. I followed the detective from his battered desk over to the ancient coffee urn on the equally battered table, next to the battered wastebasket. Did the city really buy all this stuff new, or did they have open contracts with junkmen to buy up badly used office furniture?

He squeezed a cup out of the urn, tipping it to increase the flow. I figured there wasn't much left, but acting on my theory that a drink in the hand meant more time with the witness, I poured myself half a cup when he finished. I even skipped the sweetener so I could follow him back to his desk without fussing around.

"Look, you're not under oath," I pointed out. "In fact, you could deny every word that passes between us. Forget about testifying, just tell me the real truth about Eddie, person to person."

"Why?"

It was a good question. *Because I need you to help me acquit a criminal lawyer you probably think of as the scum of the earth* didn't strike me as a viable answer.

Then I remembered the photograph on the piano in Dwight Straub's living room, the picture in which Stan Krieger had sat slightly apart from his younger squad colleagues. The picture in which he looked like a disapproving uncle dragooned into playing with the children.

"Because you hate the man's guts," I shot back, firing on instinct, "and you want somebody to know what a piece of shit he is. You want it so bad you can taste it. You want to see Eddie Fitz brought down. You want to blow the lid off, to—"

"What I want and what I have to do are two different

things," Stan broke in. His voice was raw, harsh. His dark eyes were bloodshot, his cheeks an unhealthy color. The summer tan was fading badly, and there were heavy bags under his eyes. He looked like a bloodhound with a bad hangover.

I pushed all the chips forward into the pot and called.

"There's going to be a book, you know," I said casually. "And a movie, too. I talked to Jesse Winthrop, and—"

"That cop-hating prick," Stan muttered. "What's he got to do with anything?"

"He's writing the book," I said. "And selling the movie rights to Eddie's story. I hear," I lied, "that they're talking about Johnny Depp for Eddie's part. I wonder," I went on, "who they'll get to play you? Somebody who's good at villains, I suppose. One of the usual Hollywood heavies. Someone who'll be believable as Stan the Man: the older, corrupt cop who leads the saintly Eddie into temptation."

"Will you shut up!" Stan jumped from his chair so fast, he knocked his coffee onto the floor.

"Fuck!" he screamed, hopping back as the hot liquid hit his pants leg. "Jesus fuck!" He slapped at his leg with a force that probably left a bruise. The look on his face was murderous; if a cup of coffee could die, that one would have—

No. The anger wasn't directed at the coffee. It wasn't even directed at me, despite the furious glance he shot me as I handed him a fistful of napkins.

"You're going to let Eddie get away with it, then?" I asked, going for a conversational tone, as if Stan had spilled his coffee in some perfectly ordinary mishap.

"Get away with it?" Stan parried. He tossed a wad of sodden, coffee-colored napkins on the desktop. Then he drew in a breath and let it out with a long, ragged sigh. "That little fuck's been getting away with it for years, you know that?"

I knew better than to say anything. In fact, I was afraid

to nod, afraid to respond in any way. Stan the Man was just bursting to talk, but if he stopped for half a second to recall just who he was talking to, the fountain would dry up.

"You know what he did when they Psyched him?" It took a moment to translate the cop-speak; when I did, I had to restrain myself from reaching for a notebook and demanding details. What Stan was telling me was that Eddie Fitz, Lazarus' key witness, had been sent to the police department's Psychological Services Unit for evaluation. One more little fact Davia Singer had neglected to include in her packet of discovery materials.

Stan kept talking, the words rushing out as if they'd been dammed up too long. "We had a racket over at Dwight's," the detective recalled. "One of the guys on the squad got a promotion to OCCB downtown," he explained. "Eddie got drunk and loud, the way he always did. He's yelling about the Department shrink, about how they're gonna twist his words around, but he's got a way to beat them. He's gonna wear a wire, go in with a tape recorder."

"Is that allowed?" I asked, daring to interrupt.

"Shit, no, it's not allowed," Stan retorted, giving me a civilians-are-stupid look. "But that's what I mean about Eddie. He got away with it. He taped the interview with the shrink, and the next thing everybody knows, he's passed with flying colors." Stan shook his head. "If I'd pulled something like that, it's dollars to donuts they'd have found the wire and hit me with a disciplinary action. But Eddie"—he paused and shook his head, reluctant admiration on his face—"Eddie waltzes into Psych Services wearing a wire and walks out with a tape of his interview and nobody down there's the wiser."

I took a shot and asked the same question I'd thrown at Dwight Straub the night before: "If you feel that way about Eddie Fitz, why not tell the truth about him?"

Stan shook his head. "You just don't get it, do you?"

he said. "If I do that, I'm dead as a cop. I may be dead anyway, which I suppose is what you're going to tell me next, but at least I go down with some dignity. I don't go down naming names of all the cops I ever worked with. I don't go down," he finished with palpable contempt, "like Eddie."

I finished my half-cup of coffee and sat with Stan for another fifteen minutes. As I questioned him, I visualized the scene that would take place if I subpoenaed him to testify in Riordan's case. He'd give name, rank, and serial number, and, as soon as things got hot, he'd intone the words of the Fifth Amendment to the United States Constitution—and that would be the end. Judge de Freitas would strike his testimony, and the jury would never hear what Stan the Man Krieger had to say.

CHAPTER SEVEN

One good thing about having a lawyer for a client: Riordan met me at the courthouse with four perfectly drafted subpoenas in hand. One was for the FBI, and essentially amended the one we'd already served to include the fact that John Doe "TJ" was deceased; the other was addressed to the NYPD and called for all police reports regarding the discovery of the body.

The other two were for Stan Krieger and Dwight Straub; I was determined to bring them into court and let them decide for themselves whether to tell the truth about Eddie Fitz or hide behind the Fifth Amendment.

Davia Singer walked over to me as I handed the subpoenas to the judge's clerk for His Honor's signature. They were useless pieces of paper unless Judge de Freitas agreed the information we wanted was relevant to Matt's trial.

Singer took one look at what we wanted and said, "You'll never get these signed. We'll oppose."

"Go ahead," I invited. "Oppose. Go get Nick Lazarus right now." I looked the younger woman in the eye and added, my tone tinged with contempt, "Go get your boss. I'm sure he'll want to argue this himself rather than trust you with it."

The charge was true enough to bring a flush of anger to Davia Singer's sallow cheeks. She opened her mouth as if she wanted very much to tell me she could argue her own motions to quash, thank you very much, but then she turned and walked away, the heels of her pumps clicking on the hard floor of the courtroom. The truth was, Lazarus would want to argue these subpoenas himself, and she didn't dare fail to inform him of what we were up to.

The Great Man himself came down within a scant five minutes. He strode to the clerk's desk without a word to me or Matt, picked up the subpoenas without asking the clerk's permission, and said, loudly enough to be heard at the defense table, "What's all this shit about a dead drug dealer, anyway?"

We all stood as Judge de Freitas entered, even though there was no jury in the room. Looking more than ever like a medieval painting of Saint Jerome, scholarly, ascetic, with an egg-shaped head and a sallow complexion, he took the bench amid a swirl of black robe. He'd presided over the courtroom like a law professor conducting an advanced seminar, and he proceeded to view the four subpoenas in the same bloodless way.

"Your Honor may recall," I began, "that the defense has already subpoenaed FBI records regarding this man TJ. We have reason to believe that TJ could have presented relevant evidence in this trial regarding Detective Fitzgerald's credibility. In fact," I went on, "the defense had every intention of calling TJ to the stand as a witness in this case."

"You speak in the past tense, Ms. Jameson," the judge said in his dry, papery voice. "Am I to assume this TJ is no longer on the defense witness list?"

"TJ is dead," I replied, "a fact the defense learned only last night."

"Then if he is not going to be called as a witness, how is he relevant?"

Lazarus stood next to me with a smirk on his face, as if the judge's statement were a direct consequence of some brilliant argument he'd made.

"He's relevant, Your Honor," I said, plunging ahead in spite of an inner misgiving that I didn't have the evidence to back up my claim, "because the defense has reason to believe that TJ had dealings with Detective Fitzgerald that might have tended to undermine his credibility." I was deliberately couching my remarks in legalese; the judge disliked emotional outbursts, and I wanted Nick Lazarus to be the one who appeared irrationally angry, while I presented a picture of cool competence.

Lazarus blustered, but in the end, the judge signed the four subpoenas. "I'll reserve decision as to the admissibility of this material," he said, "until after I've seen the reports themselves."

I thanked the judge and hastened out of the courtroom, eager to place the subpoenas into the hands of my investigator. Angie was under instructions to get them served at the earliest opportunity. They were "forthwith" subpoenas, which meant the information could be in court as early as the next day.

"Don't worry, Carmelita," she said in a stage whisper in the corridor outside the courtroom. "I'll get these served pronto. This is the Angelina express leaving right now."

But the Mean Streak kept moving, its pace inexorable. I needed sleep; I needed coffee; I needed a viable defense. But what I got was a parade of secondary witnesses: waiters at the Chinese and Italian restaurants Eddie Fitz and Fat Jack had frequented; Paulie the Cork Corcoran, who admitted handing over grand jury minutes in return for cash.

On cross, Paulie admitted he'd never actually taken

money from Matt, nor had he handed the manila envelope with the grand jury minutes to my client. All his dealings had been with Fat Jack; at most, he'd exchanged a little courthouse gossip and Chinese noodles with Riordan. I breathed a little easier when the disgraced court clerk stepped down; he hadn't laid a glove on us.

The real damage would be done after the lunch break, when Eddie Fitz would step up and take the oath.

I was stopped on the way out of the courthouse, not by the usual reporter, but by Annie Straub.

"I have to talk to you," she said in a low voice.

Matt, standing next to me on top of the stone steps, said, "I'll grab lunch and meet you back here at two." He strode down the stairway before I could respond.

I'd sensed that Annie and I could talk more freely woman-to-woman, and now I was going to have my chance.

"Shall we have lunch?" I asked.

She nodded. She turned and began the hazardous walk down the steep stone steps that had no railing. She wore a rayon print dress in royal blue, with an antique lace collar. It tied in the back like a little girl's dress, but the hemline was high enough to reveal shapely legs in caramel-colored hose.

I followed, making my way through the crowd with difficulty.

A voice behind me caught my attention. It was one of the print reporters from the trial. "Ms. Jameson," he called as he raced toward me, his steno pad open. "Can you answer a question for me, please?"

I nodded. Much as I would have liked to brush him off, I was under orders from my client to maintain good relations with the press. I gave him a quick summary of the morning's activities, then turned back to Dwight Straub's wife.

"Sorry about that," I said with a self-deprecatory shrug.

"Maybe we should start walking, get away from this crowd."

"I have an idea," she said. "But it will only work if you're not really hungry."

"Hungry? Me? Not at all," I lied. It was more important to put Annie at ease than to take in calories.

"Then come with me," she said. She walked purposefully toward the little church that lay hidden behind the skirts of the federal courthouse. It was a tiny brick building, dwarfed by the huge public edifices that towered over it. I glanced up at the portico above the simple columns and resolved to ask Riordan, the former altarboy, to translate the Latin motto: *Beati qui ambulant in lege Domini.*

I decided to ask Annie Straub instead.

She gave a small, indulgent smile. "It means 'Blessed are they who walk in the law of the Lord,' " she translated. "It's not a real beatitude or anything, but I always liked walking past it."

She turned right at the church and walked down the little alleyway that separated it from the Federal Correctional Center, which also housed the United States attorney's office. When she reached a gate leading to a side door, she pulled it open.

"We can go into the church?" I asked, surprised.

"There's a meeting room back here," she explained. "I have a key." She fished in her purse and pulled out a single key on a ring; there was a triangle within a circle on the emblem. She unlocked the door and pushed it open so we could enter.

The room was functional, undecorated. Perhaps fifty folding chairs were set up in a casual grouping; there was a table at what would have been a focal point of attention, and on another table in the back there was an unplugged coffee urn. It didn't take much imagination to figure out what kind of meetings took place here.

"I didn't know you were AA," I said as I lowered myself onto one of the folding chairs.

She nodded. "Almost two years. I'm in charge of opening the room for the Tuesday meeting," she explained. "Because I work so close by, I guess. And it's one of the things you do in the program—you do service."

"Where do you work?" I asked, still trying to put her more at ease.

"I work for General Services," she replied, naming the New York City agency responsible for purchasing. It was housed in the Municipal Building, on the other side of the plaza. "My office is all the way up on the nineteenth floor," she added. "My boss has a great view of the harbor from his window."

"It was a good idea, coming in here," I said.

She gave a small laugh that echoed hollowly in the big room. "I guess I picked it because I've said a lot of things in these rooms that were pretty hard to say to another person. I thought maybe it would help me talk to you if I was in a place where I felt safe." She took a deep breath and said the words I'd hoped to hear. "I don't want Dwight to take the rap for Eddie."

My conscience gave me a little stab; in truth, she wasn't really safe with me. I had a client and an agenda, and I had just arranged to serve a subpoena on her husband. I decided it would be all right to continue this conversation if I made these facts as clear as possible.

"Look, I represent Matt Riordan," I reminded her. "I can't give you legal advice, but I can sure as hell advise you to find an attorney you can trust, and put yourself in his hands."

"You really think Dwight needs a lawyer?" She might as well have been asking a doctor if her husband needed brain surgery.

"Yes," I said. "Especially if he's thinking of coming forward to testify against Eddie."

"I'll tell Dwight what you said," Annie replied. She

gave a small sigh and went on. "He was so excited when he got the promotion and the assignment to Narcotics." Her voice softened at the memory. "I got all dressed up and went over to the ceremony at One Police Plaza."

She stopped and looked down at the chapped hands in her lap, then glanced up at me shyly. "I've been going down there ever since I was a kid," she explained. "When my dad made sergeant, my mom dressed us kids up and we took off school to see him in his uniform, shaking the police commissioner's hand. I forget who it was back then, but it was a good long time ago. Then we all had lunch over in Chinatown with one of Dad's buddies and his family. It was a real high point; Dad has the promotion photo on his desk at home to this day."

"Is your father still on the job?" I asked, careful to word it the way an insider would. Annie Straub was a cop's daughter; that meant something, but I wasn't sure what.

"My dad retired six, seven years ago. But he was real proud of Dwight when he made detective. He liked for Dwight to bring his buddies over for barbecues and football games. He liked Eddie—liked him a lot." There was a wistful quality to her voice; had her father liked Eddie Fitz, the outgoing party boy, better than his own son-in-law?

It was worth a shot. "How does your husband get along with your dad?"

"Fine." She said the word quickly. Too quickly. I said nothing, hoping the silence would become uncomfortable enough for her to want to fill it.

"He likes Dwight," she finally said, lowering her eyes as if ashamed to betray her husband, "but I think Eddie reminded my dad of the way he was when he was a young cop. Eddie took chances, whereas Dwight is more—I don't know, careful."

"And careful is not something your father values?"

Her lips twisted in rueful disdain. "Oh, he says he respects Dwight. He talks about how different it was in the old days, how a college guy couldn't hope to be a good cop back then, but now they need all the education they can get. But underneath, he thinks balls are better than brains. And if there's one thing Eddie Fitzgerald has, it's balls. Big brass ones that clank when he walks.''

Something in the set of her jaw put me on the alert. I took another wild shot. ''Did Eddie ever come on to you?''

Her hand jumped to her bosom in an instinctive, protective gesture. ''How the hell could you—'' She broke off and gathered herself together. ''It was at a party at our house. It was in honor of some guy's promotion. Eddie was at least half in the bag. He was drinking more than usual,'' she said, raising her eyes to meet mine, ''because he was being sent to Psych Services and it was making him crazy.''

My own eyes must have reflected something of what I was feeling, because Annie gave a quick, mirthless laugh and said, ''Why am I making excuses for him? He was drunk and he came into the kitchen and started groping me. What really pissed me off was that he made damn sure Dwight saw what he was up to. He cornered me in the kitchen and stepped too close and put his hands all over me. And all the time Dwight was in the living room, right where he could see what was going on.''

''What happened?'' I had visions of the night ending with .38 specials at dawn. The way many a cop party has ended.

She saw where my thoughts were going and shook her head. ''Dwight came in and said something to Eddie. Eddie just laughed and said he couldn't help himself, I was so beautiful he had to make a move or Dwight would have felt insulted. It was total bullshit and I could see Dwight didn't like it any better than I did, but he laughed it off and the two of them went out into the yard with a bottle and two glasses.''

''Eddie sounds like a real prince,'' I remarked.

"Prince of Assholes," she muttered, then grinned like a teenager.

"If you feel that way about him," I said, echoing Matt's words of the night before, "why not help bring him down?"

"That's just what I want to do," she said with a grim smile. "But I have to be sure it doesn't hurt my Dwight," she added, her jaw tight.

I couldn't honestly see a way that this whole situation wouldn't hurt her Dwight, no matter what he did or didn't do, but I didn't tell her that. What I did instead was repeat my earlier advice. "Get a lawyer. Right away."

She nodded and swallowed hard. "I never thought the day Dwight was promoted that it would end like this."

The food booths were right outside the church; I decided I had time for a quick slice of pizza before I met Matt. I got on line and in short order had a triangle of crust dripping with cheese in my hand. I leaned well forward as I bit into it, not wanting oil spots on my new designer clothes.

I decided I also had time to serve my own subpoena. I finished the slice and strode across Centre Street to 26 Federal Plaza.

Warren Zebart looked up with a scowl when I walked into the bullpen office where he sat in his shirtsleeves. "What do you want?" he said in a tone that could only be called a growl.

I gave him an innocent stare. "What's the matter?" I asked. "Aren't you used to dealing with the public in here?"

"You're not the public, Ms. Jameson. You're a lawyer and you ought to go through the proper channels."

"Proper channels are for lawyers with money," I replied with a smile I tried hard to make conciliatory. "I thought I'd save time and bucks by serving my own subpoena." I set my briefcase on the edge of his desk without asking permission and clicked open the brass fasteners. His scowl deepened; every move I made signaled my intention to stay as long as I wanted.

I pulled out the subpoena and handed it over. He could have taken it without glancing at the documents called for, but I was banking on his natural curiosity.

He skimmed the subpoena. "What do you want this stuff for?" he asked.

"At the risk of sounding rude," I replied, "all you have to know is that the judge signed it earlier this morning."

I pushed my luck. "Hell, we both know TJ was killed because of his involvement with Eddie Fitz. The NYPD was called off the investigation on the grounds that TJ was a witness in a federal case. I'm going to get this stuff; the only question is when. I guess I'm wondering why I can't have it now—if the Bureau has nothing to hide."

He gave it some thought. His lower teeth reached up and grabbed the ends of his graying mustache. He nibbled a bit and then stood up. "I'll have to make some phone calls," he said.

"I can wait," I replied, making ready to sit down in the straight chair next to his desk.

"Not here," he said firmly. "You can sit in the waiting room."

The waiting room consisted of one row of welded-plastic chairs in royal blue and a glass coffee table laden with outdated magazines. It looked like the office of a singularly unprosperous dentist. I picked up an ancient *New Yorker* and thumbed through it, looking for the cartoons.

Zebart summoned me back into the sanctum some fifteen minutes later. "Lazarus said I should give you everything," he told me, his tone considerably more affable.

"He also said he wouldn't mind if I shared my own theory of the case with you," he went on.

"That's very generous," I said, my mind racing to figure out what the catch was.

It wasn't long in coming. "See, the thing you've got to remember," Zebart said, his tone still eerily conversational, "is that when this TJ character was killed—not when his body was found, you understand, but when he was actually killed—your client had more reason to worry about him than Eddie did."

"Riordan? Riordan didn't even know there was a TJ until we started hearing rumors."

Warren Zebart's mouth grimaced into a nasty smile. "That's what he wanted you to think, Counselor," the FBI man said, "but TJ worked for your client's client, remember. He was Nunzie Aiello's front man in the ghetto. Do you really believe your client didn't know Aiello had a partner?"

I got the point. I knew I was getting the point because my stomach sank into my pumps. "You were going to put the squeeze on TJ to nail Riordan for suborning perjury in the Nunzie Aiello case."

"No, Ms. Jameson," the agent said with a mock-mournful shake of his head. "I was going to put the squeeze on TJ to nail your client for murdering Nunzie Aiello."

"You can't seriously believe—"

"Oh, but I can," Zebart cut in. "I can and I do. Nunzie Aiello was killed in almost the same way Donatello Scaniello bought it three years ago. Maybe you didn't take much of an interest in the case at that time. Maybe you don't recall the particulars. Let me refresh your memory." Zebart was enjoying this; there were little flecks of spittle at the edges of his mouth.

"See, Donatello was killed the same way. Two bullets, one in the head, one in the mouth. And they mushroomed inside the body like hollow-points. Makes it hard to get a match. The bullet deforms as it travels. Only in Donatello's case, the bullets weren't hollow-points, they were hollow-base. The killer put them in backwards; the damned things exploded in the body and left Ballistics with a lump they couldn't possibly match. Same thing with Nunzie. Hollow-base bullets put in backwards. Now,'' Zebart continued, warming to his theme, ''this was a little fact the Bureau managed to keep from the press. We didn't tell a soul about those bullets, just said they were deformed. Any citizen reading the account would have thought 'hollow-points.' Only someone who knew the precise details of the Scan-iello hit would have known to reverse hollow-base bullets. It was a copycat hit, and that means only someone who really knew the inside story of how the Don died could have copied it.''

''Fine,'' I replied, ''but how does that lead to Riordan?''

''We have tapes,'' the FBI man said with an affable smile, a smile that told me how much he was enjoying this. ''Tapes of Frankie Cretella and his goombahs sitting around shooting the shit. Somebody brings up Nunzie, asks Frankie C. what he's going to do about Nunz talking to Lazarus, maybe bringing down Matt Riordan. And you want to know what Frankie says?''

I wasn't sure that I did, but I nodded anyway. ''He says, 'So the feds take down my lawyer. Big fucking deal; lawyers are a dime a dozen—no, make that a nickel a dozen. Fuck, a nickel for two dozen. So I'll hire me another boy. What do I care a mick like Riordan takes a bath?' ''

Zebart's smile showed cigarette-stained teeth. ''Some loyalty, huh? That's what Riordan got for twenty years of getting Frankie C. out of jams. And that left your client high and dry; Nunzie was going to put him away, and Fran-kie the Crate wasn't going to do jackshit about it. See,'' the agent went on, ''as far as Frankie was concerned, Nun-zie was just a gofer. But one of his little jobs was to carry messages between Frankie's goombahs and their lawyer, meaning Matt Riordan. Put those messages together and you have solid proof that your client wasn't just a lawyer representing individuals—he was the lawyer for an illegal organization.''

"House counsel for the Mob," I murmured, echoing the damaging words Judge Schansky had used when he bounced Matt off the last Cretella case. This was sounding too plausible for comfort.

"So there was only one thing for Riordan to do," Zebart continued, "and he did it. He hit Nunzie himself, and he made it look as much as possible like a Mob hit."

"You can't really believe this," I protested. Some corner of my mind was aware that this was a truly weak defense, but I hadn't had time to assimilate all the information and innuendoes that were piling up around me.

"As I said, Counselor, I can and I do. And what's more, I believe that Riordan was so pleased by his success in wiping out the Nunzie Aiello threat that he did the same to TJ. And there may not be anything I can do about it," he went on, "but it might interest you to know that I'm not the only one who's noticed the similarities between the two murders." He smiled his wolfish smile and popped a cassette into the tape player on top of his desk. He whirred it on fast forward, then pushed the Play button.

". . . really pisses me off when guys think they can pin a lotta shit on us, do things our way, mislead the public." The voice was raspy, a caricature Mob boss.

"Yeah, I can see where that would roast your chestnuts, all right. Some asshole making that nigger's death look like a hit."

"I find out that sleazebag lawyer's behind this, he's gonna pay. That's all I'm gonna say. He's gonna know what it means to be on the business end of a hit, I find out he whacked Nunz. And if he did the nigger, too—"

Zebart stopped the tape. "Just a taste of what your client can expect when we try him for murdering a federal witness," he said.

I wasn't about to leave with defeat in the air. "If you

had the evidence to indict him," I said firmly, "you'd do it. And since you haven't indicted him, I can only conclude that you haven't got the evidence."

The FBI man's last word chilled the air: "Yet," he said.

Eddie Fitz was good. The way he averted his eyes just a little when he was about to tell the jury how he'd slipped behind his corrupt partner's back to do a favor for the shop-owner who'd given his partner a kickback. As if he didn't want to seem like too much of a saint. Or the way he cleared his throat and spoke up manfully when admitting that he'd twice given drugs to an informant. On both occasions, according to Eddie, the junkie in question was "really sick." The gray-blue eyes pleaded with the jury to understand how things are on the street, to set aside their middle-class prejudices and see the sweating, shaking remnants of humanity begging Eddie Fitz for just enough heroin to get them well.

It was *NYPD Blue* without the television screen between the jury and their hero. A street-smart cop, just corrupt enough to get along with his brothers in blue, just hard enough to survive in the concrete jungle, not hard enough to sit still while a junkie sobs for his medicine. They'd seen it all before, in prime time.

This time it was being brought to them by U.S. Attorney Davia Singer and her executive producer, Nick Lazarus.

Lazarus knew was the thought that kept chugging through my brain as I watched Singer take Eddie Fitz through his paces. Eddie Fitz had done more than just turn the other way while TJ sold drugs in his precinct: Eddie Nino, Eddie Bigmouth, was TJ's full partner in the heroin business.

And Lazarus had known.

But could we prove it? Could we prove it, now that TJ was dead?

"Detective," Davia repeated, her throaty voice going all

earnest, "you admit you gave narcotics to a known drug addict in violation of the Penal Code of the State of New York on two occasions. Is there any other act of misconduct in your tenure as a police officer that this jury should know about?"

He hung his head for six seconds. Six precisely; I had my eye on the dial of my watch. Then he raised his head and I swear to God there were tears in the altarboy eyes.

"No," he said in a low whisper. He cleared his throat again. "No, and I wish to God I'd never—"

"Objection," I rapped out, jumping to my feet. "Unresponsive to the question, Your Honor."

Judge de Freitas smiled a dry little smile; his black eyes narrowed behind his half-glasses as he considered the objection. "Overruled," he said in a tone so soft I had to lean forward to hear him. "You may proceed, Ms. Singer."

She was magnanimous in victory. "Thank you, Your Honor," she said with only the tiniest smile of smug triumph.

"Detective," she continued in a tone of high portentousness, "I ask you to search your soul. Is there any act of misconduct, any criminal act, any unethical behavior in your past besides the two you have forthrightly reported to this court?"

I had to object to the "forthrightly." Once my objection was disposed of in the usual manner, Eddie Fitz gazed at the jurors, one by one. I timed it: twenty seconds. Over one second each, including alternates. It was all I could do to keep from shaking my head in admiration. If there were Oscars for Best Performance by a Corrupt Cop Turned State's Witness, Eddie Fitz would have—

Who cared? It was working. That was the problem—it was fucking working. Without TJ, the jurors would never know the truth behind the Hero Cop façade.

Eddie surveyed the jurors one by one, the look in his pale eyes one of hope and concern. He looked at each of them the way he might look at his grandmother or a favorite uncle, after confessing to something he knew they'd disapprove of. Do you still like me? he seemed to ask. Please like me; I'm really good underneath.

"I was a good cop," he said. He swallowed; his Adam's apple jumped in his skinny throat. "I wanted to be a cop more than anything in the world. And I'm so ashamed—"

His voice broke. He dropped his head; his shoulders heaved. The straight, fine hair fell over his forehead, making him look even more like a teenager confessing to having gotten his best girl in trouble.

"More than anything in the world," he said, his tone ragged, his eyes red with unshed tears, "I wish I could have my reputation as a good cop back. That's what I regret most about all this. That when people hear my name, they won't remember the good things I did. All they'll know is that I took part in corrupt acts. They won't know why. They won't care that I was trying to help people who were really hurting."

"Thank you, Detective," Davia Singer said. She said the words softly, like an Amen in church. As if to raise her voice would be to intrude on this intensely private moment.

An intensely private moment I had no doubt had been rehearsed for several hours in the U.S. attorney's office.

CHAPTER EIGHT

As I stood up to cross-examine Eddie Fitz, I felt as if the Mean Streak lurched at 100 miles per hour, then plunged down a canyon of steel, rocketing me faster than I'd ever gone before. This was a make-or-break cross; either I damaged Eddie's credibility in the eyes of the jury or I reconciled myself to watching de Freitas bang Matt away for several years for something I had become increasingly convinced he hadn't done.

Eddie had just repeated, in ringing tones, his allegation that Matt had given him a thousand dollars in return for a manila envelope containing secret grand jury minutes.

A thousand bucks. That alone, I thought as I gazed into Eddie's cool blue-gray eyes, should have been enough to acquit Matt Riordan. He wore suits that cost more than that every day of the week; he drove a silver Jaguar and ate at the finest restaurants. He was a man of taste and class; he did not take manila envelopes and hand over a fistful of cash to crooked cops.

It was a bush-league crime, and my client was major league all the way.

But did that concept constitute a winning summation?

Looking over at the twelve citizens, plus two alternates, sitting in the jury box, I decided reluctantly that it didn't.

"Some nights I went wired," Eddie Fitz said, using a laconic tone that could have come straight from a Clint Eastwood movie. It was a tone that implied a great deal of worldly wisdom, a lifetime of seeing horrors he would spare us civilians.

"And how did your boss decide when you should wear the wire and when you could go to the meeting without it?" One thing I'd noticed from my review of the tapes was that whoever made the decision had an unerring instinct for knowing when Eddie would be searched and when he wouldn't. I was willing to bet the decision was Eddie's, not a deskbound lawyer's.

He bit the bait. "He didn't. I made all those decisions." The boast lurked under his deadpan pose.

"Oh, you decided," I said in a tone that conveyed admiration. I laid on a little more butter. "I guess I assumed that decision would be made by Nick Lazarus, or by the FBI agent who 'handled' you. That is what it's called, isn't it?" I went on innocently. " 'Handling' the informant?"

He gave a curt nod; just as I'd suspected, he didn't want to talk about someone else handling him; he wanted to take the credit. So I shifted back to the wire, deciding to give him some rope and see how close he came to hanging himself.

"But on the night Matt Riordan allegedly handed you money in return for a manila envelope containing grand jury minutes, the night of the most important event in this entire undercover operation, the night you were going to participate in the crime itself, you just happened to go to the meeting without a wire, didn't you?"

The answer should have been yes. That was all: yes. I'd carefully crafted the question so that yes was the only possible answer.

But that wasn't the answer I got. "Look," the Hero Cop retorted, "after what almost happened to me the time before that, I sure as hell wasn't gonna wear a wire to that meet. I nearly got killed."

"Objection, Your Honor," I shouted, trying to drown out the altarboy voice. "Unresponsive to the question."

Singer weighed in. "Your Honor," she proclaimed in ringing tones that carried through the courtroom, "the answer was very responsive. Just because counsel doesn't like the answer doesn't make it inadmissible."

"Agreed, Ms. Singer," the judge said. "Overruled. You may proceed, Ms. Jameson."

I proceeded. I proceeded to ask Eddie Fitz questions all over the lot, dredging up the names of every junkie I intended to call to the stand, mentioning TJ's name too, as if I could somehow convince Eddie the dealer was going to rise from the dead, step into the courthouse, and call him a liar. I was laying the groundwork for what I knew would be a futile attempt to undermine the Hero Cop's credibility. I was also hoping to bury the memory of Eddie Fitz talking about his life being in danger.

But the problem with cross-examination is that it's followed by redirect. The other side gets to stand up and repair whatever damage you've done. Which was what Davia Singer hastened to do.

She asked about the night Eddie had mentioned, the night he said his life was in danger. I objected. I approached the bench. We even took it outside into the corridor behind the courtroom and argued on the record for fifteen minutes. But in the end, the judge ruled that I'd opened the door on cross.

The little smirk Singer gave me as we returned to the courtroom told me I'd walked into a trap. Eddie Fitz had been coached to answer my question the way that he had, to sneak in a reference to the incident on cross so that Singer could make a big splash on redirect, tell the jury something they hadn't heard before.

It was a nice trick, and I felt a fool at having fallen for it. I wondered, as I walked back to counsel table, whether Riordan would have let it happen, or if he would have found some way to close this door I'd inadvertently opened.

It didn't matter. What mattered was that Eddie Fitz started telling the jurors how he almost lost his life because he'd gone wired to the meeting just prior to the one at which he said Riordan paid him off.

"See, they heard talk," Eddie explained. "Paulie says they heard a rumor in the precinct about a cop turned bad, a cop who was working for Lazarus, helping put a rope around other cops' necks. And somehow they heard that cop was me."

Singer asked just enough questions to keep the flow coming. Eddie sat at his ease in the witness chair, shooting the breeze the way he would have at a cop bar. Only instead of cop stories told to impress the groupies, this was testimony under oath, guaranteed to put my client behind bars.

"So this one night, Paulie says to me, 'Nobody likes a rat, Eddie.' I say to him, 'Who you callin' a rat? Are we back on that shit again, Paulie? You think I'm a rat, search me,' I tell him. 'Open my coat. What the fuck,' I say— excuse me, Your Honor, but that's what I said—'what the fuck, open my pants, take out my dick and see if I got a wire wrapped around it. And while you got my pants open, you can kiss my—' "

I objected. No grounds, just general principles. Overruled, but at least I broke the spell. For a second and a half.

"The thing that had me nearly shitting my pants—pardon the expression, Your Honor—is that I was wearin' the wire. I was bluffin' all the way with that talk about how I was gonna open my coat."

I jumped to my feet. I'd listened to every tape in the prosecutor's arsenal; why hadn't I heard this one before?

In the hallway, out of the hearing of the bewildered jurors, I made my pitch strong and hot. "Your Honor," I argued, fueled by a passion for fairness that was all too real, "the defense moves for a mistrial. This evidence was never turned over to the defense prior to trial; I've heard every single tape and I have no copy of this one."

De Freitas turned to Singer, whose answer tripped off her tongue with a swiftness that said she had all the bases covered. "Your Honor," she said, "the truth is that the recording equipment failed on the night in question. There is no recorded evidence of this incident; if there had been, it would most certainly have been turned over at arraignment along with the other tapes."

"Do you really expect me to believe that?" My voice cracked; I was too furious to think about the consequences of my words. "You waltz in here at the last minute and fill the jurors' ears with a load of crap about Eddie nearly getting killed, and you haven't even got it on tape?"

"Ms. Jameson," the judge intoned, giving me a black look, "if you're accusing the United States Attorney of something dishonest, I warn you I don't take kindly to tactics like that in my courtroom."

"What about tactics like letting a witness testify to an uncharged crime, Your Honor?" I protested. "There isn't one shred of evidence that Matt Riordan was present on the night in question, and nothing to indicate that he knew about the alleged incident, and yet the jury is being allowed to speculate that he had something to do with this so-called threat to Detective Fitzgerald's life."

"Your Honor," Singer explained in a voice that held no hint of doubt about the rightness of her own position, "this evidence is not being admitted for the truth of the allegations. It is admitted for the sole purpose of disproving Ms. Jameson's theory of why Detective Fitzgerald wore no wire on the night the money changed hands."

"Oh, that's beautiful," I countered. "You want the jury to disregard the testimony about Eddie Fitz nearly buying the farm. That's not supposed to prejudice them against Matt Riordan by association. They're only supposed to listen to the part that says why Eddie didn't go to the next meeting wired for sound.''

In the end, Eddie was permitted to continue his story. I had a motion for a mistrial on the record; I'd have to bone up on federal appeals. Although if my friend Lani was right, my chances on appeal were about one-fifth as good as they were at the trial level. And we were getting creamed at the trial level.

''So Fat Jack said, 'We heard you were talking to Lazarus, that you're going to rat out a bunch of cops you work with,' '' Eddie Fitz said. The jurors hung on every word; this was at least as good as what they saw every week on television.

''So I said, 'Hey, the whole squad is acting crazy. Everybody's lookin' at everybody else, wondering who's going to bring who down. So I try to lighten things up a little, make a joke out of it.' '' Eddie Fitz turned his guileless eyes on the jury and gave a sheepish little shrug. ''I'm trying to talk my way out of it,'' he explained, ''like I always done. Only this time, they're pushing me around. I'm on the street with the two of them, and Fat Jack is pushing me down the street. It's late, I'm alone out there, and I'm really getting scared.

''I tell them, 'You think a guy who's really working for Lazarus is going to go around making jokes?' Then Fat Jack says, 'Some things you don't make jokes about, Eddie. Like things that could put our asses in a sling.' ''

Singer slid another question into the monologue. Eddie paced the story nicely; the jurors were glued to his every word.

''Paulie pushed me into an alley near Fat Jack's office,'' Eddie went on. ''He tried to get under my coat. I told him to stand back or I'd shoot his pecker off. He laughed. 'You never carry a gun off-duty, Eddie,' he says. 'Everybody knows that.' And the truth was, he was right. I had no gun. But Paulie did. He had it and he pulled it out and I swear I thought I was gonna die right there, only a uniformed cop came around the corner and asked if everything was all right. I don't know where the hell my backup was, but I followed that cop out of the alley and walked away. I felt lucky to be alive, that's all I can say.''

I glanced at the jurors. They were eating it up. Mouths hung open, eyes avidly took in the sight of the Hero Cop downplaying his courage under fire.

Before I could begin recross, the judge banged his gavel and adjourned for the day.

I had to walk. I had to get out of that courthouse before I exploded into a thousand red-hot pieces. If someone had handed me a machine gun, I would have held it at waist-level and mowed down everyone in my path. I wanted Judge de Freitas dead, I wanted Nick Lazarus pinned to the ground with fire ants crawling all over his writhing body. I wanted Davia Singer's head on a Thanksgiving turkey platter. I wanted—

I wanted to turn back the clock to that night at Tre Scalini and tell Matthew Daniel Riordan to get another lawyer.

I had to walk. My pumps had two-and-a-half-inch heels (a compromise; Matt had wanted three-inchers to shape my calves, and I'd told him two inches was my limit) and a skirt that clung to my hips. I was wearing a silk blouse that cost more than the outfit I'd previously considered my best suit. I was not dressed for a hike, but I had to walk.

I said as much to Riordan. His failure to protest clued me into the fact that I was wearing the facial expression of a Fury; nobody with any sense of self-preservation was going to get in my way. I sped past the press, plastering a smile on my face.

My legs hurt already. I didn't care. I had to walk. I strode past the Municipal Building and crossed the street at the light. Halfway across, I walked along the traffic island until I came to the walkway to the Brooklyn Bridge.

The Eighth Wonder of the World, they'd called it when it was finished in 1883. The tallest edifice in New York City, or any other city at the time, it spans the East River in a graceful arc. Its huge, weathered Gothic arches created a cathedral effect that calmed me the minute I stepped onto the planked walkway in the middle of the bridge. On either side, traffic sped by in opposite directions. To my left, the Manhattan Bridge stood in all its pedestrian glory, a monument to what engineering looked like without the poetry.

I stopped abruptly, causing the backpacker behind me to glare as he walked around me. I turned back. I was just far enough away from Manhattan to get a glimpse of skyline through the intricate webbing of the bridge's cables. The summer sun was still high behind the jagged towers. The Woolworth Building added a wedding-cake touch to the angular skyline, and City Hall was a tiny jewel box amid the taller spires. God, it was lovely. New York through the Brooklyn Bridge was once again the city of my dreams, the city I'd chosen to call my own.

I gave a huge sigh, expelling stale air from my lungs as if draining all the poison trapped inside me. My anger began to melt. My shoulders dropped two inches; I gave a good shrug and let my arms swing back and forth. I did a quick series of yoga breaths to purify my lungs, then laughed aloud as I realized I was breathing exhaust from hundreds of cars.

I was free. Just for a moment, just for now, I was free. Free of the trial and Eddie Fitz, of Dwight Straub and Matt Riordan.

I spread out my arms and whirled around, like Julie Andrews at the beginning of *The Sound of Music*. A jogger sweating and panting ran by and gave me a grin; I grinned back. Behind him came another jogger—this one was juggling as he ran. Three balls floated in the air; he caught them one by one and tossed them back up, running and juggling. Bicyclists passed me on the other side of the walkway, puffing and grunting as they made their way up the incline. They'd coast on the other side, going downhill, but this side was work.

I wasn't the only pedestrian in a business suit, but I was the only one with heels. Anyone with brains wore athletic shoes to walk the bridge, leaving the dress shoes back in the office or carrying them in a briefcase. My legs were cramping up. I looked down at my feet, at the newly laid replacement planks in the walkway, and made a decision. I reached down and slipped off my pumps, letting my stockinged feet touch the wood. I had to watch for splinters, but already my calves thanked me.

The pumps dangled from my fingers as I walked. The wood was hot, but not too hot for comfort. It felt good, like walking on the boardwalk at the beach. I was almost to the first set of columns, the one with the plaque in honor of Mrs. Roebling. I always stopped at that plaque and thought about the woman who'd helped her ailing husband finish his dream.

I turned back toward Manhattan; the sun was a touch lower in the sky; golden light bathed the river and glinted off the windows of the city. Uptown, the Empire State and Chrysler buildings seemed like toys, tiny and delicate.

I looked toward Brooklyn, where the huge Watchtower sign dominated the skyline. Closer to the bridge were the piers. Moored to one was a barge that offered classical music concerts every Sunday.

Manhattan and Brooklyn had been sister cities when the bridge was begun by John Augustus Roebling; they'd become boroughs of the unified city once it was finished. But the separate entities they had once been still existed, and nowhere more sharply than in the court system. Not only were the state courts different, not only did each borough cherish and foster those differences, but there were two federal courts as well. The Southern District, in Manhattan, was the jewel in the crown of federal courts. Its United States attorneys made headlines. The Eastern District, in Brooklyn, was the plain stepsister, always playing catch-up. Not even the trial of John Gotti had brought the Eastern District the notoriety it felt it deserved.

I acknowledged Emily Roebling's plaque with a nod and kept moving. My nylons were snagged irreparably and my feet were beginning to blister. I stopped and put my shoes back on, deciding that cramped calves might be an improvement. They weren't, but I kept walking, anyway. Limping, holding onto the railing, I made my way to the Brooklyn side, to the home side, of the Great Bridge.

The Eastern District courthouse was right across from the park that began where the bridge ended. I could stop on the way home. I could stop and see whether Dominic Di Blasi was in. And even if he wasn't, I could pick up some information about Fat Jack Vance's case.

Two sister cities. Two sister court systems. Two federal prosecutors who both wanted Matt Riordan's scalp on their belts. And Lazarus had won and Di Blasi had lost. But Di Blasi was still a player; his recommendation on Fat Jack's sentence made that clear. Instead of the easy walk he'd been promised, the bail bondsman was going to do time. Why?

Why was Di Blasi throwing a monkey wrench into Nick Lazarus' careful plans? Was it just sibling rivalry between the sister cities, or was there something more sinister going on? And what about TJ? He'd had things to get off his chest. He'd gone to Lazarus and Lazarus hadn't listened.

Had he taken his information across the river? The more I thought about that possibility, the more I liked it. It made sense.

But would Di Blasi admit he'd talked to the dead drug dealer? Would he admit he'd intended to use TJ to bring down his rival in Manhattan?

Thinking about Di Blasi and Lazarus kept my mind off my feet. Or so I fondly believed. By the time I reached the Brooklyn side of the bridge, I had bleeding blisters on the backs of both heels. I slipped the shoes off again and walked down the stairs, eager for the touch of grass on my burning soles.

The walk across the little park was sheer heaven. My toes dug into the lush grass; its coolness soothed me. It was the first time since Riordan's trial began that I'd been anywhere near green, growing things. My whole life had become interiors: courtrooms, offices, apartments. I didn't know until I stood in the park how much I'd missed nature.

It was a short vacation. I was on the other side of the park in no time, facing the Disneyland castle that was the main post office. Next to the castle stood the undistinguished office building that housed the IRS and the Eastern District courthouse.

My feet hated me for it, but I thrust them back into the shoes. I hobbled across the street and made my way into the building, showing my lawyer's identification to the guard at the door. I bypassed the metal detector and walked over to the directory, resisting the impulse to find out how good the cool marble floor would feel on bare feet.

Dominic Di Blasi's office was on the third floor. I walked to the elevator and pushed the button. On the way up, I thought about what I was going to say, how I was going to approach the situation. One thing was certain: No matter how much Di Blasi hated Lazarus, he hated Riordan more. He wasn't going to help me without a damned good reason. I had two minutes to think of one.

I stopped in the Ladies' Room on the way, a choice I regretted the minute I looked in the mirror. The walk across the bridge had disheveled me beyond belief; my face was red and my hair was a tangled mess. I ran a comb through it and dabbed on some lipstick. I put on my suit jacket and raised my skirt, pulling the blouse down under the waistband. I'd done what I could, and I still looked like a rag doll who'd been run through the washing machine too many times.

Di Blasi was in. Whether or not he would see me was something the receptionist had to inquire about. I gave my name and added that I was Matt Riordan's lawyer. If that didn't open the door, I'd take my aching body home and put it into a cool bath. In fact, the cool bath sounded like such a good idea that I was tempted to get up and walk out before the receptionist came back. I could always talk to Di Blasi some other time, call him on the phone, maybe.

It was too late to leave. The hennaed receptionist was followed by her boss, who thrust a meaty hand toward me and introduced himself. "Dom Di Blasi. I've been following the trial. You should be proud, Ms. Jameson," he said with a politician's grin. "You're doing one hell of a job over there. One hell of a job."

Flattery will get you everywhere. I stood up with renewed vigor and took Di Blasi's proffered hand. I followed him into the recesses of the office complex, ignoring my blistered feet. The air conditioning was nice and cold; I felt myself coming to life again after the blazing heat outside.

"What can I do for you, Ms. Jameson?" Di Blasi asked as he made his way to his oversized leather chair. He was a Great Dane of a man, big and hefty, but without fat. Solid, yet with the ability to move quickly and gracefully. He seemed a man who carefully curbed his tendency to dominate with his physical presence, always monitoring his effect on others, sensing that too much intensity could be read as intimidation. Some men would have worked that intimidation, would have gloried in their ability to push people around. But not Di Blasi; in the world he'd chosen, you dominated through brains, not brawn. By holding back, he gave people a chance to see his intelligence at work.

It was working now. He leaned back in his chair and waved me into an equally comfortable chair on the other side of his desk. "Would you care for some coffee?" he asked, then really won my heart. "I have some in the fridge; in the summertime, I can't get enough iced coffee."

"Me either," I said. My throat felt parched; my taste buds eagerly anticipated the rush of mocha. I gratefully accepted the glass he handed me and let the first sip roll around in my mouth, then sat back in the chair and heaved a contented sigh.

Di Blasi had won the first round, hands down. I didn't mind; the coffee was worth it. But I had to win round two, or admit it had been a major mistake to face him on impulse, without scripting the encounter in advance.

Should I start with TJ or Fat Jack? Which would he be less likely to expect? Which would he be more reluctant to talk about? I wanted Di Blasi off-balance, but so far he was the one in control of the interview. That had to change.

"When did you first see TJ?" I asked. I held the cold glass with both hands, swirling the coffee around a little, hearing the clink of ice cubes. "Was it before or after he went to Lazarus with his accusations?"

His answering smile was a well-crafted piece of armor. "What makes you think I saw TJ at all? I don't talk to every street-level drug dealer that makes his way to this office."

"You would have seen this one," I retorted, projecting more confidence than I felt. What if the whole explanation was that some brainless assistant spoke to TJ and never bothered to tell the boss? That assistant would probably be parking cars in Bensonhurst, but Di Blasi would have plausible deniability.

"You would have seen anybody who told you he could bring down Nick Lazarus," I went on. "And from what I've been hearing about TJ, he could have done it. Lazarus blew him off because he had too much invested in Eddie Fitz. Now TJ's dead. Very conveniently dead, since if he were alive he'd be in a position to cause Lazarus a lot of problems with the judge and the ethics committee. What I can't bring myself to believe is that you'd let a guy like that get away from you without making a detailed record of everything he knew.''

''Assuming *arguendo*,'' Di Blasi answered, a complacent smile on his lips, ''that I had such a record, I can't think of a theory of evidence under which it would be admissible.'' His dark eyes twinkled at me; he resembled an oversized, younger Mario Cuomo, delighting in argument for its own sake. ''Can you, Counselor?''

''Let me worry about admissibility,'' I shot back. ''Right now I just want to know that such a record exists. And if it does exist, I'd like to see it.''

''I'm sure you would,'' Di Blasi replied. His voice was a purr. ''But can you think of one good reason why I should let you?''

''Because you'd like nothing better than to see Nick Lazarus grovel in front of Judge de Freitas?'' I said the words with a cheerful lilt. ''Because you wanted Riordan on trial over here and Lazarus beat you to it? Because you let Davia Singer leave your office and now she's a star in the Southern District, getting the headlines you wanted for yourself? How about all of the above?''

The mention of Davia Singer wiped the smile off my host's face. For a brief moment his control slipped and I saw a glint of rage in the hitherto inscrutable eyes.

''Don't mention that little bitch to me,'' he said with feeling. ''She spent three years sucking up and then walked out and took everything she'd learned about Matt Riordan over to Lazarus. I taught her how to gather evidence, how to try a case, and now she's using everything she knows for the greater glory of Nick Lazarus. I can't tell you how much I'd like to see her fall on her face over there.''

''Then let me see the stuff you have on TJ,'' I urged. ''I promise to use it to nail Singer to the wall. You get what you want, and I get what I want. Where's the downside?''

While he considered the proposition, I swallowed the rest of the iced coffee.

His answering grin was half-amused, half-exasperated. ''You know better than that, Counselor. I can't be party to screwing a fellow prosecutor in the middle of a case. When it's over, one way or the other, I can and will make public whatever I know about TJ, but before that, none of this can come back to me. Nobody likes a sore loser, and that's what I'll look like if I sabotage Lazarus while he's going after Matt Riordan.''

''So what you're saying is you'd like to see Lazarus and Singer get theirs, but you don't want your fingerprints on the weapon.'' I pretended to give this dilemma serious thought. ''That's doable,'' I said with cheerful insouciance. ''I don't have to tell Judge de Freitas where I got this stuff.''

''You forget that Ms. Singer will know immediately where you got it,'' Di Blasi pointed out.

I pursed my lips. ''Not necessarily,'' I replied. ''Not if there was someone else in the room, someone else who could have told me all about it. Maybe another assistant, maybe the court reporter or the videotape operator. I'm assuming you made a record that includes either a transcript or a video or both. Why couldn't my investigator have found that person and made it worth their while to get us a copy of the record?''

''You have a devious mind, Ms. Jameson,'' the United States attorney for the Eastern District of New York replied. ''Are you sure you've never been a prosecutor?''

''Never,'' I said with a mock shudder. ''Don't even suggest such a thing. It makes me ill to think about it.''

I limped home along Court Street with a huge smile on my face in spite of my bleeding feet. I carried a bulging accordion folder and shopping bag containing videocassettes of the late TJ telling all to Dom Di Blasi. My plans included a cool bath with lemon soap and an evening in front of the VCR, air conditioner on high.

CHAPTER NINE

What TJ had to say to Dom Di Blasi was hearsay, pure and simple, since TJ was no longer available to be cross-examined. Judge de Freitas was never going to let the jurors hear the man's firm, uncompromising statement that he and Eddie Fitz had sold drugs together in Bedford-Stuyvesant. The information was useless as far as impeaching Eddie was concerned.

But it would go a long way toward achieving Matt's goal of destroying Nick Lazarus. How could he explain blowing off a man Dom Di Blasi had taken seriously, a man who'd given detailed accounts of corruption that would have brought down Eddie's entire precinct if the Mollen Commission had heard it? How could he justify letting Eddie tell the jury under oath that he'd only crossed the line twice in his career as a street cop?

I walked to court with a bounce in my step, having had a good night's sleep for the first time since the Mean Streak had left the starting gate. We were in the home stretch, and I was going to make it to the end without losing my lunch or my dignity.

Davia Singer's accusing eyes met mine as I approached the door to the courtroom. She pushed it open for me; it slid slowly and quietly, like the door to a secret passage in a twenties mystery novel.

"Did you hear?" she asked. It wasn't said in a gossipy tone; she sounded like someone with very bad news.

"Hear what?"

The solemn look on her pallid face was joined for a split second by the unholy glee of being the first to pass on information. "Dwight Straub killed himself this morning."

The front car of the Mean Streak hurtled right off the tracks and into the wide blue sky above the whitecapped lake.

"My God," I whispered. My hand flew to my mouth. "I can't believe it."

But I could. God help me, I could. Dwight Straub had been a man on the edge, and it wasn't all that surprising to find out he'd toppled over.

"How?" I asked, my voice a croak. It was probably the least relevant question I could have asked, but it seemed important to know.

Davia Singer's answering tone was hard as coal. "He drove his car to Orient Point, out on the Island. He sat in the front seat, then put his gun in his mouth and pulled the trigger."

He ate his gun. That was the way other cops would tell the story: He ate his gun.

Singer twisted the knife a little deeper into my guts. "He left a note on the passenger's seat," she informed me. "Right next to the subpoena you served on him."

I had a quick flash of myself sitting in the Straubs' living room, trying to convince Dwight that his only hope lay in the truth.

And now the truth had killed him.

Or was it only the truth that killed him? Had I helped push him over the edge? If I hadn't gone after him with that subpoena, would he be walking around today?

Maybe. That was the only honest answer: Maybe.

But walking around for how long? The net was closing in on Stan and Dwight. It was only a matter of time before the Hero Cop nailed his buddies in the grand jury.

Singer strode toward the back door of the courtroom, the one behind the bench that led to the rear corridors where the public never went. "I have to inform His Honor," she muttered to no one in particular.

I made my way to counsel table and sat down, shivering as if the temperature had plunged twenty degrees. I felt sick; for a panicky moment I was afraid my half-digested breakfast was going to come up and land right on my case folders.

I'd known we were playing for keeps. Lazarus wanted Riordan professionally dead, and he was willing to do whatever it took to see that his old adversary was not just convicted of bribery, but ruined. Riordan stood by his motto: Lazarus *delenda est*.

But now a man was dead. A man who'd stood in the doorway to his living room and looked at me as if I were the angel of death come to claim his firstborn had put a gun in his mouth rather than come to court and face my questions.

Hell, I do a mean cross, but this is—

The bile rose in my throat again. No amount of sick joking was going to erase the memory of Dwight's pale blue eyes begging me for mercy, his voice faltering as he refused to rat out the man he'd considered a friend.

He'd seen the inevitable, and he couldn't face it.

It was a hell of a way to admit guilt.

And it wasn't admissible.

There was no way I could say to the jury: *Dwight Straub killed himself so he wouldn't have to take the stand and admit the truth about what he did with Eddie Fitz. Consider that when you deliberate upon the guilt or innocence of Matt Riordan.*

A man was dead, and I was mentally rewriting my summation to include his suicide.

The law is a cold business. Dwight Straub was dead, but my client was alive and he needed me on top of things.

I glanced at Riordan, who'd slipped into the courtroom and now sat silently beside me in the defendant's chair. Was he thinking along the same lines? Had I become him, in my quest to make it to the big time?

The door behind the bench opened and Nick Lazarus strode into the courtroom. He was followed by Judge de Freitas, who stepped up to the bench and signaled the court reporter that we were about to go back on the record. The jury remained outside; this matter was not for their ears.

Someone told the press people out in the hall, and in a matter of seconds the first row filled with reporters and sketch artists. Everyone wore an air of subdued expectation; Straub's suicide was hot news, but it was also a sobering reminder that this case involved real people who could bleed and die.

"It appears," the judge began in his dry, thin voice, "that a witness the defense intended to call has become unavailable. I am told that Mr. Lazarus, of the United States attorney's office, wishes to make a statement for the record. Mr. Lazarus, you may proceed."

Lazarus' tone was heavy with irony. "The witness is more than unavailable, Your Honor," he began. "The witness is dead. The witness is dead because the defense chose to go on a fishing expedition, interrogating this man without a shred of evidence that he had anything to contribute to this trial. The defense showed itself both irresponsible and ruthless in its efforts to deflect the attention of this jury from the facts and to distract it with forays into irrelevant matters. Your Honor may recall that this office opposed the issuance of subpoenas for Detectives Stanley Krieger and Dwight Straub.''

Judge de Freitas shook his head. "Mr. Lazarus, all that is water under the bridge. The only thing this court intends to concern itself with is the progress of the trial before it.''

But Lazarus wasn't about to let himself be dismissed so cavalierly. "Your Honor, this office demands that Ms. Jameson be admonished that in future she is to—''

I leapt to my feet. Lazarus wanted *me* admonished. The man who had listened to TJ tell him all about Eddie Fitz's street action wanted *me* admonished. The man who'd had every intention of indicting Dwight Straub as soon as he was finished with Riordan's trial wanted *me* blamed for Straub's suicide.

"Speaking of dead witnesses," I began, not bothering to modify the sarcasm in my tone, "this court should hear about a man known as TJ, a man the defense had every intention of calling to the stand. Your Honor may recall that I asked Detective Fitzgerald more than once if he knew TJ; his name is in the record. Well, Your Honor, the defense has reason to believe that Mr. Lazarus met with TJ, that TJ told Mr. Lazarus things about Detective Fitzgerald's conduct as a police officer that would have had an adverse effect upon his credibility as a witness in this case. And the defense has reason to believe that Mr. Lazarus deliberately suppressed this information, that he permitted Detective Fitzgerald to testify under oath and deny wrongdoing when the prosecution in fact knew he had engaged in many acts of misconduct. In addition, the prosecution never turned over information about TJ to the defense in spite of the fact that it constitutes *Brady* material.''

This last contention was a serious allegation. *Brady* v. *Maryland* was an old case involving deliberate withholding of exculpatory evidence by a politically ambitious district attorney. To accuse a prosecutor of holding back *Brady* material was tantamount to calling him a liar and a cheat who would convict an innocent man on evidence he knew to be false. It was an accusation not to be made lightly—and I was making it with the full knowledge that I'd have to back it up.

Lazarus jumped in. His face was a mottled red; he looked ready to explode. "If Ms. Jameson has any proof whatsoever, Your Honor, she should be made to present it to this court. If she doesn't, she should be held in contempt of court for even suggesting such a thing."

"Do you deny that you met with TJ on at least one occasion?" I shot back. The judge frowned; one of the rules of etiquette in court is that lawyers do not address one another directly. But I was too angry to play Miss Manners. All the pent-up fury and sick rage I felt at the death of Dwight Straub fueled me as I stood toe-to-toe with the man whose overreaching ambition had started this whole mess.

"Ms. Jameson, kindly clarify the relevance of this TJ," the judge commanded.

I backed up, and started with the rumors I'd heard about a Brooklyn cop who'd cut himself in on a drug dealer's street action. I named TJ as the dealer and Eddie Fitz as the cop. I went on to say that I now knew that TJ had visited Lazarus, and when he'd gotten no satisfaction in the Southern District, he'd taken his story across the river. As corroboration, I pulled out the internal memorandum from Di Blasi's office, recording TJ's visit. I handed the document to the nearest court officer, who proceeded to walk toward the bench. "Show it to opposing counsel," Judge de Freitas ordered. As if programmed, the uniformed man wheeled and headed toward the prosecution table.

Lazarus gave the memo a quick glance and tossed it onto the prosecution table. "Your Honor," he began, "defense counsel is making a mountain out of a molehill here. This man TJ was a self-confessed narcotics dealer and convicted felon. He came to my office with a cock-and-bull story about Detective Fitzgerald. I had his story checked out by my top investigators, Your Honor, and found that there wasn't a shred of truth in any of his allegations against the detective.''

"You checked him out?'' The words burst out of me, but this time I caught my mistake and turned my attention to the judge. "Your Honor,'' I amended, grabbing onto my self-control with both hands, "if the prosecution checked out TJ's allegations, then we not only should have been informed about the existence of TJ, we should have been provided with the results of the investigation. This entire matter has been swept under the rug by the prosecution in an attempt to keep vital information from the defense, information that would have seriously undermined the credibility of the chief witness against Mr. Riordan. This calls for a mistrial, Your Honor.''

My voice was shaking, a combination of rage and nerves and sick regret. Dwight Straub was dead, and my response was to castigate Nick Lazarus for withholding evidence. But somehow it seemed right to open up all the closets, to let all the skeletons dance through the courtroom, to strip away the façade of civilized justice and reveal the bull walruses butting their heads against one another until the blood ran down their faces.

I'd seen that once on Channel Thirteen. One of those nature shows where the camera lives with the animals, showing in grotesque detail everything from birth to carnivorous mealtime. The walruses had all gathered on a frozen island; breeding was about to begin. And the males fought for the prize females, banging their heads together horribly. Armless, they threw themselves at the bigger males, drawing blood and grunting. The loser slunk off and died of shame and exhaustion; the winner went on to impregnate as many females as he could find.

It was one hell of a way to insure more walruses.

Somehow the spectacle this trial had become reminded me of those walruses. Lazarus and Riordan were both bloodied, both charging at one another, roaring their masculine pride as each attempted to destroy the other.

"This is nothing more than a smoke screen, Your Honor," Lazarus pronounced by way of reply. "This TJ has nothing to do with the matter at hand; Ms. Jameson is trying to divert attention from her client's guilt and put Detective Fitzgerald on trial in his place. I am outraged at her suggestion that this office would deliberately suppress evidence. She has all but accused me of suborning perjury in this case, and I demand an apology at once."

You could hear a pin drop. Or a pen scratch; behind me, a sketch artist drew swift lines on an oversized drawing pad.

"Ms. Jameson," Judge de Freitas said in his dry, inflectionless voice, "I am going to proceed with this trial in a moment. But I am ordering you to produce before this court any and all evidence you have indicating that Mr. Lazarus has committed any act of wrongdoing in this case. I am also," he went on, turning toward Lazarus, "going to require the United States attorney's office to produce all memoranda, including internal work product, that involves this TJ."

There was a distinct rustling in the press seats behind me. The reporters were eager to race out of the courtroom toward the public phone banks. But the judge wasn't finished.

Fixing Nick Lazarus with a basilisk eye, the former law professor said, "And if I find that the United States attorney's office has withheld *Brady* material or otherwise conducted itself in a manner inconsistent with the Canons of Professional Ethics, I shall take whatever steps I deem necessary."

A surge of elation swept through me; we were on our way toward achieving justice at last. But then the judge turned his attention to me.

"If, on the other hand," he went on, "I am satisfied after

perusing such evidence that the defense allegation is unfounded, then I will consider holding Ms. Jameson in contempt and imposing sanctions accordingly. Do I make myself understood?''

I stood up a little straighter and answered "Yes, Your Honor" with just a hint of defiance.

I'd just put my own career on the line; either I proved my allegations against Nick Lazarus and beat Matt's case, or the two of us went to jail together.

The reporters swallowed us up the minute we stepped outside the courthouse onto the stone steps. There was no time to position ourselves for maximum photo opportunity; microphones were thrust at Matt and Lazarus, Singer and me, with seemingly random abandon. They wanted a sound bite, and it didn't much matter who uttered the words.

The questions peppered me like buckshot: "Are you really calling Lazarus a liar?" a black reporter asked. "What's this about a cop killing himself?" another demanded. Ginger Hsu, a concerned look on her photogenic face, wanted to know how it felt to have a witness commit suicide rather than face my questions in court.

That one I answered quickly and emphatically. "It feels like hell," I said.

"What do you think Dwight Straub could have contributed to this trial?" Ginger persisted.

I took a deep breath and weighed my options. I could go public with all my suspicions about Eddie Fitz and his partners, or I could tell the reporters to wait and see what turned up in court, or I could—

Lazarus' piercing voice cut through my thoughts. "Not all the police officers in this city deserve the name New York's Finest," he said. "It's an unfortunate fact, but it's true." For a wild moment, I thought he was about to admit to the city press corps the truth about his Hero Cop, but instead he said, "And I'm sorry to have to admit that

Dwight Straub, who worked closely with Detective Fitzgerald at the Seven-Four precinct, was apparently one of those officers who succumbed to the temptations of the street. My office, as you know, has been investigating corruption in the police precincts, and I can say now that an indictment will be filed shortly, and—''

''Are you saying,'' Carlos Ruiz jumped in, ''that you were about to indict this Straub guy?''

''Does this mean,'' Tom Delaney of Channel Four cut in, ''that your star witness was a corrupt cop, too?''

''No, no,'' Lazarus replied. ''Detective Fitzgerald was the one man in that precinct who refused to go along with what was happening. He was the one man who blew the whistle on the drug dealing, and Ms. Jameson and her client should be ashamed of themselves for suggesting that he has anything to hide. As for Dwight Straub,'' the prosecutor went on, ''all I can say is that a man who disgraces his badge by acts of corruption has reason to be afraid when an honest cop speaks the truth.''

The reporters lapped it up. They flocked around Lazarus like hungry pigeons falling on a crust of bread, pecking and scratching and begging for more.

I felt sick. How the hell was Annie Straub going to feel, watching this performance on the six o'clock news? And was there anything I could say to counter it, or should I hold my fire until I had all my ammunition ready?

At the edge of the clutch of reporters stood Jesse Winthrop. His face was drawn and pale; he looked as nauseated as I felt. He knew, thanks to me, that his Hero Cop was the real disgrace to the badge. I wondered whether he would finally write everything he knew.

The court clerk had given me an envelope containing subpoenaed material; I ripped it open and glanced through the police reports. The final item caught my attention: TJ had been in the Brooklyn House of Detention shortly before he died. He'd been released on bail posted by Jack Vance.

• • •

The sign in the window said ''Jack Vance, Bail Bonds, All Hours.'' On the sign there was a cartoon drawing of a man in a striped prisoner suit behind bars; underneath was the slogan ''A Friend in Need Is a Friend Indeed.'' There was an 800 number for those too panicked to enter the 212 area code lest the warrant fall and they spend the night in jail. It was a sleazy little office on a sleazy little street, the kind of street that hides behind the skirts of courthouses everywhere. A service-providing street: bail bonds, investigations, cheap-copy stores, lawyers with signs offering everything from divorces to name changes to notary services at five bucks a pop. The kind of street a self-respecting lawyer didn't step into without making the sign of the cross: Please, God, please, don't ever let me sink this low.

There was a For Rent sign in the corner of the window, no sign of activity within. No ''girls'' answering phones, no phones ringing. No clients' families sitting on the edge of chairs, sipping bad coffee from plastic cups. No Jack Vance, come to that, but he could be in his office in the back. I knocked on the window and waited.

Fat Jack lumbered toward the door, listing from one side to the other as his weight shifted from leg to leg. His belly was an enormous burden, lopping over his pants, straining against the huge expanse of white shirt-front. Beads of sweat stood out on his domelike forehead; the effort of walking from his office to the door had taken a lot out of him.

I hoped we could finish the interview before he had the coronary that was so clearly in his future.

''Ms. Jameson?'' he asked, his voice weakened by a wheeze. Asthma, on top of everything else. I nodded; he motioned me inside, opening the door just wide enough to let me slip through. As if he were afraid someone or something bigger and stronger would follow me in.

The desks were clean. Not a paper in sight. No telephones either. Jack was closing down, winding up his business. Getting ready to face the sentence soon to be imposed by the Eastern District judge.

Who had his papers?

I decided to ask, to open discussion before we sat down, before Fat Jack reached his office, his turf.

"Did Nick Lazarus subpoena your records, or did you just turn over anything he wanted?" I addressed my question to Jack's broad back, which was crisscrossed by suspenders that were fashionable back in his grandfather's day.

All I got for an answer was a wheeze. It hadn't occurred to me that he couldn't walk and talk at the same time.

His office was as stripped as the rest of the place. There was a battered wooden desk that looked as if it had been purchased at a city auction. On the top sat a multiple-line phone, one pristine yellow legal pad, and a Far Side coffee mug filled with sharp yellow pencils. Gone were the stacks of papers that must have buried the desk at one time.

The only decoration left on the wall was a framed copy of the *Post*'s famous headline about an early Riordan case: LOUIE NEEDS A WITNESS, the banner screamed. Matt had been defending a low-level mobster, a Nunzie Aiello clone, who'd told the jury he was playing poker with his pals at the Little Flower Social Club on the night of the crime. When the D.A. asked Matt's alibi witness how and why he'd come forward to testify the man had shrugged and told the jury, "Because someone told me Louie needed a witness."

The city had had a good laugh, and Matt's client had gone down in flames, but the style and grace with which Matt had laughed along with the press and the public helped forge his reputation as a class act.

The clipping was still on the wall. Was that because it held some meaning for the fat man, or did he intend leaving it there when he moved out, as a signal that his friendship with the man who'd engendered the headline was a thing of the past?

I sat in the straight-backed chair and tried not to stare as Fat Jack lowered himself, inch by inch, into the sagging leather chair behind the desk.

"Now, Ms. Jameson," he said, his needy voice edged with something I couldn't identify. Sarcasm? Triumph? Something not quite pleasant, something I'd better figure out before I left this place.

"You ask whether or not I betrayed the man I worked for." His restatement of my question was meant to elicit a protest: Oh, no, that's not what I meant at all.

I didn't protest. I stared straight at him and gave a small nod; *yes, that's exactly what I meant. Did you give ammunition against Riordan to Lazarus, or did you make him work for it? And is there anything you held back, anything Lazarus doesn't have that might help us? And what happened after you met TJ at the Brooklyn House of Detention on the last night of his life? Did you drive him to Lazarus' office? Did you shoot him in the head and hide the body in the trunk of a car?*

It occurred to me that there were a few land mines on the ground that stretched between Fat Jack and me. He was not being called as a witness for the other side, so there was technically no reason why I couldn't talk to him in the absence of his lawyer, but I was definitely searching for evidence of a crime, evidence I might have a legal obligation to turn over to the authorities.

I opened my mouth to rephrase the question; a small smile at the corner of Jack's thin lips told me he'd followed my train of thought with a swiftness that could only have come from years of association with lawyers.

The direct approach was not, I reflected, always the best one. I stepped back, shifted ground, went for the conversational instead of the confrontational. The course I should have taken in the first place.

"Looks like you're closing down," I remarked, looking around at the empty shelves, the clean desk.

"Doesn't take a rocket scientist to figure that out," Jack said. He sat back in his chair, which rocked under his weight. "Nick Lazarus set out to break the Baxter Street Gang, and I guess he succeeded."

"The Baxter Street Gang," I repeated. The sleazy little street outside was probably the least desirable section of Baxter Street. "Who else on this street did he go after?"

Jack gave a shrug. "It's kind of like a figure of speech. Matty started out here, had an office two doors down. So even though he's been gone from Baxter Street a long time, Lazarus still thinks of him as part of some kind of gang, some kind of conspiracy to make him look like an asshole. Personally," Fat Jack confided, inclining his head forward an inch or two, "I never thought Nicky Lazarus needed any help in looking like an asshole."

The use of the nickname gave me an opening. "In Brooklyn, we call Nick Lazarus, Jr., Nicky. He's an assistant D.A.—and a real pain in the ass."

Jack nodded. "Chip off the old block. Just like Nick trying to fill his father's shoes. Sid Lazarus was maybe the best prosecutor this city ever saw. Between him and Hogan, anyway. Don't even mention Tom Dewey in the same breath, you ask me."

"Tom Dewey became governor," I said. "And almost president."

"Yeah, and Rudy Giuliani's the mayor now," Jack commented. "Seems like being a U.S. attorney for the Southern District is a ticket to a political future."

"And Nick Lazarus? What job is he angling for?" I asked. "Would mayor be enough, or does he want to go higher?"

"What he wants and what he can get are two different things," Fat Jack pronounced.

"He's been getting a lot of ink on this Riordan case," I pointed out.

"Counselor," Jack said, his thin voice weary, "you didn't come to the ass-end of Baxter Street to talk politics. Why not cut to the chase here, okay?"

"You could testify for Riordan," I said, giving the fat man the blunt truth he'd asked for. "Unless, of course, that was part of the deal you made with Lazarus. Did they let you plead on the condition that you stay off the stand during Matt's trial?"

Vance shook his head; his jowls waggled. "I could testify if you want," he said. Then the thin little smile returned. "But you don't want. Trust me, Ms. J., you don't want."

Why the hell not? I wanted to shout. *What could you possibly say that would make things any worse than they are now?*

And then he told me. "See, you gotta understand, once I found that memo, everything changed. Everything turned around."

"What memo?" I leaned forward on my chair, not bothering to conceal my eagerness. "Jack, what memo?"

"You didn't get the memo?" The bondsman's eyes widened with surprise. "I thought for sure Lazarus would have to turn that over to the defense. It was a memo from Nick Lazarus to some undercover cop, and I found it in an envelope Eddie Fitz gave me. So it didn't take a rocket scientist," the fat man continued, using a favorite expression, "to figure out that Eddie was working undercover for Lazarus. I nearly shit my pants," he confided. "I was that fucking stunned. I just looked at the damned thing like it was gonna explode in my face, and then I realized he must have taped our conversations. We were fucked, me and Paulie and Matty."

"When was this?" Fat Jack's legal instincts were correct; the defense absolutely should have been told about this. I was going back into the courtroom loaded for bear.

"I don't know, sometime after I gave Paulie the money for the grand jury minutes, though. In fact," he admitted after a moment's thought, "it was after the Riordan thing was over with. I was trying to get some information on a wholly different matter at the time, nothing to do with Matty."

"But at some point, you knew about Eddie working for Lazarus, and you never told Riordan?" I persisted.

"Hey, it was after the fact, you know. It was after I paid the money. And I wanted to tell Matty, I really did, but Lazarus had my balls in a wringer. He said, 'You breathe a word to Riordan, I'll see to it you do heavy time in that Brooklyn case.' So I had no choice. I had no fucking choice."

"But you have a choice now," I shot back. "You could come to court and tell the jury that you paid Paulie for those minutes on your own hook, that Matt had nothing to do with it."

"No, I can't, Ms. J.," Fat Jack replied, his voice a mournful dirge. "Because when I gave that money to Paulie the Cork, I was just doing what Matt Riordan told me to do."

This was not the answer I wanted; the only thing that made it tolerable was that I didn't believe it for a second.

"How about when you posted bond for a man named TJ?" I countered. "Were you just doing what Nick Lazarus asked you to do?"

If the question hit a nerve, Fat Jack didn't let it show.

"That's what I do," he said simply. "I write bonds. I must have wrote a thousand bonds this year, and it's only summer. So maybe I wrote one for a guy known as TJ. I could have done that."

"And maybe you could also have gone to the Brooklyn House of Detention to post the money in person," I went on. "And maybe you also walked out of BHD with TJ.

And maybe you were the last guy to see TJ alive.''

The fat man shook his head; the jowls waggled again. ''No, I wasn't, Ms. J.,'' he said in his wheezy voice. ''I wasn't the last man to see TJ alive. Because I delivered TJ to the man who actually paid the bond-piece.''

''Nick Lazarus,'' I guessed. ''Did you take him to the U.S. attorney's office, or did you—''

''Who said anything about Lazarus?'' Fat Jack cut in, his huge face wreathed in a smile meant to convey innocence. ''I took him to the cops who registered him as an informant. I took him to Stan Krieger and Dwight Straub.''

CHAPTER TEN

"I can't believe the way those reporters turned that poor guy's death into a feeding frenzy this morning," I said morosely. Matt and I had agreed to meet in the cool interior of McSorley's for a much needed drink. "How do you suppose Straub's wife is feeling?"

"You can't let yourself worry about that," my companion replied. "You were brilliant back there," he went on. "The way you shifted the focus in the courtroom from Straub to TJ, the way you had Lazarus on the defensive. You really came out slugging, Cass—just the way I would have done."

"Praise from Riordan is praise indeed," I murmured, savoring the irony as much as I savored the vodka and cranberry juice he'd ordered for me. "I'm glad you appreciate my sacrificing my career on the altar of your acquittal."

"Your career is safe, babe," Matt assured me with an indulgent smile. "We've got Lazarus on the run and he knows it."

"Meanwhile," I mused aloud, "poor Dwight Straub shoots himself because he thinks I'm about to pin TJ's murder on him, when the truth is I had no real evidence until Fat Jack gave me the whole thing on a silver platter."

"Somebody would have found out sometime," Matt replied. He placed his warm hand over mine and gave a gentle squeeze.

We sat in silence for a moment, a silence that might almost have been a moment of remembrance for the terrified man who'd left my subpoena with his suicide note. Then Riordan said, "And we still have to cross Eddie tomorrow on that bullshit about Jack nearly killing him."

"I'd forgotten about that," I admitted. It was partly the nature of trials and partly the nature of life: What had seemed so vitally important earlier now meant little or nothing, in the context of Dwight's suicide. But Matt was right. The trial would continue, and we'd have to wipe from the jurors' minds the image of the Hero Cop narrowly escaping with his life.

"There's something off about that, don't you think?" Matt said. He leaned forward on his chair, a predatory look on his face. "He's got Fat Jack going on about killing him if he rats them out, but then when Jack has real evidence that Fitz is a rat, he just stands there and makes more threats. Why didn't Jack pull the trigger in that alley?"

"Are you really asking why your former associate didn't kill this guy?" I asked incredulously. "That would make a nice comment for the jury. Besides," I went on, "are you saying you think Fat Jack is capable of murder?"

"To save his own ass? Of course he is." Matt lifted his glass of Irish whiskey and held it in the air. "And what I'm wondering is, why didn't he take advantage of a perfectly good opportunity to plug the little shit and walk away?"

"Because that uniformed cop came along," I replied.

"Not for a good ten minutes," my client countered.

"Jack had plenty of time to kill Eddie if he really wanted to. I can't help but wonder if the whole episode wasn't a show."

"A show for the jury?" I was thinking aloud.

Riordan shook his head. "A show for Paulie the Cork," he said.

I thought about it. "You think Jack and Eddie planned the whole thing? You think Fat Jack pretended to threaten Eddie? Then what about—"

I broke off as a sudden revelation hit me. What had Zebart testified to about Eddie? That he'd never seen anyone with such an unerring sense of when to wear a wire and when to leave the equipment back in the office. It was as if Eddie had radar, the FBI man had said. It was as if he'd known in advance when Fat Jack was going to search him.

It was as if he'd known in advance.

What if he *had* known in advance? What if he and Fat Jack had orchestrated their little dance, the ballet of trust and distrust that led to the damning tapes?

But why?

Because Eddie Fitz was a liar. He was no hero cop; he was a crooked cop who wanted to cut a deal that would let him walk away from his misconduct while his buddies served time. And the best way to do that was to turn state's evidence before anyone else thought of doing it.

"Jack found a memo," I remarked. I told Matt what the bondsman had told me about the internal memorandum from Lazarus to an undercover cop. "So at least part of the time he was pretending to believe Eddie, Jack knew the truth. He was on the prosecution's payroll."

"That's why they didn't call Jack to the stand," Riordan said in an authoritative tone. "If they presented him as a witness, they'd have had to give us that information."

"I don't know where this gets us," I continued. "I feel as if every time I acquire another piece of information, it turns to garbage. I mean, we know for a fact that Eddie

Fitz is a crooked cop, and that Nick Lazarus knew it and put him on the stand anyway, and let him lie through his teeth—and we have no more concrete evidence of any of that than we did the day we first learned about it.''

We sat in McSorley's until the sun made its way below the horizon. As I walked with Matt toward the subway that would take me back to Brooklyn, I watched the huge red ball slowly descending into the Hudson, hanging in the sky like a Japanese lantern, sending long, slanting rays of orange light along the streets. There was a wispy breeze off the East River. The street was alive with people. Lovers of all ages and gender combinations strolled hand in hand, lazing their way along Third Avenue past Indian restaurants and boutiques devoted to leather in all its various forms. Musicians plucked guitars or played South American pipes or fiddled in front of open cases with a buck or two lying inside to encourage passers-by to toss in more cash. In front of the Ukranian restaurant a mime imitated people as they walked by; I smiled as he picked up Matt's intense stride, jutting his head forward as though to cut his way through the very air around us.

There was a doleful little tune playing in my head. It had been there ever since McSorley's, nagging at me until I managed to identify it. It was a folk song, something about a boat. Something about a big lake they called Gitche Gumee.

I gave a wry little laugh when the title came to me: "The Wreck of the *Edmund Fitzgerald*." It was a long, lugubrious ballad about the sinking of a Lake Superior barge, sung by Gordon Lightfoot.

The wreck of the *Edmund Fitzgerald*. Was I thinking of the wreck Eddie Fitz had made of his own life, or of the others he had taken down with him to the bottom of the lake?

Back in Brooklyn, I had messages on my answering machine and a spew of faxes to read through. I was about to toss them into the pile I'd mentally marked "After Trial," when a reference to Eddie Fitz caught my attention. I sat down on my red leather office chair and began to read.

"Do you really think Eddie is that stupid?" the fax began. "Do you think he'd talk to Nick Lazarus without protecting himself? Well, he wouldn't. He wore a wire and he made a tape of everything he said. He kept the tape in the barbecue in his backyard so no one would find it. Only I found it, and I can give it to you in return for two thousand dollars. Meet me tonight in front of St. Andrew's Church at 11:00. Don't be late—and bring all the money."

There was no signature. The heading identified the sender as a public copy shop in the courthouse district of lower Manhattan. It was not the first such offer I'd received since the trial began. It seemed as if the entire population of Manhattan wanted to help me win Matt's case—for a small, eminently reasonable fee, of course. But this was different. For one thing, whoever had written this knew Eddie's penchant for taping his own conversations. For another, we needed all the ammunition we could get to make good our promise to show the judge that Lazarus had bent the rules.

I called Matt and read the fax to him over the phone. "I'll be right there," he said in a tight, excited voice. "A half-hour at the most."

I walked upstairs to my apartment and stripped off my working clothes. After tossing the sweat-damp pantyhose into the sink for a quick wash, I slipped into jogging shorts and put on the fish-on-a-bicycle T-shirt. Then I trudged back downstairs and left a note for Matt to ring the apartment bell instead of the office. It was too damned late and too damned hot to keep it professional. I opened a diet soda and stretched out on the couch.

I was half-asleep by the time my client rang the bell. I buzzed him up, and set the fax on the coffee table for him to read. I met him at the door with a cold beer.

"Where is it?" he said by way of greeting. I gestured toward the coffee table and stood back.

"This could be good," he said after a minute. "This could be very good."

"This could also be a complete crock," I pointed out. "A wild-goose chase, a waste of time, a scam, a fraud, a blackmail scheme, a—"

"I know all that," Matt interrupted, "but it could also be just what we need. Think about it," he urged. He tossed the fax back onto the coffee table and began to pace the living room. "We know Eddie Fitz made a tape of his Psych Services interview, in defiance of Police Department regulations. So is it wholly out of the realm of possibility that he sneaked a tape recorder into Nick Lazarus' office and taped his conversations there?"

I shook my head. "Not completely," I replied, giving Matt what he wanted. "That does sound like something Eddie might do."

"Of course it does," Matt said approvingly. "Because if we manage to nail Eddie Fitz as a liar, you and I both know Lazarus is going to turn on him. He'll tell the court he never had a moment's suspicion about Eddie, but now that he knows the truth, he'll rush straight to the grand jury and indict the former Hero Cop. And Eddie's just smart enough to know that the best way to guarantee that won't happen is to have his own insurance policy; namely, a tape of Lazarus listening to every horrible thing Eddie ever did on the street."

"I understand all that," I said, not liking the excited undercurrents in Matt's voice. "What I don't believe is that this anonymous faxer has any such tapes. Why would Eddie leave them around where someone else could find them that easily? And who is this person, and what does he really want?"

"He wants two thousand bucks," my client retorted.

It came to me as I contemplated Matt's too-smooth skin

that he'd had plastic surgery. He'd had a face lift. And maybe an eye job. And a tummy tuck—Was that why his stomach still looked flat as a washboard?

"Is that all he wants?" I asked in a soft voice. "Can you be sure he doesn't want something you're not going to want to give?"

"All I know," Matt replied, "is that come eleven P.M., I'm going to be standing in front of St. Andrew's Church. If I'm wasting my time, so be it. It's my time."

We agreed to meet at 7:15 the next morning, outside the courthouse at the round metal tables next to the food booths, to discuss the results of his night's activities.

It was late. And hot. And the air conditioning felt good and so did the gins and tonic I made and so did sitting on the couch tucked neatly into Matt's sinewy arm, the television soothing us with a meaningless flow of images we scarcely noticed. He smelled so good; he had always smelled so good: a combination of male sweat and citrusy after-shave that roused something inside me.

His hand brushed the front of my T-shirt and stiffened my braless nipple. The arm around my shoulders squeezed me close to him. I gave a contented sound and let my hand travel across his shirt. The hair on his broad chest felt springy under my fingertips; I wanted to reach in and pet him like a dog.

He reached down and covered my mouth with his lips. His meaty hand crept under my T-shirt and cupped my breast as he thrust his tongue into my willing mouth.

A hot rush of desire flooded me; I wanted the release, the closeness, the sound of his breath as he lay on my bed next to me, the touch of his manicured hands on my skin, the give and take of good, strong sex, the—

I wanted him.

And in very short order, I gave myself what I wanted.

The sex was great. Raw, animal passion that released a lot of the tension I'd been under. I lay on sweat-soaked sheets, my fingers idly roaming through the hairs on Matt's chest, the cool blast of air conditioning wafting over my satisfied body.

"It's too bad you have to go," I said. "But I guess you're right. You have to go meet this guy, whoever he is. You won't be satisfied unless you—"

His hand grabbed mine too tightly. "Ah, babe, let's cut the shit. It doesn't matter what this guy has. I'm finished, and we both know it."

I sat upright in bed. "What are you talking about? We have Eddie Fitz on the ropes and Lazarus in the hot seat. You have a really good chance of winning this thing."

"I told you from the beginning," he said, his deep blue eyes focused on my face, "winning wasn't going to be enough."

I was getting nettled. "Then what would be enough? A public apology from Nick Lazarus? A medal from the mayor?" I smiled; there used to be a judge in Brooklyn who said that to all the criminal lawyers when they argued bail motions. *What does your client want, Counselor, a medal?*

But Matt wasn't smiling. He heaved a sigh. "There's an old courthouse story I used to tell," he began. "Always got a laugh with it, too. There's a criminal lawyer on trial with a dead loser of a case. But he cross-examines, he objects, he argues—he puts on a show. And when he's finished, his client looks at him and says, 'This is wonderful. We're really doing great.' "

I knew where this was going, but I kept quiet and let Matt go for the punch line.

"The lawyer turns to his client and says, 'No, moron. *I'm* doing great; *you're* going down the toilet.' "

"But you're not going down the toilet."

"My life is," he replied, in a voice that wavered. He turned his face away, not quite burying it in the pillow, but with a decisiveness that told me not to come any closer.

Part of me figured he was just crashing from his earlier high, which had been fueled by alcohol, adrenaline, and optimism. And part of me knew exactly what he meant.

"You'll get your life back," I promised, working to exude a confidence I didn't entirely feel. "Once all this is over, you'll be turning clients away, just like you used to."

He cleared his throat and swallowed the phlegm in a throaty gurgle. His voice was thick with what I hoped to hell weren't unshed tears. "No, babe," he said. "Clients like the ones I had don't give replays. When they're gone, they're gone. And as far as they're concerned, I'm yesterday. Kurt's their lawyer now. And maybe he can keep Frankie C. happy and maybe he can't, but I'll never see a Cretella case again."

"So you'll—"

Now his voice was back to its full, round timbre. It rang with authority as he cut in: "Save the locker-room speech, Cass. I know what I know."

He reached over and stroked my naked flesh, raising goose bumps as his fingers touched sensitive spots. "I've got to go. Thanks, Cass," he said. "Thanks a lot."

"I hope you get what you need," I replied. It sounded inadequate as hell, but it was what I hoped.

It was only later that the irony of those words came home to me.

The F station at East Broadway was deep underground; it was the first stop in Manhattan, and the sense of having been underneath the East River was overwhelming. The station was deep and damp and cool, as if I were stepping out of the subway car straight into riverbed.

I climbed toward the sunlight and emerged from darkness at the corner of East Broadway and Canal Street, on the northern edge of Chinatown. It took a moment for my eyes to adjust to the light. It was going to be another hot day, and the sun streamed down on the tenement houses, glinted off windows and fire escapes and the triangular gold top of the federal courthouse, visible along the straight line of East Broadway.

From Canal Street, the courthouse looked like a castle, gold and remote and beckoning. It was a place of fantasy, a place to spin tales about.

As recently as last week, that courthouse had been a place of mystery to me. And now I walked up the smooth stone steps every day, stood under the high ceilings and addressed a judge on the high, polished bench.

It was only seven in the morning, but the street was already bustling. Delivery trucks were double-parked in front of Chinese restaurants and groceries; huge plastic bags filled to bursting with bean sprouts and tofu cakes sat on the sidewalk, leaking water in little rivulets that ran toward the curb. I stepped gingerly around the puddles, taking in the exotic sights and smells. I passed a Chinese herbalist, with unlabeled glass jars in the window. One jar held flat, dried lizards. *Take two lizards and call me in the morning*, I joked to myself.

I passed underneath the huge brown bulk of the Manhattan Bridge, grateful for a temporary respite from the sun. On the opposite side of the street I noticed a building that still had Hebrew letters carved above the door. A former synagogue, perhaps; this was part of the legendary Lower East Side of Manhattan.

There were little hole-in-the-wall eateries with whole smoked ducks hanging in the windows; juices dripped into pans directly under the ducks, which were destined to be wrapped in rice pancakes and smothered with *hoisin* sauce. There were newspaper stands with Chinese papers and bright red greeting cards with gold calligraphy. There were tourist stores with dusty Buddhas in the windows and back-scratchers hanging outside. Asian schoolgirls in plaid uniform skirts walked three abreast, cradling books in their arms like babies. Old women shuffled by in cotton slippers, wearing sweaters in spite of the growing heat. In the street, horns honked and drivers swore at one another.

Although the restaurants were closed, the smells of soy and duck hung in the air; I would have to prevail upon Matt to eat Chinese for lunch. A dim sum parlor, perhaps; my mouth watered in anticipation of little dumplings served from rolling carts trundled through the restaurant by women who seldom spoke English. You pointed and took your chances.

I was meeting Riordan at the little round tables near the food stalls. As I stepped past the Federal Correction Center, which also housed the United States attorney's office, I found myself hoping one of the booths would be selling hot coffee to early risers.

I ducked down the little alleyway that separated the federal jail from the tiny church that sat among the larger public buildings like a sparrow among hawks.

Most of the food stalls weren't open yet, but Ferrara's was doing some business in coffee and Italian pastries. I stepped up and ordered a double cappuccino. When I had the steamy, foamy drink in my hand, I carried it gingerly to one of the metal tables chained to the paving stones.

Too nervous to sit, I shaded my eyes and looked up and down Centre Street, waiting to see Matt Riordan's purposeful stride heading my way.

The plaza seemed peaceful, in sharp contrast to the bustling activity that would fill it in less than an hour. It was a crossroads of civic life; within a half-mile there were five courthouses, the Municipal Building, One Police Plaza, the Federal Correctional Center, and, across the street, the federal building.

Where was Riordan? I had things to tell him and he had things to tell me. Had he come away with evidence, or had the anonymous fax been, as I'd loudly predicted, a waste of time?

There was someone on top of the courthouse steps. A

figure huddled beside one of the huge smooth stone columns that topped the long staircase. Probably a homeless guy catching a few extra winks before the court officers showed up for work and shooed him away. I dismissed him from my thoughts.

Then I looked back. Could the huddled figure be Matt Riordan? Could he be sitting at the top of the steps, waiting for me to join him? Sitting on cold marble in his designer suit didn't sound much like Riordan, but I decided to hike up the steps on the theory that I'd get a good view of Foley Square from atop the stairs.

I swallowed the last of the cappuccino and tossed my cup into a wire trash bin. Then I crossed to the courthouse and trudged up the steep steps, half-expecting to hear Riordan's voice behind me, asking me where the hell I was going.

The huddled figure made no move as I approached. I supposed that sleeping outdoors meant being able to sleep in spite of people passing by.

As I drew closer, my first thought was that the man had made a hell of a mess out of the pristine marble wall behind the austere columns. There was a huge brownish-red stain behind where he lay. Graffiti was my first thought.

My second thought was that the color was dumb and there was nothing artistic about the scrawl that ran from head level down to the floor.

My next thought was that it was strange that the huddled man had so much of the brownish-red paint all over his head and clothes.

The cappuccino came halfway up my throat in a great burning rush as reality finally dawned on me. I leaned against a cool marble column to prop up my suddenly rubbery knees.

The man was dead. The brown-red stains were blood.

I focused my eyes on the face—could it be Riordan who

lay there, his blood and brains splattered against the granite wall?

Relief surged through me as I realized that the remaining hair on the half-shattered head was a light color. The clothes were wrong, too—a navy blazer, gray summer-weight slacks, and black loafers. And there was an ankle holster strapped to his right leg.

Eddie Fitz. The dead man was Eddie Fitz.

He'd been shot. You didn't have to be a forensics specialist to see that. He'd been shot the night before he was due to finish testifying against Matt.

I hoped to hell that my ex-lover and present client hadn't been the one to pull the trigger.

CHAPTER ELEVEN

"Oh, my God," a man behind me said in a strangled voice. I turned; a blue-uniformed federal court officer stood nearby, his face as white as the granite columns on the portico.

"I'm gonna call 911," he said in a croak.

"The Fifth Precinct would be better," I pointed out. "He's been dead a while. There's no emergency here."

I sounded far cooler than I felt.

The court officer turned and made for the heavy doors. He opened them with his key. I decided to go back down the stairs and wait for the cops by the picnic tables. My knees shook badly as I hobbled down the steps, and I cursed the lack of a railing; I could picture myself falling, and finishing the trip on my—

I saw Riordan as I was halfway down. He gave his watch an ostentatious glance. When I got close enough to be heard, I told him to shove it.

He raised an eyebrow and I explained what I'd found at the top of the stairs. His face showed surprise. I was glad.

I was glad I wasn't telling him something he already knew.

"Oh, God, Matt," I finished, putting a shaking hand over my mouth, "it was horrible. Half his head was missing. He—"

"Don't think about it, babe," Matt said. He placed his hand over mine and gave a squeeze. My hand felt cold and fragile, as if it might shatter if squeezed too hard. I swallowed and lowered myself onto a bench at one of the tables in the plaza. My client had a warm hand on my shoulder. I wanted very much to bury my face in his starched white shirt-front and cry.

I bit my lower lip to keep from doing just that, and took in a long, ragged breath.

"Matt, I have to know," I said, deliberately refusing to look into his eyes. "Did you—"

"Did I put a hole in Eddie Fitz?" His tone was harsh. "Is that what you're asking?"

"I have a right to know," I replied in a trembly voice. "I have to know if I'm representing you on a bribery charge or a murder charge, after all."

His smile was half-amused. "I assure you, Cass, I'll get another lawyer if they charge me with murder. I won't ask you to stay with my case if you—"

"Oh, shut up," I cut in, my voice rising to what even I recognized as a hysterical shriek. "Just shut up and tell me the truth."

"I did not kill Eddie Fitz," my client replied in a solemn tone. "Since I don't know when he was killed," he went on, "I can't be certain where I was when he died, but—"

"You were home, weren't you?" I asked, surprised there could be an issue on that point. "You left my house to go meet this anonymous faxer, and after that, you went home."

He shook his head. It seemed to me that a slight blush tinged his tanned cheeks. "I came here to Foley Square at eleven or so," he said. "I waited for over an hour. No one showed. I'll tell you more about that later. Then I left and went to Taylor's for the rest of the night."

He'd gone from my bed to hers. From his old squeeze to his lemon-haired lady.

I clenched and unclenched a fist. He'd slipped out of my bed and ended the night in hers. He'd betrayed me in the worst way a man can betray a woman. There was a lot I could have said—wanted to say—but now was not the time.

We had a lot more to talk about, but before we could get to it, the cops rolled up. Blue-and-whites screamed into Foley Square, rolling right up onto the broad sidewalk in front of the federal courthouse. Cops jumped out, ran up the steps, and went to work. A plainclothes detective team walked over to Matt and me, deceptively pleasant expressions on their faces.

The black detective's name was Martha Rodney; her Asian partner was Harold Lam. They separated us. I went with Rodney, while Matt followed Lam to the church steps. My client was out of earshot, but not out of sight. I couldn't keep my eyes from wandering in that direction as I answered the detective's questions, wondering whether Matt needed his lawyer by his side.

"I understand you found the body," Detective Rodney said in a noncommittal voice. I nodded.

"Did you recognize him?" She had a steno pad in one hand, a ballpoint pen in the other. I felt uneasy speaking for the record, answering questions without knowing how those answers might be used. This probably wasn't exactly what Rodney had in mind, but I could have bet that she wouldn't be happy to learn how anxious she'd made me.

"Not at first," I said. My gorge rose again as I remembered the horror of Eddie. "I don't know if his mother could have recognized him in all that blood," I added.

"I know what you mean," Rodney replied in a soothing tone. "It never gets to be what you'd call easy."

But underneath the velvet glove, the iron fist lay in wait. "Could you tell me who you recognized the corpse to be?"

I joined her in speaking police jargon. "I recognized him to be Detective Edmund Fitzgerald of the Seven-Four Precinct in Brooklyn."

"And exactly how did you recognize him?"

"He's a witness in a case I'm defending," I said.

"Could you tell me where you were last night?" she asked. Then she flashed a bright, white smile that lit up her dark face. "It's just a routine question, Counselor," she explained.

"Then I'll give a routine answer," I said, deliberately echoing the words and the smile. "I was home in bed."

"And was anyone there with you?"

No, the person who could and should have been there with me jumped out of the sack and went away. He either shot Eddie or he didn't, but either way he went from me to Her, so why don't you put that in your little detective's notebook and—

I took a deep breath. "No," I replied.

Before she could ask another question, her partner was back, with Matt in tow.

Detective Lam made a gesture with his thumb toward Matt. "He says he won't say another word without talking to his lawyer first." Lam nodded at me. "I guess that's you," he added sourly, as if the word "lawyer" hurt his mouth.

"I'm his lawyer," I confirmed.

Lam pointed toward the church steps. "Then go over there and talk," he demanded. "When you're finished, come back here."

We obeyed. When we reached the steps leading to St. Andrew's, I turned on Matt and asked, "What the hell happened last night?"

"I got here at exactly eleven-oh-three," he replied. "I checked my watch and made a note of the time. If somebody did show up and hand me something I could use as evidence," he explained, "I wanted to be prepared to give accurate testimony about the meeting. I waited for over an hour. No one came up to me, no one brought me anything. But," he added, a glint in his eye, "I saw some very interesting things just the same."

"Like what?"

"Like at eleven-fifteen on the dot, Davia Singer came out of the U.S. attorney's office and walked toward that ugly piece of junk." Matt pointed toward a giant sculpture of three huge circles enmeshed in one another. It had originally been a rusty metal color; the city had painted it bright red in vain hopes of improving its aesthetic quality.

"She stood by that damned thing for a good twenty minutes," Matt continued. "And every two minutes she looked at her watch and tapped her foot and craned her neck to see who was coming. She acted, in short, like she'd been waiting for someone who stood her up."

"Do you think she had an anonymous fax, too?" I asked.

"Who knows? All I know is she left before I did, and she left without anyone turning up to meet her. But the important thing is, she was here. Here in Foley Square at about the time Eddie was killed."

"Yes, but you were watching her," I protested. "Did you see her walk up the courthouse steps?"

"I wasn't watching her every minute," he replied. "She walked toward the sidewalk and back, she walked to One Police Plaza and back. There could have been three, four minutes there where she slipped around the back of the church and climbed the steps to the courthouse without my seeing her. She could have shot Eddie when I wasn't watching her."

"But did you hear a shot?" I demanded. "I can't believe whoever killed Eddie did it without making a noise."

"I didn't hear a shot," Matt answered. "But the killer could have used a suppressor." *Suppressor*. Most people, including me, said "silencer." But suppressor was the term of art, the term a real gun person would have used.

I nodded, refusing to consider the implication that my client knew more about firearms than I'd realized. "Okay. Singer could have killed Eddie. But why?"

"Leave that for a moment. She's not the only person I saw. Nick Lazarus left his office ten minutes after Singer came out. He walked along Centre Street, toward Worth; I wasn't watching every second, and he could easily have gone up the steps to meet and kill Eddie while I was over here by the church."

"Lazarus," I said, thinking aloud. "What if he got the news that I'd been to see Di Blasi? What if he knew I had a smoking gun ready for today's testimony? I'm willing to bet he'd rather see Eddie Fitz dead than properly cross-examined in a way that could prove he knew Eddie was crooked. He had a lot to lose if we destroyed Eddie on the stand."

"True," Matt replied. "It's hard to cross-examine a corpse. There's one more player who was here last night," he went on. "I was right here in this church doorway," he explained. "I had a perfect view of the plaza, but I don't think anyone saw me here in the shadows. And who should I see walking toward One Police Plaza but Stan Krieger?"

Stan Krieger, who was very probably going to be indicted on Eddie's say-so as soon as Matt's trial was over. Stan Krieger, who had no way of knowing I had the ammunition to destroy the witness who could put him away. Stan Krieger, who rightly blamed Eddie for Dwight Straub's suicide.

It flashed through my mind that there was something extremely odd about the fact that four people, all with good reason to want Eddie Fitz dead, just happened to be hanging around the plaza at the time he was shot. Before I could remark upon this apparent coincidence, Detective Lam gestured at us to come back to the food-stall area.

"What do you want to do about them?" I asked Matt.

"I don't mind telling them I was here," Matt replied. "For one thing, someone may have seen me. Why get myself hung up if I don't have to? Might as well cooperate."

But when we walked back toward the table where Rodney and Lam waited, we discovered they'd been joined by a third law enforcement officer: FBI Special Agent Warren Zebart.

Zebart was all iron fist; if he'd ever owned a velvet glove, he'd mislaid it years ago.

"For a lawyer," he said heavily to Matt, "you sure as hell don't like letting the system do its job."

I gestured to Matt to keep quiet, but he pretended not to notice. "Just what do you mean by that?" he demanded.

"I mean it's amazing to me how many cases in which you're involved end up closed on account of murder."

Matt shrugged. "When you represent a certain type of individual," he replied, "murder is just part of the package."

I tuned out for a dangerous minute as the full implication of Zebart's remarks sank in.

Closed on account of murder.

You can't cross-examine a corpse.

The case against Riordan was effectively over. Judge de Freitas would have no choice but to grant my motion for a mistrial; without a full opportunity to cross-examine Eddie Fitz, Riordan couldn't get a fair trial. And with Eddie dead, there would be no retrial.

I'd just won the case.

And Matt's motive to kill Eddie loomed as large as the massive Municipal Building that overshadowed the plaza.

"Stop," I said, holding up a warning hand. "Whatever you two are saying to one another, please stop."

Of course Riordan was way ahead of me. He'd understood from the moment I'd told him Eddie was dead that this meant he'd be acquitted. I'd still been in shock from the grisly discovery I'd made at the top of the stairs. I hadn't been parsing out the legal implications of a New York City detective with his brains splattered all over the white granite of the federal courthouse.

"You," I said to Zebart, putting a finger closer to his face than politeness permitted, "stop interrogating my client. I haven't heard Miranda warnings, and yet it's obvious you consider him a suspect. Either arrest him or leave him alone."

Then I wheeled on Riordan. "And you," I continued, moving the finger in his direction, "shut up. Stop showing everyone how cool you are in the face of intimidation. These people, in case you've forgotten, are not jurors you have to impress. They're law enforcement officers who'd like nothing more than to march you away in handcuffs."

I took a deep breath and looked up at the top of the courthouse steps. Bright yellow crime-scene tape surrounded a large square area; the cops had brought blue sawhorses for crowd control. The reporters and minicams had arrived; they stood at the foot of the stairs, waiting for someone to come down and give them sound bites.

"One thing about working for the Bureau," Zebart said with a wolfish grin, "they've got one hell of a support staff. Anything you ask for, you can get in record time."

I wasn't sure where the big FBI man was going with this, but the complacent look on his face told me it wasn't going to be anywhere I wanted him to go. I was certain of this when he pulled an official-looking paper out of his jacket pocket and handed it to me.

"What's this?" I asked. I opened it, read it, and handed it to Matt.

"It's a search warrant," I said in a tone dulled by shock. "It authorizes Agent Zebart to search you for a weapon."

Matt opened his silk-lined suit jacket to reveal a shoulder holster. Zebart reached in and gingerly pulled out the sleek black gun in a practiced two-fingered hold that was designed to preserve any fingerprints.

"We'll just take this along to the lab," the agent said. "See if it's been fired recently, see if the bullets match the ones that blew Detective Fitzgerald's head to bits."

I felt like a prize idiot. Why hadn't I asked my client if he'd come armed to the plaza the night before?

Was it because I was afraid to hear the answer, afraid to acknowledge that Matt's rage at Eddie Fitz could very easily have driven him to the top of the courthouse steps? That to a man who viewed a criminal trial as nothing less than war, acquittal wasn't victory enough?

Only death would do.

"I'm not getting your point," Lani protested. I'd broken through the gantlet of reporters and made my way to her office for a little coffee and sympathy. Coffee, I had. Sympathy, I was still waiting for. "The ballistics people will test Matt's gun and they'll realize it's not the one that killed Eddie, so what's the problem?"

"Lani, don't be naive. Of course Matt's gun didn't kill Eddie. At least," I amended, "the gun he carried in that holster didn't."

"I repeat, if Matt's gun didn't kill Eddie, then—"

"Matt Riordan is one of the smartest people I've ever met," I retorted. "Of course he's not going to kill the chief witness against him and then carry a smoking gun around with him the next day. If he killed Eddie, then he did it with another gun. A gun that can't be traced to him. A gun he got rid of as soon as he used it. A gun that—"

"Why wouldn't he just throw the gun down next to the body?" Lani asked. "I've heard of Mafia guys doing that. They use an untraceable gun and then just leave it for the cops, knowing it won't do them any good."

"Hell, maybe the killer *did* toss the gun," I replied glumly. "I wouldn't be surprised if someone saw it lying there and stole it." Then I remembered Eddie's ankle holster. It would be hard to accept a thief stealing the murder weapon and leaving a perfectly good gun on the corpse.

"So the FBI has Matt's gun," Lani persisted. "It'll come back clean, and Matt will be in the clear."

"Your simple faith is so touching," I remarked. "In the first place, who's to say the Bureau isn't going to fudge the results to nail Matt? But even if they don't, Zebart stood there in the open plaza and searched him. They treated him like a mutt. I know at least one of the reporters saw what they were doing. I won't be surprised to see pictures spread over the front page of the *Post*. If they can't destroy Matt with real evidence, in a courtroom, they can ruin him in the media. How many people want a criminal defense lawyer who's been searched in public by an FBI agent?"

"You don't think his future clients will feel a bond with a man who's been the victim of mistaken suspicion?"

"I do not. And neither do you, if you think about it. Hell, Frankie Cretella already has a new lawyer, and I don't think he's coming back to Matt no matter what happens."

"So even though you've won," Lani summed up, "you've lost."

"And you can finish that thought and say you told me so," I went on. "You can remind me that you warned me I'd be tarred with the same brush if I defended Matt. You can—"

"What I *can* do," my old friend said in a tone that could slice day-old pumpernickel, "is let you in on the latest courthouse gossip about Nick Lazarus. That ought to put the roses back in your cheeks."

"Only if the latest courthouse gossip says that Nick Lazarus walked out of his office late last night packing a gun and used it to blow away his star witness," I retorted.

"Almost as good," Lani promised. I perked up. She sat at her desk in a characteristic pose, nyloned feet propped up on an opened drawer, Bass loafers on the floor beside the desk. Her dark hair was an uncombed mop; she raked her short fingers through it, making an even bigger mess, then began her tale.

"Word is that Lazarus threw one of his famous shit-fits last night," she said. "The whole courthouse heard him. Or at least," she amended, "those who were still here at about ten or so. Which, before you ask," she added, holding up a warning hand, "didn't include me. I was home in the bosom of my little family."

"How is Lil?" I asked. Lani's lover was a civil court judge.

"She's fine," Lani said. "Now stop interrupting and listen. This is going to make your day."

I complied. A kind of calm settled over me, the first peace I'd felt since I'd stumbled upon Eddie's corpse that morning. I'd get through this, I decided; I had friends, and with friends all things were possible.

"I heard he ripped Singer up one side and down the other for not telling him about Eddie—and that she screamed back that he'd known all along and if he thought he was going to hang it all on her, he had another think coming because she had contemporaneous notes." Lani gave a conspiratorial grin and said in a wry voice, "Isn't it amazing to hear a fight between lawyers? Even when we're threatening one another, we do it within the rules of evidence. 'Contemporaneous notes,' " she mocked, " 'past recollection recorded.' As if in the very moment she's defending herself against Lazarus, she's got one eye on admissibility of evidence."

"Well, hell," I protested, "there's every reason to think this will end up in court. And Singer's too smart not to realize Lazarus would try to dump it all on her. I can hear him now: 'Your Honor, I didn't know what my assistant was up to. I never would have countenanced such a thing if I'd been informed.' "

"Well, in any case, it was a shouting match that was heard three floors away. And the upshot of it was that Lazarus started screaming that he ought to indict Eddie for perjury."

"There's a three hundred and sixty degree turn for you," I observed. "Lazarus indicts his star witness."

"That would be one way to distance himself from Eddie's corruption," Lani suggested. "It would be telling the world he didn't approve of Eddie's lies, and that he didn't cover them up."

"But it would also open a huge can of worms," I argued. "Judge de Freitas would take the U.S. attorney's office apart, making sure there was nothing in there that pointed to Lazarus or Singer's having known the truth about Eddie. No judge wants to be made a fool of, and if Lazarus put Eddie on the stand knowing he was a liar and a scumbag, de Freitas is going to flay Lazarus alive. What Matt's just been through will look like a Sunday school picnic," I added, with more than a touch of relish.

"There is, believe it or not, more," Lani said. She smiled, and her plain face lit up with mischief. "I was going to tell you this earlier, but I didn't get a chance. I wasn't sure what you could do with it, but I thought you ought to know, anyway. Guess who was shacked up with Eddie every night?"

"Not Davia Singer!" I was genuinely shocked. When will women lawyers learn not to sleep with witnesses?

Then I dropped my eyes, remembering Matt and me the night before.

When we learn not to sleep with defendants, I answered myself in a rueful inner voice.

Lani nodded. "And my sources tell me this had been going on for a while. They also tell me Eddie, who you may recall was married, was about to break it off, and that Singer was pissed as hell. I'm not sure it qualifies as a *Fatal Attraction* situation, but it is nice and messy."

"So that's who Singer was waiting for by the sculpture," I mused aloud. "She must have stood there every night, waiting for Lazarus to let Eddie go home. Then the two of them would waltz off to her place and—''

"And do the horizontal mambo," Lani finished. "Like I said, I don't know how this helps, but—''

"Does she have a gun?''

"She *could*," Lani pointed out. "U.S. attorneys are authorized to carry weapons. And I know Lazarus has one; remember, he was attacked a few years ago, and went very public about buying a gun and learning how to use it.''

I nodded. So now we not only had four suspects wandering through Police Plaza the night Eddie died, all four of them had the right to carry a weapon—and the means to find a weapon that couldn't be traced to them. And they each had motives: Lazarus would find it considerably less messy to kill Eddie than to indict him; Singer was the classic dumped woman; Krieger knew Eddie could send him to jail; and Matt Riordan wanted not just to win his case, but to destroy his enemies.

I made a token visit to Judge de Freitas' chambers on the way out of the courthouse. He'd adjourned the case to give the prosecution time to respond to my motion to dismiss, but there was little real doubt that with Eddie dead he'd have no choice but to throw out the charges against Matt. We hadn't finished cross-examination, and without a full cross, Matt wouldn't have received the fair trial guaranteed by the Constitution.

Afterwards, I dragged myself back to Brooklyn, emotionally and physically exhausted. I walked into the Morning Glory and told my troubles to Dorinda—who began explaining to me why I shouldn't be upset that Riordan had deserted me for his lemon-haired lady the night before.

"Stop pouring oil on troubled waters," I muttered, poking a newly unwrapped straw into my cherry milkshake. "I *like* my waters troubled.''

"Yes, but how do you like the milkshake?" Dorinda countered, her hands on her hips. Her apron sported giant shadow-print cherries on a sky-blue background. It was one of her many Lassie's-mom vintage aprons.

"Sweet," I replied after a hefty swallow. "And thick. It's hard work to get this stuff through the straw."

"I think you have a piece of cherry stuck in the bottom," she remarked with an air of expertise. "That happens a lot with fresh cherry shakes."

I was drinking a cherry milkshake in honor of the Morning Glory's Second Annual Cherry Festival. Dorinda had grown up in the lakeside town of Traverse City, Michigan, and she had fond memories of her hometown's annual early July homage to the red fruit. She had drawn the line at serving the cherry meatballs that had won her mom a third prize one year in the entree category, but her menu overflowed with cherry shakes, sundaes, pies, tarts, danishes, muffins, and scones. She had even mashed up a cherry-and-cream cheese concoction for spreading on a bagel, and she had tried to interest me in a cherry-flavored iced tea instead of my usual iced coffee. Fat chance.

She'd been trying to jolly me out of my anger at Matt Riordan; now she just laughed. "That must be what kept you two together all that time," she said. "I think you both like troubled waters better than calm ones. Who knows?" she went on. "Maybe this trial will bring you together again."

I shook my head. "Not if he's going to make a practice of hopping from my bed to Taylor's." I pulled the straw out of the thick liquid and set it on the counter. Then I lifted the glass, tilted it and let a large glob of shake fill my mouth. Little flecks of fruit hit my taste buds; she'd used deep, dark cherries and the flavor was intoxicating. Her folks back in Michigan had shipped her a selection that included sour and sweet, Bing and yellow.

"Great stuff," I said when I'd swallowed.

She rewarded me with a smile. "My very first date was at the Cherry Festival," she recalled. "Bobby Anson was the only boy in school who was taller than me. He was skinny as a string, but he had an inch on me, so he asked me to the Festival and bought me a shake. A whole one just for me. I carried it around till it melted into mush, just so the other girls could see me with it and know I was on a real date. He kissed me on the Ferris wheel.''

Her big blue eyes had taken on a dreamy look. This was a Dorinda I'd seldom seen; by the time we met at Kent State, she'd been a full-blown hippie with long Indian skirts and flowers in her hair.

"Where is he now?" I asked.

"Lansing," she replied. "At least that's what my mom said. With a wife and three kids."

"Do you ever wonder," I began, "what your life would have been like if you—"

"Not really," she said. She turned her back and began to fuss with the danishes she'd made with yellow cherries.

I wasn't buying that. "Of course you do," I persisted. "Everybody does. Don't you think I wonder sometimes what my life would have been if I'd stayed in Ohio, gotten married, had kids, joined the PTA?"

"You'd have been miserable," Dorinda said. "And what's worse, your kids would have been, too. You'd have no outlet for your energy, your anger."

"Do I really have that much anger?" I wasn't sure I wanted to know.

Dorinda laughed. It was a nice laugh, a laugh that said she liked me and was going to keep on liking me no matter how she answered that question.

"The first time I met you, you were ranting about some injustice on campus. I don't remember what it was, but I remember thinking you needed to mellow out, smoke a joint or something."

"Yes," I said, deliberately choosing a tone as sweet as Dorinda's cherry shake. "As I recall, that was your all-purpose remedy for everything in those days. Hell, you thought the war would end if Nixon and Ho Chi Minh would just pass a doobie back and forth.''

"And you thought it would end if you marched on Washington enough times. We were both wrong.''

Yes, but I was righter, I wanted to say. Marching accomplished something. Marching told the country to stop and think it over. Marching was action. Smoking dope was passive, self-involved, self-indulgent.

Protesting, of course, was never self-indulgent.

Neither was anger.

My milkshake had melted into a sticky pink puddle. I pushed it away, suddenly sickened by its childish sweetness. "Got any more iced coffee?'' I asked.

Dorinda walked toward the sun tea container where she kept the cold coffee. "Coffee,'' she pronounced, "is a drink of anger.''

I gave this piece of wisdom some thought. "Anger is good for the blood,'' I pronounced back. I could play Wise Woman as well as Dorinda. "Anger tones you, puts you on your mettle, makes you feel alive. Without anger, I'd be a blob. I'd have nothing but contentment, and, contrary to the belief of those of you who spent the sixties in a haze of marijuana smoke, contentment is not enough.''

"I may have to take it back,'' my friend remarked.

"Take it back about what?''

"About Riordan. You and he may have been made for one another after all.''

CHAPTER
TWELVE

" 'So what do you think of your blue-eyed boy now, Mr. Death?' " I tossed the words onto the table like a gauntlet and waited for the Grand Old Man of New York muckraking to pick them up.

He did. He saw my e. e. cummings and raised with Kenneth Rexroth.

" 'You killed him,' " he intoned, with a nod of his lion head. " 'You killed him in your God-damned Brooks Brothers suit.' "

He heaved a sigh and let his gravel voice rumble on. "Only it wasn't true about Dylan Thomas. Nobody, in or out of a Brooks Brothers suit, killed Thomas. He drank himself to death, and no amount of poetry can shift the blame to someone else. I met him once or twice, back in the old days, at the White Horse Tavern. He may have been the finest poet in the English language, but he was a mean, sloppy drunk. He died. Nobody killed him."

"But somebody killed Eddie Fitz," I reminded Winthrop. "Somebody iced him. My question to you is: By the time he died, was he still your blue-eyed boy? Did you still believe he was incorruptible?''

Another sigh. Jesse Winthrop seemed to be carrying a load as heavy as the one that burdened the statue of Atlas in Rockefeller Center. ''No,'' he said at last. He looked away, focusing on the huge cappuccino urn in the back of The Peacock. This time we didn't have a coveted window table; we sat in the middle of the coffeehouse. At the table next to us, three first-year law students from nearby NYU argued about the Rule Against Perpetuities. I smiled in recognition, seeing my younger self as a passionate but deeply confused law student (any law student not confused by the Rule Against Perpetuities instantly became an expert in wills and trusts; the rest of us moved on to other specialties).

''No,'' Winthrop went on, heaving another sigh, ''those tapes you sent me of that drug dealer convinced me. But I still don't approve,'' he added, his tone sharpening, ''of your client's methods of dealing with witnesses he doesn't like.''

''You don't seriously think Matt Riordan killed Eddie?'' I seemed to be asking that question of far too many people lately.

''Believe it or not,'' Winthrop assured me, ''I know better than to accept as gospel everything I read in the *Post*.'' As I'd predicted and feared, a photo of Matt with his hands in the air, being searched for a weapon, had been plastered on the front page of the tabloid under a bloodred headline that read MOB LAWYER KEY SUSPECT IN COP KILLING.

In much smaller letters underneath the picture, the *Post* admitted there had been no arrest.

''Since you have such an open mind,'' I said, trying hard to suppress the sarcastic edge to my voice, ''why don't I tell you the whole story of what went on in the plaza last night?''

I did, starting with the anonymous fax and Matt's determination to meet the sender and see what dirt he could get on Lazarus. I continued with Matt's account of what he'd seen in the plaza, of the three other suspects who'd been in the area at the same time.

"So it seems clear," I finished, "that whoever this faxer was, he probably lured Stan Krieger to the plaza with the same kind of bait. Something that would help Krieger in his own troubles with the police. Davia Singer was already there, but it seems equally clear that whoever killed Eddie knew she was in the habit of meeting him at the sculpture after work. And Lazarus has a reputation for working very late hours, so it wasn't much of a stretch to think he'd be around at midnight."

"You think the murder was premeditated, then," Winthrop said. "Not a spur-of-the-moment thing, an impulse."

"Not with four prime suspects all on the scene at a time when at least two of them, Riordan and Krieger, would ordinarily have no reason to be there. Not with three out of four of those suspects standing alone at different landmarks in the plaza, none of them really able to alibi the others for the whole time. Not with—"

"You make this killer sound like a real manipulator. A chessmaster," Winthrop cut in.

"Yeah, I guess so," I agreed. "I don't know what ploy he used to get Krieger to the plaza, but I can guess."

"You say 'he,' " the journalist pointed out. "Are you ready to eliminate Davia Singer as a suspect?"

"No," I admitted. "But I do have my eye on Lazarus. He's the one whose balls are on the line here. He'd have access to the kind of inside information that could bring Stan Krieger to the plaza. He'd know how to jerk Riordan's chain as well, how to bait the hook that brought him to the plaza. And I can't believe he's ignorant of the little affair between Singer and Eddie."

"Doesn't it occur to you that the same could be said for

your client?'' Winthrop's eyebrows rose, and he held up a hand to forestall my protests. It was a workingman's hand, calloused and hard-fingered. I decided he was a woodworker in his spare time.

"Hear me out before you start preparing your defense, Counselor," he urged. "Don't you think Matt Riordan is smart enough to plan Eddie's murder and cover his own ass by making sure he committed the crime at a time and place when Lazarus and Singer would be on the scene? And don't you think he knows enough about cops to set a trap for Stan Krieger? Don't you think he's capable of faxing himself an anonymous message, to explain his own presence in the plaza? Everything you've said about Lazarus is equally possible for Riordan."

"But Lazarus is the one who really benefits from Eddie's death," I protested. "Matt had no reason to kill Eddie; he wanted to destroy him in court."

"No reason other than revenge," Jesse Winthrop said in a deceptively soft tone. "No reason other than to wipe off the face of the earth the man who'd humiliated him, who'd almost cost him his professional life. And to put a frame around his old enemy Lazarus at the same time."

"Then why drag in Krieger?" I countered. "Why not tighten the noose around Lazarus instead?"

The waitress hovered next to me, waiting for an order. One thing about The Peacock, it was possible to sit there for a half hour before anyone mustered enough energy to walk over and see what you wanted. I ordered iced cappuccino, Winthrop a double espresso with lemon peel.

After she walked away, it occurred to me that I'd defended my client and sometime lover, not on the grounds that he wouldn't commit murder and frame an innocent man for it, but on the grounds that he'd have done it more efficiently, without muddying the waters with bitter, crooked cops and jilted lovers.

"I've heard a little something through my police

sources," Winthrop went on. "I've heard they're comparing the bullets that killed Eddie with the bullets that killed TJ and Nunzie Aiello."

I dismissed this with an airy wave of my hand. "That's just Warren Zebart's wishful thinking," I said. "He'd like nothing better than to nail Riordan for every mob crime going back to Judge Crater's disappearance."

"What if there's a match?"

"Well, I still have my suspicions that Lazarus had TJ eliminated, so a similarity of ballistics there won't shake me up much. And I read the police reports on both TJ and Nunzie, and as I recall, the bullets mushroomed pretty badly. I'm not sure they can get a match in any case."

We stopped when the drinks came. I sipped cappuccino and watched my companion taste his dark, bitter brew, lifting the tiny cup to his lips as if he were the guest of honor at a tea party for dolls.

"All my life, I've hated guys like Eddie Fitz," he mused aloud. "I've hated the bully boys and the big dicks and the fascists. Because to me they're all the same thing. They're all variations on a theme: 'I've got power and you don't.' That's what they're all about, guys like that. And I was the kid on the playground fifty years ago who'd stand up against those guys and defend the kids they picked on. I was strong and big enough that I could have been a bully too, but somehow I wasn't. Somehow I stood between those guys and the fat kid, the retarded kid, the girl they called the class slut."

I could see it. I had a sudden image of Jesse Winthrop as a boy, standing in an old-fashioned schoolyard with his legs apart, chin thrust out, eyes blazing with anger. Fighting back with logic and with words, with fists if he had to. And when he'd graduated from the playground, he'd fought back with his column. Instead of bloodying the noses of the bullies, he'd exposed their scams, revealed their petty political machinations.

Until now. Until he'd fallen under the spell of Eddie Fitz.

"So what changed?" I asked. "How did you miss the fact that Eddie Fitz was just another bully?"

"I'm not sure I did miss it," he replied, his grating voice as soft as he could make it. "I'm not sure, but I think I ignored my gut on this one. I met Ike Straub, you know. I met him and I saw the way Eddie treated him, and I ignored it. I chose to believe they were friends, equals, but the truth was right in front of me: Eddie had that kid buffaloed. Straub was the little sycophant all bullies like to keep at their sides. A one-man cheering section, a guy who can always be counted on to play yes-man and butt."

"Like Paulie the Cork," I said, recalling the tapes of Eddie's meetings with Fat Jack.

"Yeah, him, too," Jesse agreed. "He was like Dwight, only older. And getting older just means the bullies dump on you even more. Poor stupid little fucker."

"You mean Dwight, I suppose," I commented.

"Hell, I guess I mean all the misguided assholes who think their dick is the most important thing in their lives. You're a woman, you know what I mean. How many guys do you know who lead with their dicks? Guys like Eddie, it's a macho thing you can see coming a mile away. But listen to these three at the next table, and what do you hear?"

I listened and gave my companion a wry smile; I heard what I'd been hearing ever since my first day at NYU Law School. Three guys arguing about whose was bigger. Oh, they thought they were arguing about the Rule Against Perpetuities; they would have sworn they were having a perfectly logical legal discussion that would help all three of them pass Property. But underneath, the refrain was exactly what Jesse Winthrop said it was. One guy was trying to prove to his fellows that he knew it all, and that his knowledge made him better, made his bigger than theirs. The others were fighting back, championing their own viewpoints, but they accepted the underlying premise all too readily: Whoever was right was King of the Hill, which meant that being right was everything and being wrong made you a eunuch.

Guys like Jesse Winthrop, who actually understood what was going on and were capable of standing apart from it, were as rare and precious as rubies.

Matt Riordan had spent his whole life becoming King of the Hill, and now he was defending his right to stay on top. He had never stopped to question that major premise, never been able to let go of the compulsion to be right, to be the best.

And if he had indeed killed Eddie Fitz, as I was deeply and horribly afraid he had, it was because Eddie threatened his position on top of the hill.

The question was: Who else was Eddie trying to knock down? Who else stood to lose if Eddie was publicly exposed as the most corrupt cop in the city?

Nick Lazarus, for one. Like Riordan, he accepted the rules of the masculine game. You're either on top or you're nothing. You're either a bully or a patsy. You've either got balls or you're a girl. Eddie Fitz had played Lazarus for a patsy. In Lazarus' world, this merited a death sentence.

"Did Lazarus know the truth about Eddie?" I asked. "I have reason to believe he did, but I want to know what you think. Did Lazarus put Eddie on the stand knowing that he was going to lie?"

"If he did, he was taking one hell of a chance," Winthrop pointed out. "There were a number of people who could have taken the stand and blown Eddie out of the water."

Playing devil's advocate was one way to get through law school without directly playing King of the Hill; you didn't exactly challenge the alpha male, but you undercut his position with little zingers that had him scrambling for territory.

"People like TJ?" I asked with a sly smile. "But TJ was dead. He was dead the whole time Riordan and I were combing the five boroughs looking for him. And if Lazarus knew he was dead, he had nothing to worry about putting Eddie on the stand. He'd know from the beginning that TJ wasn't going to pop up and tell the world Eddie was his partner in crime."

Jesse made the logical leap I had every confidence he was going to make. "You want me to write a column accusing the United States attorney's office of having a drug dealer killed so he wouldn't tarnish their chief witness."

"Face it, Jesse," I replied, "your book deal is down the tubes unless you change your premise from Eddie the Hero Cop to Eddie the Guy Who Screwed Everyone and Got Away With It. Why not start with a column raising a few questions about what Lazarus knew and when he knew it?"

"I don't suppose you have any information you'd care to contribute to this column, Counselor," my companion said. "In the interests of journalistic integrity, of course. No benefit whatsoever to your client."

I brought Winthrop up to date on everything I'd learned from Dom Di Blasi and Fat Jack Vance.

"So here's the prosecution rushing to judgment to nail Matt Riordan for Eddie's murder," I concluded, "when the truth is we wanted Eddie alive so we could discredit him. The only people who benefited from Eddie's death are Nick Lazarus and Davia Singer."

"Nice try, Counselor," Jesse's gravel voice replied, "but what about Stan Krieger and the other cops? Aren't they getting a reprieve, what with Eddie out of the way?"

"Yes," I agreed crisply. Always concede what you absolutely have to. "Yes, but why now? Why kill Eddie now? Why not before? Why not later? The only reason to kill him right now is that he was on the verge of being unmasked before Judge de Freitas."

"As I recall, you were the one he threatened with disciplinary action,'' Winthrop countered. ''It seems to me Lazarus just had to sit tight and watch you go down in flames.''

''But if I didn't go down in flames, if Matt and I managed to prove to the judge that Lazarus deliberately suppressed evidence that Eddie had committed crimes, the judge would have turned his wrath on Lazarus. He still will; he'll have no choice. No judge wants a lawyer from either side parading perjured testimony in front of a jury and getting away with it. De Freitas would have to discipline Lazarus, and if he does, there goes Lazarus' political career.''

Winthrop stood and gave a little bow, then walked with a heavy, old man's tread toward the door of the coffeehouse.

I watched him go, then ordered a second cappuccino.

He'd left me with a great deal to think about. Underneath my ringing defense of Matt, there was an uneasy suspicion that Winthrop and Zebart might just be right about Matt. He'd wanted Lazarus destroyed; he had to feel the same way about Eddie Fitz.

Had Matt gone from my bed to the stone steps of the courthouse instead of to St. Andrew's Church? Had the man who'd held me in his arms, made hot, sweet love to me, gone from me to the killing ground where Eddie Fitz lay in his own blood?

That would be worse than going to Taylor's.

Or would it?

I needed to know. I needed to know whether he'd betrayed me with Taylor or with murder. Either way, it was betrayal, and I wasn't sure which I hated more, but I had to know the truth.

One way, of course, was to ask the lemon-haired lady in question.

The doorman let me up without a second glance. Apparently I was dressed well enough for the Upper East Side;

the designer briefcase didn't hurt either. My low-heeled Ferragamos clicked on the tile floor. The lobby was decorated in black and white, with silver accents and not a speck of color. It was as cold and unwelcoming a place as I'd ever seen in the five boroughs. But it was chic as hell.

Her apartment was directly under the penthouse, which meant she had almost the same million-dollar view for considerably less in monthly maintenance. Shrewd, but then I'd never thought Riordan was a man who liked dumb broads.

She opened the door with a wide but puzzled smile. She invited me in with the same cool grace she'd probably used on the *New York* magazine people when they'd come to photograph her apartment. As I recalled, the theme of the article was "Country Life in the Heart of the City."

What people in the Midwest think of as country: mass-produced wooden doodads with little carved holes in the shape of hearts. Dried flower arrangements with the flowers dyed Federal-blue. Cute sayings in calligraphy with folk-art designs around the border. Anything with geese on it, especially if the geese are wearing ribbons around their necks.

What Taylor Fredericks considered country: a Shaker chair, just one, against a white wall, an authentic shawl draped over the little rod on the back. A sampler, dated 1823, framed, next to a doll's quilt with yellow and pink butterflies. A warming pan of highly polished brass, a hand-embroidered footstool next to a rocking chair hand-carved in mellow yellow wood. A dry sink with a painted china basin.

In short, a very high-class antique shop—with modern touches: a print (or was it a print?) of a painting by Leonor Fini, a glass-and-brass coffee table with a big book on the Wyeths lying invitingly on top, a Noguchi lamp next to the rocking chair.

I could live here. I could really live here.

For the first time, I saw Taylor Fredericks as a person. If she lived in a place that appealed to me, a place I could see myself living in, then she had to be somebody I might actually like if I got to know her.

I didn't want to get to know her. I didn't want to like her. All I wanted was to find out if Riordan had said anything important to her the night that Eddie Fitz had three bullets pumped into him.

She asked if I wanted tea.

Tea, yet. I withdrew the notion of liking her; this was all too civilized for me.

I nodded; tea meant I'd be staying a while, and I wanted all the time I could get with her.

I explored the bookshelves while she went into the kitchen. The kitchen I didn't have to see; I remembered that very well from the magazine piece. Copper everywhere. A stripped pine table with turned legs. A pie safe.

I'd always wanted a pie safe.

Her books were hardcover, lots of modern fiction, mainly by women. A whole shelf of heavy picture books on American antiques. Some pop history, no pop psychology. No genre fiction. All hard-core quality. I thought of my prized collection of Dell mapbacks and wondered if she had a softcover in the place. Maybe the bedroom; I wondered how I could catch a glimpse of—

The old bathroom dodge. I could peek in on the way to the powder room. And then I could sneak open the door to the medicine cabinet and wipe out my entire day's stock of self-respect.

The prescription bottles were in the name of Sarah T. Fredericks. The ''T'' had to be for Taylor, which she'd taken as her first name, dumping the too prosaic Sarah.

Hah. I knew a name like Taylor Fredericks was too good to be true.

What else about her was phony? Her ash-blond hair? I didn't expect to find any telltale Clairol bottles; that kind of color you pay a fortune for on Fifty-seventh Street.

There were no paperbacks in the bedroom. The book on her night table was the latest Alice Walker. And the quilt on the bed was to die for. A friendship quilt, with the names of all the ladies who'd worked on it sewn into the border. The design was log cabin, with rich colors and odd squares depicting buildings that seemed taken from life: a schoolhouse, a church, a barn, a—

"What are you doing in here?"

"God, what a fantastic quilt!" This was not cleverness on my part; I coveted the quilt, and the fact that I'd originally opened the door to spy on her was wholly forgotten. Who cared what she read or what her real name was? She had wonderful taste and the luck and money to indulge it.

"It's from Pennsylvania," Taylor said, a hint of pride creeping into her voice. "It's called a friendship—"

"I know," I interrupted. "Because a group of women make it for a friend, usually someone who's going away. They were often made for minister's wives, when their husbands moved on to a new congregation."

She nodded agreement. "This one was made for a doctor's wife," she explained. "The buildings in the odd squares were real buildings in the town of—"

"God, it's gorgeous. How ever do you find a thing like that?"

"I spend a lot of time antiquing," she said. She turned toward the bedroom door, a subtle sign that I should follow.

I did. "I apologize for going into your bedroom," I said. "I just saw that quilt and I had to get a closer look."

"Matt didn't say you were an antique buff," Taylor remarked.

"I'm not. Not like you. I have a few pieces given to me by clients on Atlantic Avenue, but nothing like this."

We talked antiques through the first cup of tea. Earl Grey, a little flowery for me. I prefer Darjeeling, but I poured two or three drops of milk into it and drank thirstily.

The china was English, bone china with tiny curlicued handles that made my hands seem huge. She had arranged little butter cookies on a plate. I took one and nibbled at it, feeling like a Sara Paretsky character suddenly dropped into a Jane Austen book.

Well, hell, if I was a bull in a china shop, it was time to start breaking crockery.

"Was Riordan with you last night?"

She choked on her tea. "Why do you—"

"Not because I care that he went from my bed to yours, I assure you," I said with a bitchy pomposity that would have gone down well on a soap opera.

"From your bed to—" Either she was having trouble keeping up or she was stalling till she decided how much to tell me. And I didn't think she was stupid.

"Look, this isn't personal. A man was killed last night."

"That policeman?" Her voice rose on the last word, but it wasn't really a question. "I heard something about it on the news this morning. But I didn't hear anything about Matt."

"Most of the newspeople in this town know better than to throw premature accusations at a trial lawyer. But the fact remains, Eddie Fitz's death means the end of the case against Matt. And that makes him suspect number one in the eyes of the police. So I was wondering how he acted when he came here. Was he upset? Did he say anything about his trip to the plaza?"

"He's been under a lot of stress," Taylor said in a thoughtful tone. "This trial has been just devastating for him." She looked at me, her eyes blazing an improbable turquoise. "But I'm sure you know all about that. Although," she went on, "if he was really in your bed before he came to me, maybe that explains why he couldn't, exactly—"

Was she telling me what I thought she was telling me? And if she was, poor Matt. Poor old Matt. If there was one thing he couldn't endure it would be for his new flame to reveal to his old flame that he hadn't been able to rise to the occasion.

I stifled my sense of outrage and said, in mock-sisterly sympathy, "Men take these things so seriously. I'm sure you were very understanding."

Her tone crept into tartness. "I probably wouldn't have been quite so understanding if I'd known he'd already given one successful performance," she retorted. "As it was, I put it down to stress. And alcohol. Matt had several drinks after he got here. But then, you probably know all about that, too. Matt's always telling me that I should drink real drinks, like you, instead of white wine."

"I don't drink any more than any other trial lawyer," I said, stung into defensiveness. It was more than a little disconcerting to realize that Matt considered my ability to down hard liquor one of my better qualities.

I had not come to Taylor's co-op for a temperance lecture.

I lowered the fragile teacup to its saucer and looked her in the eyes. Tinted contacts, I decided, looking at the improbable shade of turquoise. "Did Matt say anything about the meeting in the plaza?" I asked. "Did he tell you that was why he was coming here so late?"

"No," she replied. She lowered her eyes. Her lashes were long, full, curled; they didn't look mascaraed but they framed her eyes perfectly. She placed a manicured hand on her thigh, smoothed an invisible wrinkle in the silk palazzo pants, and looked up again.

"You know how it is with a man as busy as Matt," she went on. "I never knew when to expect him. It could be as early as eight or as late as one A.M. He even"—she gave a throaty little laugh—"kept me waiting on his birthday. I'd made reservations at Le Cirque, and he made me sit for a full hour, with everyone giving me pitying looks because it was so obvious I was being stood up. But then he came in, sat down, and explained he'd been with a witness and couldn't get away. So I was used to his coming in at strange hours.''

"Did he say anything about meeting someone downtown?" I persisted.

"He *said*,'' she replied, putting a wry spin on the verb, ''that you and he were working on the case.''

Working on the case in my bed. The one that didn't have a thousand-dollar quilt on it.

Nothing Taylor had said could be used in evidence, but I left the Upper East Side wondering whether Matt's inability to perform could have arisen from the fact that he'd just killed a man.

CHAPTER
THIRTEEN

"She doesn't actually *sleep* under that quilt, does she?"

Of all the questions I could have asked my former lover and present client, this one took the cake for sheer irrelevance, but I wanted to know. I truly wanted to know.

"What difference does that—" he began, then broke off as he realized I wasn't going to quit until I got an answer. "Sometimes," he admitted.

I nodded, satisfied. Taylor was a woman who could pay a fortune for something beautiful and insist on using it, not just having it. Interesting.

I changed the subject with an abruptness that would have earned me points on cross-examination. "Whoever killed Eddie," I said, "had to get past you, standing in front of the church. Assuming that the killer is someone connected with this case, then why didn't you recognize the person walking past you toward the courthouse steps?"

"Because the killer went around the back way," Matt replied. "The killer sneaked up the courthouse steps from the other side, the one behind the church, where neither Krieger nor I would have seen him.''

''Good answer,'' I said. ''That's what I was thinking, too. And that thought leads to Nick Lazarus. We don't go back to court on your case for another day, but I think I'm going to pay a visit to the U.S. attorney's office anyway.''

I was in enemy territory. Inside the belly of the beast. Wandering through the United States attorney's floor of the corrugated-concrete building that also housed the Federal Correctional Center, a state-of-the-art facility for federal prisoners awaiting trial.

I was looking for Davia Singer. If Stan Krieger had been lured to the plaza to serve as cover for the true killer of Eddie Fitz, then he wasn't that killer. But who was? My money was on Davia Singer or her boss, and I wasn't particularly interested in which one had pulled the trigger. What I wanted was a lever with which to pry a little truth out of one of them, and I didn't much care which of them opened up first.

I'd never been a prosecutor. I simply wasn't born on that side of the courtroom. My instincts, my strategic abilities, were all defensive. But one trick I'd learned from twenty years of doing combat with Brooklyn district attorneys: Find a weak link and put pressure on it till it cracks.

There had been little in Davia Singer's courtroom demeanor to indicate that she had potential as a weak link, but I decided she was a better bet than her canny boss.

I went through more layers of bureaucracy; I'd already announced myself at the reception desk downstairs and been given a color-coded plastic badge to wear. Now I was ushered into a taupe-carpeted sanctum where I was told to wait for Ms. Singer.

Her mascaraed eyes widened a fraction when she saw me. ''Come in,'' she said in a curt tone and turned without watching to see if I followed. I trailed her down a carpeted corridor and followed her into a cubicle the size of a freight elevator. It was on the inside of the building and had no window. A framed poster of the Joffrey Ballet company dominated one eggshell-white wall; a black-and-white blowup of Peter Martins suspended in midair hung on the opposite wall.

Davia walked with her toes pointed out, duck-fashion. Dancer-fashion.

So she was a frustrated ballerina. How was that piece of information going to help me?

I wasn't sure, but I filed it away in a corner of my brain just in case. You never knew.

I considered opening with a world-weary rhetorical question about why women lawyers continued to sleep with witnesses, but realized it would open me to a charge of hypocrisy, since my own relationship with Matt Riordan was not unclouded by sex.

Besides, that wasn't the issue. I was certain that if Davia Singer had had anything whatsoever to do with the death of Eddie Fitz, it had been professional and not personal motives that had driven her.

"See, the thing is," I began, jumping in as if we'd been having this conversation for twenty minutes, "guys like Eddie have a way of conning other people into holding the bag for them. Which is why Stan Krieger is on record as having registered TJ as an informant."

There wasn't even a flicker in the dark eyes that watched me with the unblinking intensity of a cat. I was fairly certain I was telling her things she didn't already know, but she wasn't about to give me the satisfaction of reacting to my words. A formidable opponent, this little sister of the courtroom.

"And guys like your boss do the same thing," I added, keeping my tone chatty. Pretending we were shooting the breeze about bosses we had known; pretending this was not an interrogation. "They keep layers of deniability between themselves and their questionable acts. Which is why I'm willing to bet that the only fingerprints on this whole mess will turn out to be yours and not Nick Lazarus'.''

Davia Singer knew perfectly well we were not chatting. "Whatever you want with me," she said in a hard voice, "you're not going to get it. So you might as well leave the way you came."

"If you wanted me out of here," I reminded her, "I'd be gone. This is your territory. All you'd have to do is call a guard, revoke my little badge here, and I'd be on the street. You invited me into your office because you want to know what I know."

"So tell me what you know and then get out of here," she retorted. The hard voice was wavering just a tad; she sounded more like a sullen child than a killer prosecutor.

"You know better than that," I chided, going for a big sister tone of voice. I settled back into my taupe chair, in an attitude of complete ease. The more on edge she became, the calmer I intended to appear. It was a variation on my courtroom strategy. "You're the prosecutor, after all. You know you can't get information without giving something in return."

She thought it over. I could see the wheels turning under the sleek black hair. "Eddie's dead," she said. "I didn't kill him. I think you know that already, so I don't know what you expect from me."

"Well, for one thing," I said, "you could tell me who told you to wait by the sculpture after you left the office that night. Was it Eddie promising you a night of passion, or was it someone else promising something else?"

"God, your generation makes such a big thing about having sex," Singer complained. "So Eddie and I had a thing going. What's the big deal? Lazarus would have been pissed off if he'd known, so I kept it quiet around the office, but—"

"You kept your affair a big secret from your boss by

meeting your lover in front of the building where you work?'' I let my voice rise in disbelief. ''That's a really clever approach, I must say.''

''Lazarus always walks the other way,'' she explained. ''He always goes to Centre Street, then turns and walks up to the subway at Canal.''

''Why Canal Street?'' I asked. ''Why not go right into the subway station in front of the courthouse?''

''That entrance isn't open at night,'' Singer said. ''Besides, he takes the Number Two train, and he says it's easier to walk to Canal than change trains at that hour,'' she finished.

''Sounds like you know a lot about his habits,'' I remarked.

''I told you,'' she said with a touch of asperity, ''I didn't want him freaking out about Eddie and me. I wanted to be sure he wouldn't see me waiting by the sculpture every night.''

''You could have found a less conspicuous meeting place,'' I commented. ''I can think of at least five in the plaza area alone, not to mention the fact that you could have met in Chinatown or at a bar on Broadway. Why did you and Eddie insist on taking chances by meeting at that sculpture?'' I had the idea that she was half-hoping someone would see her and Eddie together; that she relished the notion of throwing the affair in the teeth of the man she worked for.

''I hope you used a condom,'' I said with wry wisdom. I was playing older sister for all it was worth—which wasn't much, to judge from the disdainful expression on the younger woman's face.

''Oh, don't give me shit about sleeping with a witness,'' Singer retorted, the cool sophisticate turning smart-mouthed kid. ''I can keep my professional life and my personal life separate. It was just sex, nothing more. Besides,'' she hit back, a sly smile playing around her dark-red lips, ''I don't believe you and your client are exactly unknown to one another in the biblical sense."

I said nothing. I didn't have to; the color rising in my face said it all. I could have explained that it was different for Riordan and me; we'd had a history before we ever became lawyer and client. But the truth was that I'd been a fool to let him into my bed in the middle of a trial, and no amount of rationalizing was going to change that. The only difference between me and Davia Singer was that I knew sleeping with a witness had been a mistake; she was willing to defend it on the grounds that it was "just sex."

"There's no such thing as just sex," I retorted, "and before you decide that's a Victorian viewpoint you don't relate to, consider what Judge de Freitas is going to say about you and Eddie Fitz. Consider what it will do to your reputation in the office, to your chances of becoming *the* U.S. attorney."

"You can't tell me there haven't been male U.S. attorneys who've screwed around," she shot back. "Why should this be different?"

"You can't really believe the double standard is dead, can you?" I asked. "You can't really think you can get away with the same things the good old boys can?" I fell back in my chair with an expression of astonishment on my face. "You really are young."

"Please don't give me that tired old feminist line," she said in a voice as cold as the air conditioning in her windowless office. "I've heard all the stories about how it was when your generation went to law school. It was different for me; women were almost half the class. I took it for granted that I could become editor in chief of the law review if I had the grades. Just like I take it for granted now that I can become *the* U.S. attorney in a few years if I work hard and make the right contacts."

In a scant few years, according to the herbal wisdom school of female aging, I'd be ready to become a crone.

Sitting in the same room as this heartless child, I felt as old as coal and twice as hard. I was already a crone in the eyes of this tough little girl who really believed there were no more barriers in her way, nothing to keep her from rising to the top. She truly didn't see the glass ceiling right above her head.

"I guess you don't know what Warren Zebart said about you out in the hall after he testified," I remarked. "If you did, you couldn't possibly believe you can become *the* U.S. attorney without a fair amount of bloodletting."

"You mean because he calls me a cunt?" Her answering smile was amused. My own teenaged face had registered the very same expression when I tried to shock my Aunt Patsy with the F-word. "That's no different from men calling each other pricks and putzes, no big deal. No giant sexist conspiracy, that's for sure."

"Is it? Is it really the same?" I shook my head. "I don't think so, myself, but it's your opinion that counts here. I just think you're in for a rude shock in a few years, when you try to step into your boss's shoes only to find out the powers that be are a lot more comfortable with wingtips than with pumps. But that's not my problem, is it? And since I'm sure you've made no attempt to join with other women in your office or your profession, you'll be all alone when you make the big discovery that women really aren't equal yet. But that's in the future. It's what's going to happen to you now that bothers me."

"What is that, Ms. Jameson? What do you think is going to happen to me?"

"I've already accused Nick Lazarus of putting Eddie Fitz on the stand knowing full well that he was going to perjure himself," I said, "and you and I both know that Lazarus is going to stand in front of the judge and deny everything. He is then going to say that he entrusted the entire process of witness preparation to his very able trial assistant, namely you. You are going to stand in front of the judge holding a very large bag. All the intra-office memoranda have your name or initials on them; all the notes on the file folders are in your handwriting. Nick Lazarus has deniability—and you don't.''

"Even assuming you're right,'' she said with that overlay of smugness that made me want to slap the blusher right off her expertly made-up face, ''isn't that one of the hallmarks of a good assistant? Isn't loyalty to the boss something that gets rewarded down the line?''

"The reward you want,'' I said bluntly, ''you have to be a member of the bar to get. Let Lazarus use you for a scapegoat, and your continued ability to practice law will be in serious doubt.''

"It will never come to that,'' Singer replied. She tossed her dark hair from side to side. ''Nick Lazarus wouldn't let it. And the judge won't want to push things that far. This is the Southern District; we act like gentlemen here.'' The implication was clear that I, a barbarian from the wrong side of the Brooklyn Bridge, couldn't possibly understand the genteel code of the jewel in the crown of federal courthouse.

Which was true, in a way. It was hard for me to understand the degree to which Judge de Freitas was committed to his rock-solid belief in Lazarus's integrity, even in the face of the contrary evidence I'd received from Dom Di Blasi. But then, Di Blasi, like me, was a Brooklyn barbarian who'd gone to the wrong schools and didn't belong to the right clubs.

"Dom Di Blasi's pissed off as hell about your defection,'' I mused aloud, ''but I still think he'd be willing to cut you a deal if you'd help him nail Lazarus. If you want, I can talk to him.''

"Don't do me any favors,'' Singer said. ''And close the door on your way out.''

I closed the door and marched out of her office with my head held high and proud, as if I'd actually accomplished something. I guessed I had, if only in a negative way. I now knew that Singer was living in a state of denial that would end only when she realized that this was one situation Judge de Freitas wasn't going to be able to ignore in the name of Southern District gentility. Someone's head was going to be on the chopping block, and Singer wasn't going to admit that head would be hers until it came time for her to kneel down in front of the executioner. And by then it would be too late to cut deals.

I walked out the back door, the one Nick Lazarus had exited from the night Eddie Fitz died. I walked along the little back street that separated the federal buildings from the venerable civil courthouse at 60 Centre Street. When I came to the alleyway between the Federal Correction Center and the church, I stopped and turned toward the plaza.

Man and women hustled through the alley, going to and from the public buildings. A tiny stream of people turned into the gated side entrance to the church's meeting room; a little wooden sign with the letters AA carved into it hung on the gate. I tried not to stare, wondering what I'd do if I recognized any of the city workers who were spending their lunch hour in the dark, dingy room.

I stood at a spot on the sidewalk where I had a clear view of the alleyway, but I didn't step onto the flagstones. I let my eyes travel to the huge red metal sculpture, which was straight ahead.

Okay. I was Nick Lazarus, leaving the office after a long night's work. I just happened to glance to my left as I walked toward Centre Street. I could see the sculpture— could I see Davia Singer waiting in its shadow?

The sun was high and bright and hot; it was hard to picture the way the now-crowded plaza would have appeared at night. But there were lights mounted on poles. I decided Lazarus could have had a good view of his assistant waiting for her lover. Could he, I wondered, have seen Stan Krieger as well, waiting at police headquarters?

I swiveled my head. No. Too many buildings in the way. Then I walked to a closer spot on the pavement. Still no. I walked into the alleyway. For Lazarus to have spotted Stan, he'd have had to walk almost to the end of the church—and if he'd done that, Singer would have seen him.

Next question: Could Lazarus have seen Riordan, who was in the doorway of the little church?

Again, not unless he'd walked almost to where Singer stood beside the sculpture.

I kept walking until I reached the side entrance to the federal courthouse, then continued on to the steps leading to the columned portico where Eddie had died.

Lazarus could easily have slipped past the alleyway, walked up the steps, met and shot Eddie, then walked back down and headed for the subway at Canal Street. While the others waited in their appointed places, he could have—

I stopped cold. A man behind me grunted and moved around me without a word. I looked back toward the corrugated building where Lazarus and Singer worked.

Why was I playing games at ground level, trying to figure out what Lazarus could have seen from the sidewalk, when his office commanded an eagle's eye view of the entire plaza?

If he'd been the mysterious faxer who'd lured Krieger and Riordan to the scene of the crime, he could have determined that they were in their appointed places before he ever left his office. And he could have seen that Singer was in her established place by the sculpture waiting for Eddie Fitz, just as she had been on the other nights they'd worked late.

With all his pieces in place, the chessmaster could have sidled up the courthouse steps and ambushed Eddie Fitz at the top of the stairs. He could have pulled him behind the stone columns, taken out a gun and blown his star witness's head half off, then walked back down to catch his train.

I stood at the top of the steps, slightly winded from the

quick climb. I looked down at the busy sidewalk below. My eyes traveled across the street to the many-windowed federal building where Warren Zebart had an office.

Could the Z-man have been the anonymous faxer? Could he have placed the chess pieces in the plaza and then strolled across the street to blow away Eddie Fitz?

Sure, he could have, I decided. But why would he?

I decided to postpone my impromptu conference with Lani and stroll across Centre Street to the FBI man's lair and find out.

He looked up with a scowl when I entered the big room with the file-laden desks. "Can't you just go to court like other lawyers?" he asked. "Do I have to see you every time I look up?"

"Anything new on Eddie's murder?" I said, sliding into the chair at the side of the big man's desk. "I know you took the case away from the city cops," I went on. "So what are the preliminary findings?"

"Anything that can be made public," Zebart replied, "will be in the newspapers. Anything not in the newspapers is not for public consumption."

"I remind you, Agent Zebart that I am not just a member of the public. I am an attorney representing a man you've chosen to treat as a suspect."

"Get a subpoena, you'll get the information," the agent said, ostentatiously turning his attention back to the paperwork on his desk.

"I guess that means that whatever you've turned up doesn't point to Riordan as the killer," I remarked. "If it did, I'm sure you'd be only too pleased to rub my nose in it."

"When I'm ready to move against your client, Counselor," the agent promised, "you'll be the first to know."

I didn't like that *when*. I didn't like it at all. "Don't tell me Matt's gun matched the bullets you pulled out of Eddie's body," I said, not bothering to conceal the note of very real fear in my voice. I didn't think for a minute Matt would be stupid enough to shoot Eddie Fitz and then walk around carrying the murder weapon, but I couldn't think what else would have filled the agent's voice with such rich self-satisfaction.

"It might interest you to know," Zebart said, "that we compared the bullets we found in Detective Fitzgerald with the slugs that killed TJ and Nunzie Aiello. And we got a nice match on the bullets that killed TJ, even with the mushrooming. I always said your client had a good strong motive for that shooting. But he made a mistake keeping the gun and using it again. It would have been smarter to ditch it. But he didn't, and I'm going to find that gun if it's the last thing I do. It won't be long before I'll be at Matt Riordan's fancy office with a warrant for his arrest."

CHAPTER FOURTEEN

Courthouses have back corridors, secret passageways, an underground railroad of connecting points that lead from chambers to private elevators to those rear doors in the courtroom that judges pop in and out of like black-robed jacks-in-the-box. I knew my own back roads, in the courthouses of Brooklyn, like the proverbial back of my hand—but this was Manhattan, and I was lost.

I had turned left three times. I was totally convinced that one more left turn would take me to Judge de Freitas' chambers. It didn't. Instead, the turn stranded me in a cul-de-sac with a window that faced onto the Chinese park behind the Criminal Court building.

It was a Chinese park because across the narrow street stood Chinatown. I looked out the window; kids played in the dusty little park; old people with wrinkled faces and almond eyes sat on the benches, dressed for winter in spite of the July heat. A band started playing a long, slow tune with lots of trumpets. I craned my neck; sure enough, a white sedan laden with flowers proceeded along the street. It was followed by people on foot, dressed in white; on the car a giant blowup photo reminded the mourners of the man they were on their way to bury. The Chinese mourned in white; I wondered idly if they wore black to weddings.

"Lost, Counselor?" a voice said in my ear. I jumped; I hadn't heard footsteps.

The voice was familiar, but it wasn't until I turned that I saw it was Nick Lazarus.

I wasn't about to admit to Lazarus that I couldn't handle his courthouse. "Just taking in the view," I replied. "There's a Chinese funeral out there," I added for good measure.

He shrugged. "There's always a Chinese funeral," he said. Then he added with a wry smile, "Either that or an Italian feast."

I'd wanted to see him. I'd wanted to confront him, truth be told. But I didn't want to do it unprepared. I didn't want to do it on his turf.

I wanted to do it when I thought I could win.

This wasn't the time.

This wasn't the place.

"Speaking of funerals," I said, "there've been quite a few connected with this case, haven't there?"

"You mean Eddie, I suppose," he replied, then added with a frown, "And that cop who killed himself. What was his name?"

That did it. *What was his name?*

"Dwight Straub," I said. Loudly, clearly, with more than a touch of ice in my tone. "His name was Dwight Straub. And I was thinking of him, but not just him. There's TJ as well. I'm not sure anyone gave TJ much of a funeral; I wouldn't be surprised if they rowed him out to Hart Island and dumped him in a pauper's grave. They still do that, you know," I added conversationally, "put people in pauper's graves. There's still a Potter's Field on this little is- land, up in the Bronx.''

"As long as you're saying *kaddish* for the dead, Ms. Jameson,'' Lazarus countered, his thin voice sharp, "you might remember Nunzie Aiello. They buried him from a little church in Brooklyn. I remember because I was there. You might think Nunzie would have had a Mob funeral, all black limos and white lilies, but you'd be wrong. He had his mother and his Aunt Marie and his retarded brother, Vito, and me. That's it. That's all the people who stepped forward to remember Nunzie Aiello. Frankie Cretella wasn't there, Matt Riordan wasn't there. Now, Nunzie wasn't what you'd call much of a citizen, but for my money, he deserved better than that. But you give your loyalty to the Mob, you give it to rats. You give it to people who use you up and throw you away.''

"The way you used up Eddie Fitz?'' I said. I said it softly, but I let the challenge hang in the air.

"What the fuck are you talking about?'' His voice wasn't raised. It was inflectionless. But Lazarus wasn't a man who used obscenities unless he was seriously rattled. He prided himself on being a gentleman. So my heart leapt a little when he lapsed into the F-word; I had struck a nerve.

"I'm talking about Eddie the ambitious little sleazebag. First he rides the gold shield express to the top of the heap as a narcotics detective, then he lives off the fat of the land, and as soon as he sees that it's all going to come crashing down on his head, he runs to you and cuts a deal. A deal that had him in the witness box while all his buddies stood to warm a seat at the defense table. He used you and you used him.''

Lazarus looked at me with the air of a man giving his enemy enough rope. He was letting me talk for only one reason: to find out how much I knew.

I only hoped I knew enough.

I plunged ahead. "You overlooked the corruption he was

into because you wanted the convictions he could make. You even overlooked the sudden disappearance of TJ; with him out of the way you thought Eddie could withstand even the kind of cross Matt Riordan could put him through.''

''I've already told the court that I evaluated this TJ as a low-level drug dealer with a motive to incriminate Detective Fitzgerald. I saw no reason to give credence to anything a man like that had to say.''

''But you told Eddie Fitz he'd come to see you,'' I guessed. The scenario became clearer and more convincing as I voiced my suspicions aloud. Zebart was wrong—Matt hadn't eliminated TJ. Stan Krieger had, and then used the same gun to kill Eddie Fitz.

''You'd have to,'' I continued. ''You'd have to see what Eddie would have to say. But what you were really doing was fingering TJ, telling Eddie that unless he got TJ out of the way, the whole thing was going to explode in both your faces.''

''This is preposterous,'' Lazarus said, going into bluster mode.

''Is it?'' I returned. ''If you hadn't told Eddie that TJ came to see you, Eddie and his cop friends wouldn't have stuffed TJ's body into the trunk of that car. You as much as told Eddie what he had to do to be safe from TJ. And Eddie did it, and you thought you were safe.''

''Ms. Jameson,'' Lazarus began, his tone patronizing, ''this is patently—''

''But then I showed up with the tape TJ made across the river,'' I finished, raising my voice to cut through his polite protestations. ''Which led to Judge de Freitas' asking questions about you and TJ. And since we know how loyal the late Eddie Fitz was to his friends, it was clear to you that Eddie was less dangerous dead than alive.''

''I can see why you're such an effective trial lawyer, Ms. Jameson,'' the prosecutor remarked. ''You have the kind of imagination that sways juries. Fortunately, Judge de Freitas is not a man who responds well to emotional appeals. You'll need solid facts for the judge, and since I had nothing to do with Eddie's death, there are no such facts."

"Is that a negative pregnant?" I asked, using a legal term of art I hadn't thought about since my law school days. "Are you denying you killed Eddie, but admitting you had TJ eliminated?" Perhaps the trigger man wasn't Krieger, but Lazarus himself.

"Of course not. I'm a United States attorney, not a hit man, Ms. Jameson. It's clear you've spent too much time with a certain type of criminal lawyer; you've forgotten the essential distinction between representing criminals and behaving like one."

"You could have done it, though," I persisted. The drone of the Chinese funeral music had subsided. "You could have walked right up the courthouse steps, met Eddie at the top, shot him in the head, and walked to the subway without anyone—"

The prosecutor's face lit up with a singularly repulsive smile. "Ah, but I didn't walk to the subway," he cut in. "At least not directly. Not that night. I had an appointment, you see," he went on. He was enjoying this. "An appointment with Warren Zebart. I walked to his office; the guard at the reception desk has a record of me signing in at precisely eleven-twenty-nine P.M. And I'm told Eddie was seen alive at eleven-forty by one of the guards from the courthouse. So you see, it would have been physically impossible for me to have shot my own witness."

I opened my mouth to argue that the sighting of Eddie at 11:45 wasn't written in stone; the cop's watch could have been off by a couple of minutes. And who was to say Warren Zebart and the FBI were above fudging Lazarus's sign-in time to give him an alibi?

But I had no chance to make my case; Lazarus turned and walked away, leaving me in the cul-de-sac. Lost.

I pretended I was in a maze. I kept turning right. No

matter what, I took the right fork every time I had a choice. And finally, I was rewarded by the sight of an elevator. I stepped on and hit the button for Lani's floor deciding I could always phone the judge later.

She was in her characteristic pose, stockinged feet propped up on an open drawer, reading glasses on her nose as she perused a transcript. Her shapeless suit was khaki-color and her blouse was a button-down Oxford in a bright white that sucked all the color from her olive skin.

She greeted me with a wry smile, put down the transcript, and waved at the coffee pot on a side table by way of invitation. I stepped over and poured out a cup of what looked like battery acid, then creamed it with powdered stuff and opened a sweetener packet.

I was vamping till ready. I didn't look forward to sitting face to face with my old buddy and conceding that she'd been right from the start, that representing Matt Riordan could only lead to big trouble. But even Lani couldn't have realized that the trouble would include three dead witnesses—two murders, one suicide. She couldn't have known that Matt would have as good a motive as anyone else for those murders.

Or could she? I looked into her hazel eyes and saw a level of amused comprehension that made my heart sink.

"Okay," I said crossly. "You were right. I've said it once and that's the only time you're going to hear it."

"For what it's worth," she replied, "I don't think Riordan killed Eddie Fitz."

All the frustration I'd been feeling welled up. "Then who the hell did?" I snapped. "I just came from talking to Lazarus, who threw his alibi in my face with the most insufferable smugness. I talked to Singer, who still thinks she's going to survive this whole mess, so she didn't have a real reason to kill Eddie. I like Stan Krieger for the murder, but he won't talk to me, so I can't be sure what's going on with him."

"But you're really worried they'll arrest Matt, aren't you?" my friend asked.

"Zebart's got a hard-on for him," I replied, lapsing into the phallic metaphors that amused me when men used them. "He'd have Matt in custody right now if he had the evidence. And the ballistics report worries me. Zebart said the gun that killed Eddie was definitely the same gun that killed TJ. I can't buy Matt killing TJ himself, but what if one of his Mob clients did it for him and then iced Eddie?"

"If that's what happened," Lani replied with a matter-of-fact air that helped cut through the miasma of despair surrounding me, "then no one will ever prove it. So why not set that possibility aside and concentrate on the others," she suggested.

"The plaza was filled with suspects," I recited. "Lazarus and Singer because they worked there; Krieger and Riordan because they were lured there by the killer."

"You don't know the killer brought them there," Lani pointed out. "It could be a coincidence that Riordan and that cop were promised—"

"Oh, come on," I interrupted. "If there's one thing that's clear, it's that someone wanted Krieger and Riordan in the wrong place at the wrong time. Someone knew exactly how to bait the hook to get Riordan there; I assume they did the same to Krieger. Someone told them precisely where to stand in the plaza so they'd be on the scene. Someone set them up to be—"

"What about Singer and Lazarus? Do you think they were manipulated too?"

"Not anymore," I conceded. "At least not Lazarus. I believe him when he says he went to see Zebart. Which means he changed his usual pattern, and the chessmaster didn't expect that, hadn't done anything to prevent it. As for Singer," I went on, thinking aloud, "it seems to me the chessmaster knew she was in the habit of meeting Eddie at the sculpture, and just took advantage of that. The killer knew she'd wait at least fifteen minutes. So he dangled some kind of bait in front of Eddie, told Eddie to meet him at the top of the courthouse steps, then blew his head off while the others waited in their appointed places.''

"This killer is someone who really knew the area," Lani remarked.

"Yeah, I've thought of that," I said. "But that applies to all of them. With the possible exception of Krieger, I suppose. He's a Brooklyn cop, but it wouldn't be hard for him to survey the area, figure out how to position people. As for Riordan, he knows that plaza like—"

"Let's make a list," Lani cut in. "The killer is a person who knew the area well," she began. She grabbed a legal pad and a pen and began to write. "The killer also has a strong motive for getting rid of Eddie."

"So far, so obvious," I commented. Lani stuck her tongue out at me and continued her list.

"And the killer knew Lazarus walked to the subway the back way, not going through the plaza. He also knew Singer would be waiting for Eddie beside the sculpture."

"I know all this," I pleaded. "Tell me something I don't know."

"How do I know what you know or don't know?" Lani replied equably. "Do try for a little patience, dear," she went on. "I am coming to the more arcane pieces of knowledge this killer had to have."

"Pray continue," I invited, echoing Lani's Victorian-novel manner of speaking.

"The chessmaster, as you call him, dangled exactly the right bait in front of Riordan," she pointed out. "The chessmaster knew Riordan would believe Eddie taped his conversations with Lazarus, and the chessmaster knew Riordan wanted those tapes so he could nail Lazarus. Which argues a pretty good knowledge of your client's character, it seems to me."

"Which the chessmaster could have gotten from a cursory reading of Jesse Winthrop's column," I reminded her.

"Yes, but how did the chessmaster know Eddie made those tapes?"

I opened my mouth and then shut it. She had a good point. Riordan and I had speculated about the tapes, particularly after Stan Krieger had told us of Eddie's boast that he'd taped his interview with Psych Services. But how did the chessmaster know Eddie had a reputation for surreptitiously recording interviews?

Unless the chessmaster was Stan Krieger.

What was Stan Krieger doing in the plaza at the time Eddie Fitz was killed? Who was he meeting and why? Had he been lured to the scene of the crime in the same way Riordan was lured—and, if so, what was the bait?

Or had he lurked in the plaza, waiting for Eddie? Had he grabbed his pal's shoulder and walked him up the steps to the federal courthouse? Had he stepped behind a pillar, pulled a gun, and blown away half of Eddie Fitz's head?

"You think Eddie put the gun in Dwight's mouth, is that it? You think he pulled the trigger, that this is some kind of dumb murder mystery?" Stan Krieger looked at me with a contempt he made no effort to conceal. I didn't blame him. I'd given up trying to get past the desk sergeant and had shown up on his apartment doorstep. He'd let me in with ill-concealed resentment, but he'd let me in. That was the important thing.

"No, Stan," I replied, echoing his tone of barely controlled exasperation, "I do not. Any more than you do. But I do think Dwight Straub would be alive today if he'd been assigned to a precinct that didn't have Eddie Fitz in it."

The light of combat died in Stan Krieger's eyes. The muscles of his face sagged a little as he let my words sink in. Ten years jumped onto his face; he looked ready for retirement, ready to pack it in and start hanging around in cop bars telling war stories.

"Ah, shit," he said at last. "Fucking kid couldn't handle it. Anybody could see that. Anybody but Eddie would have let the kid alone, work whatever he was doing around Dwight, make sure he didn't know what was going down."

"But Eddie didn't do that," I volunteered.

"Hell, no. He made sure Dwight was in it all the way. He teased Dwight a lot, gave him that stupid nickname."

"Ike," I repeated. "So tell me about Ike," I invited.

"Don't call him that!" Stan's voice was harsh; his left eyelid twitched uncontrollably.

"Someone made sure you were in the plaza the night Eddie was killed," I pointed out. I sat in a sagging armchair; Stan perched on the edge of his couch like a bird about to take flight. "Were you meeting someone?"

"Why should I tell you?" Stan shot back. He shifted back in his seat, as if trying to add to his bulk and solidity. Sending me a message that he was not to be moved.

"Why not? Somebody made damned sure you were in a position to be suspected of killing Eddie. Someone set you up. Doesn't that make you mad?"

"Lady, I've been mad since the day Eddie Fitz first walked into my precinct."

"So why did you let him get away with it? Why did you let him call the shots?"

His mouth twisted into a sneer. "In the first place," he replied, "the money was good."

"You knew there were investigations pending," I guessed. "I suppose whoever lured you to the plaza promised inside information."

"One of the guys who used to be in this precinct works at Headquarters now," Stan explained. "I had a message from him, said to meet him in front of One Police Plaza. Said he'd be working late, and he could tell me when charges were going to be filed."

"Which means whoever set you up knew the name of

someone in Headquarters who might help you," I mused aloud.

"Lazarus would know," I pointed out. "And Singer. I imagine the U.S. attorney's office would keep close tabs on an internal police investigation of cops who worked with their undercover."

And Riordan wouldn't know, I thought, but didn't add. Or would he? How hard would it be for a man with his connections to find a detective now working at Headquarters who'd once shared a desk at Stan's old precinct?

"I suppose your old friend at Headquarters says he never sent you a message," I remarked.

"Hell, yes," Stan replied. "He cursed me out when I called him, said I was jamming him up by even making a phone call. He said he sure as hell wouldn't have put his career on the line to help me out. I believed him."

"How did Eddie talk you into registering TJ as a confidential informant?" I asked, shifting back to the heart of the matter.

"Hey, that was a good idea," Stan replied, stung into defending the man he'd hated. "If anyone started nosing around, they'd find out TJ was on our side, that any dealing he was doing was for the sake of making cases. It was a perfect cover."

"At first," I agreed. "But that meant that when TJ became a liability instead of an asset, your name was on the paperwork. You were the one who stood to lose when the Department found out what TJ was all about. So when it came time for TJ to die, you took him out and—"

He'd started shaking his head in the middle of my recitation, and now he broke in. "No," he said in a hard, decisive tone. "No, that's not how it was. I didn't want it to come out, but now everything in the fucking world is going to come out, and, besides, the poor schmuck's dead, so—"

I caught on at last. "Dwight," I said. I sat back in my chair. "Eddie conned Dwight into killing TJ with him."

"Not *with* him," Stan objected. "It was worse than that. He had Dwight kill TJ *for* him. Eddie had an alibi all set up; he talked Dwight into taking out TJ all by himself."

"And the alibi was . . ." I let my voice trail off, trusting Stan to finish the sentence for me.

"A poker game with half the guys in the squad. Good guys," Stan explained. "Guys whose word would be believed. I was the only one there who knew what was going on. I was the only one who knew that when Dwight got there late, it was because he'd just come from killing TJ."

He shook his head at the memory. "Fucking kid looked sick as a dog," he recalled. "His face was pasty-white, and I thought he was gonna heave. In fact," he went on, "I think he did heave. Said he was coming down with stomach flu and left the game early. But it wasn't the flu, it was the fact that he'd just killed a guy in cold blood."

"Sounds like Eddie, all right," I said, feeling a little sick myself. It was all too easy to visualize Dwight Straub trying to macho his way through his first murder—and failing miserably. "Conning someone else into doing his dirty work for him."

"Ah, shit," Stan said through a long, exhaled breath that should have been blue with cigarette smoke but wasn't. He had the raspy voice of an ex-smoker; I wondered how long it had been since he'd put out his last butt. "The trouble was, Dwight married a ball-busting bitch," Stan pronounced. "That was the whole fucking trouble in a nutshell. You know who he should have married?"

I said nothing. I had no idea who Dwight should have married.

"He should have married a gum-chewing bottle blonde with a high-school diploma and a job at the Key Food checkout counter, is who he should have married. Some girl from the neighborhood who thought he was hot shit, who'd sit in the audience and clap her fucking hands off when he made detective. Trouble with Annie," he said, as much to himself as to me, "is she always wanted Dwight to be something he couldn't."

"I got the feeling she would have been happier if Dwight had left the Department," I said, keeping my tone neutral. I'd liked Annie Straub and I didn't buy the idea that any woman who didn't idolize her man was a ball-buster.

"Is that right?" There was a challenge in Stan's dark, angry eyes. "Is that the feeling you got from meeting Dwight and Annie for, what, a whole fucking six minutes? That is bullshit, Counselor, bullshit pure and simple. Annie wasn't nearly that straightforward with the poor bastard. If she had been, he might still be alive. No," Stan went on, "underneath it all, she wanted him to be the same kind of guy, the same kind of cop, as her precious father, Sergeant Mick Cohagan. She wanted him, when it came right down to it, to be Eddie Fitz."

"But she loathed Eddie," I protested.

"That's what she *said*," Stan concurred, undercutting any real agreement with his tone of voice. "And maybe that's what she really believed in some part of her twisted brain. But make no mistake," he went on, fixing me with his intense eyes, "Annie got turned on by Eddie. He may have been a prick, but he was a man, and she was a bitch in heat around him. What she really wanted was for Dwight to punch Eddie's lights out, then take her to bed and fuck her brains out. She wanted—"

"Give me a fucking break," I muttered, but my words didn't even slow Stan down.

"She wanted her husband to show he had bigger balls than Eddie. Which the poor sap never had and was never going to have. A woman without Annie's smarts wouldn't have seen all that, would have appreciated Dwight without comparing him to the macho cops. But Annie was Mick Cohagan's daughter, and she knew Dwight didn't have the balls to make it, and she let him know she knew it. Even more so after she got sober."

Balls. It came down to balls, always. Who had them, who didn't, whose were bigger. As someone who'd gotten through forty-some years without any, I had a hard time understanding how they could have dominated Dwight's thinking.

"Dwight killed himself because he was afraid of being charged with TJ's murder," I said.

Stan shook his head. "It was more than that," he explained. His face wore a mournful expression. "It was Annie. Not only would Dwight stand naked as a murderer, he'd be revealed as a jerk who was set up by a man he thought was a hero. He'd be a schmuck. And the last thing in this world a schmuck can stand is for everyone to know he's a schmuck. It wasn't so much that Dwight couldn't face the music, it was that he couldn't face Annie."

It was only after I left Stan's Bay Ridge apartment and rode the subway train through the dingy little stops along the way to Borough Hall that I let myself understand the relief I was feeling. If Dwight killed TJ, then Warren Zebart was wrong about Matt. He was innocent of TJ's murder, and, by extension, of Eddie's.

But why was that such a relief? Hadn't I always believed in Riordan's innocence?

CHAPTER
FIFTEEN

I stood outside the church, waiting for the meeting to end. There was a light drizzle, the kind of rain that makes you feel foolish whether your umbrella is up or down. If it was up, you felt that you were overreacting because it was, after all, only a mist. But if you kept your umbrella furled, you felt like an idiot because you were getting wet while holding an umbrella you weren't using. A can't-win kind of rain.

My umbrella was up. I needed protection, not so much from the rain as from my thoughts. I'd spent a long, sleepless night running through my list of suspects, and I thought I knew at last who'd killed Eddie Fitz.

I'd known it longer than I'd admitted the truth to myself. In some corner of my mind, I'd known it even as I'd confronted Lazarus, lectured Singer on her moral choices, hunted down Stan Krieger. I'd wanted very much for the killer to be one of them. To be anyone other than who it was.

To be anyone other than the person who was going to

walk out of St. Andrew's in five minutes.

People began streaming out of the little room at the side of the church. I walked to the stone portico of the Federal Correctional Center and stood under it, folding up my umbrella now that I was no longer being rained upon.

The meeting was almost over. People were leaving. Why didn't I see the person I was waiting for?

At last I gave up and dashed across the alleyway, going through the gate with the little wooden AA sign on it. I ducked into the doorway.

She was alone in the room. She held a red banner with gold letters that read "One Day At A Time"; she was getting ready to put it away in a cupboard.

"We have to talk," I said, my voice echoing in the empty room. Chairs sat where people had left them, in ragged rows grouped around a scarred wooden table. There were empty paper coffee cups and an occasional brown paper bag wadded up on the floor. I wondered if it was Annie's job to clean it all up, or if a janitor came in.

"No, we don't," she replied, rolling the banner up as if I hadn't come in. "We have nothing to talk about."

"We have Eddie to talk about," I replied. I moved toward her. I picked one of the chairs, turned it around so it faced her, and sat myself down in it.

"Eddie's dead," she said. "And if you want me to shed tears about that, you've come to the wrong person. But that doesn't mean I had anything to do with it."

"But you did," I countered. "You were the chessmaster." She gave me a blank look that had nothing to do with pretending. I realized the term was my own; there was no reason it would mean anything to her.

"You were the one who made sure all the suspects would be in the right place at the right time," I explained. "You were the one whose boss's office overlooked the plaza, the one who could see the possibilities from twenty stories up."

She hugged the furled banner to her chest as if it could warm her. The day was dank and cool, but she was dressed for sun. "I'm right, aren't I?" I asked in a tone I kept carefully conversational. "The Department of General Services is on the twentieth floor of the Municipal Building, isn't it?"

She shook her head. "Nineteenth," she corrected in a flat tone of voice. Then she smiled a one-sided smile and added, "but who's counting?"

"People must look like chess pieces from up there," I mused aloud. "Easily manipulated, easily put in whatever place you want them to be in. Not," I added, "that you needed to manipulate Nick Lazarus or Davia Singer to be in the plaza at the right time. You knew Lazarus worked killer hours, and that Singer worked almost as late as he did. All you had to do was get Eddie to the top of the courthouse steps while Singer waited for him at the sculpture."

No reply. She stood with her arms folded, making me spin it out, making me lay all my cards on the table. I kept talking, in hopes something I said would force her to respond.

"So all you had to do," I continued, my voice growing strained, "was arrange for Stan Krieger and Matt Riordan to be on the scene."

She turned away abruptly and walked toward the cupboard. She put the banner away and headed for the window, where two large cardboard signs had been propped up for the meeting. One listed the Twelve Steps, the other the Twelve Traditions. She hefted the Twelve Steps and walked it over to the cupboard.

"Let's take Stan first," I said, trying not to let her lack of response interfere with my train of thought. "Whoever baited the hook for Stan had to know he had a buddy at Police Headquarters. At first, I thought that pointed to Lazarus or Singer. I knew they were monitoring the internal investigation into the squad.''

Annie stood beside the cupboard where she'd stored the huge poster. She looked thin, hungry. Sad. I forced myself to keep talking, to keep making my case, setting out my indictment.

''But the more I thought about it, the more I realized anyone who knew the squad would know that. Then I realized this cop wouldn't just be an old pal of Stan's—he'd be an old friend of your husband's, too. You knew him, you'd had him over to your house for a party to celebrate his promotion to OCCB. So it was no problem to use his name to lure Stan to the plaza that night.''

There was still no spark of comprehension in her face, but at least she'd stopped fussing with the posters.

''As for Riordan,'' I continued, ''he was a little harder. But it was at the same party that Eddie bragged about taping his Psych Services interview. You knew he'd probably worn a wire when he spilled his guts to Nick Lazarus, and you knew he'd keep the tapes as insurance. So when you let Riordan think you had the tapes Eddie made, you were acting on what you knew about Eddie.''

I cleared my throat. ''And you were acting on what you'd read about Matt. You knew he'd do anything to destroy Lazarus, and you knew he'd do anything to get those tapes.''

Still no response. Her eyes seemed to drift away as she listened to me. ''The guy I married was a really good person,'' she said at last. ''He was a good cop and a good guy. And then he met Eddie.''

In her mouth, the name was a curse. ''He met Eddie,'' she went on, ''and he became somebody I didn't know anymore, somebody I didn't like very much.''

She pulled herself up and faced me, her eyes burning with a need to convince me of something. ''They killed him,'' she said. ''The goddamn squad killed my Dwight, turned him into someone else. Eddie killed him with his macho bullshit and his dirty money. Stan killed him with his indifference. Lazarus and Singer killed him with their ambition. You and Matt Riordan killed him with your lousy subpoena. So when it came time for me to do what I had to do, I wanted all of you to suffer. I wanted all of you to be suspected.''

''But Riordan and I were going to destroy Eddie,'' I pointed out. ''He wasn't going to get away with it, not really.''

''He was going to be alive, wasn't he?'' she replied. ''That's getting away with it from where I sit. Because Dwight's dead, and I couldn't stand to live one more day in a world where Dwight was dead and Eddie was alive.''

Her voice shook slightly, whether from grief or rage I couldn't be sure. She clamped her jaw shut, but not before I realized she was very close to falling completely apart.

''It must really have torn you up to hear Nick Lazarus trying to put the blame on Dwight for everything Eddie did,'' I said.

''Don't patronize me, okay?'' Annie said. The tears that had been lurking in her eyes dried up; her voice was firm and hard and angry. ''Lazarus was a complete shit, but none of the rest of you were any better. All any of you cared about was your goddamned egos. Eddie was going to get away with it one more time, because he had balls and my Dwight had too much of a conscience.''

''So you took the gun Dwight used to kill TJ and you brought it to the plaza to kill Eddie Fitz,'' I said. ''Only you didn't realize it was the same gun, did you? You didn't realize Dwight killed himself because he was worried about being indicted for murder, not just corruption. Corruption he probably could have lived with, but he didn't want the world to know Eddie had conned him into murder.''

''Stan should have stopped it,'' she said in a low voice. ''He was older, he was a guy Dwight could have looked up to, would have listened to. Only Stan was too busy being cynical. He could have stopped Eddie, or at least helped Dwight to see Eddie for what he really was. But he didn't care enough. He let Dwight kill that drug dealer.''

''I hate to sound harsh,'' I said, ''but all Dwight had to do was say no. You can blame everyone else in the world if you want to, but the truth is, nobody forced Dwight to rip off drug dealers or to murder TJ. He could have said no.''

''You don't understand,'' she cried. ''You don't know what it's like for a man like Dwight. How he always had to prove himself, how he was never sure of who he really was. The other guys laughed at him, made him feel like a wimp. He needed to show them. Oh, God,'' she said. ''If only I'd been able to convince him to move away, to leave the Department.''

''Is that what you really wanted?'' I prodded. ''Or did you want Dwight to show Eddie what a big man he could be? Did you maybe let Dwight see that if he left the Department, it would be because he wasn't man enough to handle it?''

''I never said that,'' she replied. ''I never in our whole marriage said a thing like that.''

''Maybe you never said it sober,'' I shot back, the thought just occurring to me, ''but how about when you were drinking?''

''If I said it then, I didn't mean it,'' Annie said, her tone sullen.

''Do you think Dwight could make that distinction?'' I asked. ''You know what they say about *in vino, veritas*.''

''Which is total bullshit,'' Annie argued. ''Any ex-drunk knows that. People say a lot of crazy things when they're drinking; it doesn't make it the truth.''

''I repeat, did Dwight know that? Or did he think the only way to get your respect was to be like Eddie?''

''Why are you asking me these things? Why do you want

to make it my fault that Dwight did what Eddie wanted him to do?''

That was one hell of a good question, and one for which I had no good answer.

Or did I? Wasn't I really seeking absolution for the crime of hitting Dwight with the subpoena? It had been no more than a fishing expedition but it literally scared the life out of him. I'd known Dwight wouldn't break, wouldn't testify against Eddie when push came to shove. I hadn't known why. I hadn't known it was because Dwight had committed a murder for Eddie, but I did know the subpoena was just a scare tactic. And I served it, anyway. I served it anyway, and it ended up in Dwight Straub's car, alongside his body.

I wanted that to be someone else's fault.

"What happens now?" Annie asked. She pushed a strand of hair from her forehead and looked at me with the weary gaze you see in Walker Evans photographs. Her thin arms, drawn face, shapeless print dress, all added to the illusion that she was a Dust Bowl wife worrying about how to feed the young'uns. "Who do you tell about this?"

"Warren Zebart, I guess. He's the FBI agent who—"

"I know who he is, for God's sake," Annie cut in. She took a deep breath, let it out in a long sigh, and asked, "Do you have to tell him?"

I nodded. "You know I do." I tried for a gentle tone, but no amount of gentleness would soften the facts.

She smiled a secret smile. "They'll never find the gun," she said in a childish voice. "I threw it in the river."

I gave that assertion some thought, then shook my head. "No, you didn't. Not that night, anyway."

Her eyes widened. "Why do you say that?"

"Because no woman is going to walk to the East River in the middle of the night, throw a gun into the water, and walk back alone. Not at one in the morning. Whatever you did with that gun," I finished, "it is not in the river."

Her smile widened but held no amusement. "It's in the water, though."

In the water. We were standing on an island. The amount of water available for throwing guns into was—

Then I had it. Where else would a grieving widow get rid of the gun she'd used to kill her late husband's best friend?

To the place where her husband had sat in his car, watched the sun come up over the bay, and shot himself in the head.

"You threw it off Orient Point," I said.

She nodded.

"Zebart will have the area dragged," I said. "He'll find the gun." I sounded more confident than I felt.

"I know," she replied. "I suppose I've always known I wasn't really going to get away with it. But I felt better as soon as Eddie was dead. I really did feel better. I stood there at the top of the courthouse steps and I looked at all that blood and Eddie's brains splashed on the white stone wall, and I felt great. I felt powerful. I felt like I could float right down without touching the steps with my feet. I felt alive for the first time since all the trouble began. Can you understand that?"

I nodded.

"You know what I hated most?" Annie went on. "That stupid nickname: Ike. That stupid fucking nickname." She fixed me with her serious gray eyes. "My husband let another man tell him what his name was. Can you imagine anything more pathetic? He let another man give him his name."

Fat Jack sat in the last booth, a doll-sized cup of espresso in front of him. The cup was flanked by a bottle of sambuca capped with an aluminum nozzle. He nodded me into the booth with the air of a cardinal granting permission to approach. Or perhaps it was the late Don Scaniello the ex-bail bondsman was imitating.

I slid into the red leather banquette and signaled the waiter for my own demitasse. I'd have preferred cappuccino, but somehow it seemed important to match the fat man drink for drink, to spice my coffee with the licorice-flavored liqueur and sip the way they did in the old country. Neither of us was Italian, but the atmosphere of Forlini's settled over us and added a layer of intricate Machiavellian nuance to our every gesture, our every word.

"Tell me again why you wouldn't testify," I said after Fat Jack had poured a shot into my cup. I lifted it to my lips; the flavors of strong coffee and sambuca lingered on my lips like a Judas kiss. I was here to get the truth about Riordan, and I'd known from the minute I walked in the door it wasn't a truth I was going to like.

"I told you," the fat man replied in a rasping voice. "I told you you wouldn't like what I'd have to say."

"And then you told me Riordan ordered you to pay off Eddie Fitz," I reminded him. "But that was a lie, wasn't it? Riordan's not stupid enough to fall for a scam like Eddie's; he never gave you money to pay Eddie off."

"So why did I pay him, then?" Fat Jack asked. His pudgy fingers enclosed the tiny china cup. The huge restaurant was all but empty; the legal lunch crowd was back in court.

"I'm not sure you did," I replied. "I know why you said you did, though. Because you and Eddie were in it from the start. You didn't jump over to Lazarus' side because you found that internal memo—you were on Eddie's team the whole time. The memo was just a pretext, a cover for the real truth."

"And just what is that real truth?"

I sat back in the booth, letting the quiet of the place settle over me, calming my nerves.

"Everyone kept saying how remarkable it was that Eddie

knew when to wear a wire and when to leave it off," I pointed out. "Lazarus said it, Singer said it, and so did the judge—hell, Eddie himself said it. But what if it wasn't instinct? What if he knew damned well when to leave the wire off because he knew for a fact he'd be searched that night?"

"How would he know that, Ms. Jameson?" Fat Jack made a good straight man. For a moment I wondered whether his willingness to let me spin my little yarn meant that I was completely wrong in my conclusions. I decided there was only one way to find out, and plunged ahead.

"Because the person responsible for conducting the search made a practice of telling him in advance," I said. "You and Eddie talked before every meeting. You told him whether or not you were going to search him, and he wore a wire or not, depending on what you said."

"Why would I do that?" The fat man's hands were still. He waited with the patience of a Buddha, his face expressionless. He was a tough room; I began for the first time to doubt the reasonableness of my own conclusions. "For that matter," he went on, "why would Eddie do that?"

That question I had an answer for. "Eddie knew his days as king of the street were numbered," I theorized. "He knew the squad was being investigated, and he knew it was only a matter of time before someone cracked and the whole bunch of them went down. He decided he wasn't going down—that his only option was to beat the other guys to the prosecutor's office and turn state's evidence. That's why he sucked up to Lazarus during the commission hearings, why he dared Lazarus to go after lawyers and judges. He saw himself as the star witness, bringing down other guys instead of being marched out of some precinct with his jacket over his head. He decided to go from corrupt cop to Hero Cop—but a hero needs an enemy. A hero needs to put himself in danger. So you played the heavy."

A flicker lit the gray eyes in the piggish face. "Pardon the pun," I said without a smile.

"Guys like Lazarus," Fat Jack said, "always fall in love with cops. See, that's the thing I always liked about Matty. He could stand toe-to-toe with the kneecappers and he never flinched. He never stood in awe of those fuckers, either—never hero-worshipped bastards like Frankie C. or cops like Eddie. Matty was a street fighter in a three-piece suit; he wasn't awed by tough guys. But a guy like Lazarus—Nicky creamed his pants whenever Eddie told a war story. He loved it when Eddie went out wired, put his life on the line to make his case. He ate it up the night Paulie and I held the gun to Eddie's throat. Eddie was golden from then on."

"And that was the point," I said. "Eddie had a closetful of skeletons, and he knew the only way to insure that Lazarus wouldn't throw him to the wolves when he found out about those skeletons was to let Lazarus think he was risking his life to make the case against Riordan. That way Lazarus would always owe Eddie, would think twice about holding him responsible for all the stuff he did on the street."

"It worked, didn't it?" Jack asked.

"You explained why Eddie did it," I said, "but you haven't told me yet why you went along with it."

"Why don't you guess?" my companion retorted with a sneer.

"All right," I replied. This was the part I was least certain about—and the part I wanted least to discuss and to face. But I'd promised myself the full truth. I'd stood in judgment on Annie Cohagan Straub for refusing to face the full truth about the man she'd loved, and I was damned if I was going to keep on doing the same thing.

"It all starts with Nunzie Aiello," I said. My espresso was cold; I took a sip anyway.

"What do you know about Nunzie?"

"I know Frankie Cretella didn't kill him," I responded. "I know the person who did went to a lot of trouble to make it look like a mob hit, a replica of the Scaniello murder."

"Nunzie's old business," the fat man pronounced.

"Maybe," I agreed. "But you drew the line at murder, didn't you? You'd fetched and carried for Matt Riordan for thirty years, but you drew the line at murder."

I wasn't certain exactly when I'd come to believe that my ex-lover and ex-client had killed Nunzie, but I knew that Taylor's story of how he'd been late to his own birthday party had something to do with it. Nunzie had gone missing in October, just about the time Matt would have been celebrating. And Frankie C. was on record as telling the world he wasn't going to rescue his lawyer from Nunzie's treachery.

"I couldn't see ratting him out for it, though," the bail bondsman said. "That I couldn't see. But when Eddie Fitz came along with his little scam, I thought, what the hell? Matty deserves some punishment for what he did to Nunzie. Why not help Lazarus nail him for bribery, when the God's honest truth is, he's bribed in his time. Which I didn't care much about then or now, but whacking Nunzie—the guy was an inoffensive little schnook who was trying to save his own ass. He didn't deserve to wind up as worm food in the trunk of a car."

"You never asked."

This was true. I had never asked. I'd plunged into Riordan's defense on the bribery case without bothering to ascertain whether he had, in fact, killed Nunzie Aiello. I'd accepted his explanation that the whole idea of his being responsible for Nunzie was a delusion on the part of Nick Lazarus, an obsession of a demented FBI agent.

I had never asked. But this didn't mean he'd had no obligation to tell.

I said as much as I stood in the parlor of Riordan's office suite. I stood because I wasn't sure I wanted to sit, wasn't sure I wanted to share an intimate chat and a drink with a man I now knew to be a stone killer.

I now knew. I now knew what I hadn't wanted to know.

From the beginning, I'd known what Matt was. I'd hopped on for the ride anyway, refusing to let his reputation deter me from pursuing whatever it was we had together.

Why?

Because I'd always loved roller coasters.

"How?" I asked. I was keeping my words to a bare minimum, as though by opening my mouth to speak I ran the risk of filling my lungs with poisoned air.

"Will you please sit?" Riordan's voice carried an edge of annoyance. "I hate the way you're standing there like the Angel of Judgment."

The exotic blooms in the blown-glass vase were shriveling. There were little brown edges on the pale-peach lilies. In the old days, Matt changed the flowers every other day, throwing out the whole bouquet and starting fresh. In the old days, there were three or four law students doing research in the library, two receptionists covering the phone, Kurt Hallengren handling the preliminary court appearances. Now it was just Matt and the decaying flowers.

His career would never recover from the body blows struck by Nick Lazarus. The people who wanted Matt to represent them wanted a winner, and Matt was beginning to carry the smell of defeat, even if he had beaten the rap.

He'd been right; winning wasn't enough. He'd won the verdict, but he'd lost in the long run.

"How?" I said again, as I slid into the armchair beside the drop-leaf table.

"Let me give you a drink," Matt said. He rose and went to the bar. "You always say it's too hot to drink Scotch in summer, but you'll like this."

He brought back a huge blown glass with a half-inch of

amber liquid inside. I sipped and let the warmth surge through me like a jolt of electricity. "Nice," I said. "Thanks."

I was drinking with a killer. A killer who wore an Armani suit and tasseled Gucci loafers with black silk socks that covered his calf.

But the bright-headed bird had lost some of his luster. The blue eyes were red-rimmed and the jowls hung loosely in spite of his plastic jobs.

"Do you really want to know, babe?" he asked. His face was impassive, but his eyes begged me to stop asking questions. "Isn't it better to just—"

"No," I cut in. "I really want to know. I think you owe me that much." Which was a stupid thing to say, since he owed me nothing besides my fee. I'd made a pretty penny representing my former lover, but beyond that, he owed me no explanations and we both knew it.

"I'd saved his ass," Riordan said. "I'd gotten him off on at least five petty beefs before the Lou Berger case. And on that one, I'd done what I could. I didn't think he'd sell me out, I really didn't. Even when I first heard Lazarus was going after him, trying to turn him against me, I didn't think Nunzie would bite. He was a soldier of the old school, Nunz, and I thought he'd stand up."

"You thought he'd stand up," I repeated. "Isn't that what Dwight Straub said about Eddie Fitz? 'He's a standup guy.' Interesting," I went on, "how that same phrase is used by both the cops and the bad guys."

"Another reason I wasn't really worried," Riordan continued, "is that I talked to Frankie C. I figured Frankie wasn't going to let Nunzie start running off at the mouth."

"You mean," I translated, "you hoped Frankie C. would take out Nunzie on his own account."

"You might say that," Riordan acknowledged.

"Look, we're not on tape. Let's just talk straight, shall we?" I picked up the glass and let a little Scotch oil my tongue. It burned like a delicious fire.

"Okay," he said. "I was hoping Frankie would take care of business. I was hoping he'd feel nervous enough about Nunzie to do something. But when he didn't, I knew I had to act. I wasn't just going to sit there like some patsy and let Lazarus roll over on me."

"So you arranged to meet Nunzie under a bridge somewhere?" I asked. "And how did you get him there? I can't believe he was stupid enough to come to a meet with you while he was busy shoving the knife into you in the grand jury?"

He shook his head. "I sent a message saying Frankie wanted to meet him. And, no, it was not under a bridge. I moved the car under the bridge later. It was over by the Brooklyn Navy Yard on a Sunday morning, very early. I had Nunzie waiting beside his car, right next to the river. I walked up behind him, pulled a gun out of my raincoat, and did it as quickly as I could. I took the keys from his dying fingers and opened the trunk of his car and hoisted him up and threw him in like a sack of dog food. And when I got him into the trunk, blood all over the fucking place, I gave him another shot in the mouth. Right in his filthy, lying mouth. And then I closed the trunk of the car and walked away. I threw the gun into a sewer on the way home."

I sat in silence. I wanted more alcohol in my body. I wanted not to be there, not to have heard the words spoken in the cruel, dispassionate voice.

"You said 'filthy, lying mouth,' " I pointed out, "but you killed Nunzie because he was going to tell the truth."

"Yes," Matt replied. I looked directly into the blue eyes in the tanned face. "Yes," he repeated. "And I'd do it again in the same circumstances. Survival, babe. It's the way we do things in Hell's Kitchen."

• • •

He was on Tom Snyder the other night, commenting about a big criminal trial going on in Florida, telling war stories about his own trial days, laughing with Snyder and shooting the breeze with the people who called in to talk to him.

He'd put on a good ten pounds. His face was ruddy and his tie was just this side of garish. The Fordham class ring sparkled on his finger as he gestured to punctuate his stories. His rich voice filled the studio; when he and Snyder laughed, it was as hearty as a good beef stew.

I could have almost enjoyed it if I hadn't known what he thought of lawyers who did the talk show circuit instead of trying cases. He'd likened them to tigers caught and caged and tamed, night after night, by some jerk in tights. They still looked like tigers on the outside, but on the inside, all the things that made them tigers had died.

I was watching a dead tiger entertaining the public.

He lifted his exquisitely manicured hand to make a point. I looked at the hand and remembered how it had felt around my breast, tracing patterns on my bare skin, pleasuring me.

The bright-headed bird was dead. Lazarus had killed him, in his Brooks Brothers suit.